KING IN HIDING

KING IN HIDING

BOOK 1 IN THE SWAYAMVARA ROMANCE SERIES

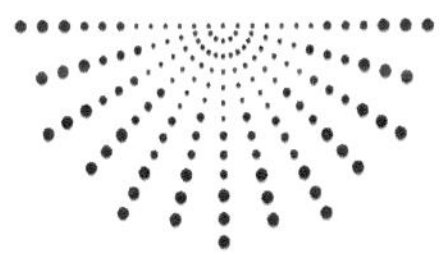

ANNA BUSHI

JULY PUBLISHING

www.annabushi.com

Library of Congress Control Number: 2023901536

ISBN 978-1-7364103-6-3 (paperback) — ISBN 978-1-7364103-7-0 (hardback)

First Printing, 2023

To Mary and Priya, who gave me something most valuable, their time

CHARACTERS

VIDARPUR KINGDOM

King Dushyant
    Princess Kanika, sister of Dushyant
    Princess Ambika, sister of Dushyant
    King Lambhodara, father of Dushyant
    King's Head Guard Jayanth
    General Ayobahu
    Minister Panini
    Advisor Upananda
    Chief Guard Samudra
    Former Commander Kanva
    Sundari, daughter of Kanva

* * *

GARTHAPURI KINGDOM

King Samrat
    Queen Padmavati, wife of Samrat

Prince Bhimasena, brother of Samrat
Princess Charulatha, wife of Bhimasena
Princess Lalitha, daughter of Bhimasena
Minister Kapila
Agamathi, daughter of Kapila
City Guard Commander Nambi

* * *

NIDHAPUR KINGDOM

Prince Giridhar, brother of the king

1

LALITHA

Princess Lalitha rode along the narrow forest path, her heart hammering against her ribs. The wind rustled against the branches as she and her tired mare advanced slowly in the descending darkness. She'd left her Aunt Chitra's house two days ago and had journeyed nearly non-stop since then. Only finding out the fate of her father kept her moving.

Something crawled on her back, and she nearly screamed. Pressing her lips tightly, she brushed her back to dislodge the insect. Where she headed, she could not be frightened.

Lalitha was visiting Aunt Chitra, her mother's sister, when news about a skirmish near Garthapuri reached them. Her aunt had worried for her safety and denied her request to return home. Lalitha had nearly laughed at her aunt's concerns. If King Dushyant invaded her kingdom, she would have no safe haven. She had to protect Garthapuri. Lalitha had written a scroll explaining her decision to seek her father and departed without her aunt's consent. Lalitha had stolen a horse from the stables and had left in the cloak of early dawn.

The path narrowed, and tree branches scraped her arms. Dew drops fell from the leaves and wet her cotton sari.

She had to find her father. With that thought lighting her path, Lalitha emerged from the cluster of tall trees. She straightened and breathed in the twilight air. She looked at the sky painted in a vibrant shade of orange by the setting sun. The sound of running water reached her, and her parched throat burned. She guided her horse toward it.

A tiny creek flowed in front, and she jumped off lightly near the shore. Leading her mare to the water, Lalitha knelt beside the animal and drank deeply. She splashed water on her face and washed her arms. After the briefest rest, she mounted the saddle again.

A pair of eyes glistened gold in the light. Lalitha pulled her reins to halt the mare. She took out the small knife she'd tucked into her waist. A lone jackal. Her stomach turned at the thought of the beast eating the carcasses of dead soldiers.

After watching her warily, the animal abandoned the water and ran into the forest. The mare trudged through the undergrowth while her eyes swept the area. Tree limbs merged with the shadows and scratched her arms. The forest opened up here and sloped down.

The warm breeze brought in a decaying odor. Her head jerked up to glimpse the meadow beyond the tree line. She was gazing at the site where the battle had taken place. Fear rose in her throat as Lalitha gazed at the frozen objects on the ground. A large shape that looked like a horse rested next to a shield that glinted faintly in the light. She heard moans and saw a few men moving about the slain warriors. Robbers? Her father might be lying on the ground bleeding to death or worse.

She edged forward as the sun sank lower, praying fervently for him.

A blinding light appeared in front of her, and her mare reared in fright. Lalitha tried desperately to hold on to the reins, but she had no support. As the horse fell, it was impossible to jump aside. Her arms and legs flailed as the horse's belly flashed above her head. A jerk, a splash into the mud, and then a painful collision with the ground. She remained horrifically paralyzed in fear as a dull ache spread from her right leg.

"Who is it?" a voice called sharply, and she bit her lip. She could not let them find her. She tried to roll, but an excruciating agony stabbed her leg. Her horse wheezed beside her as the animal tried to regain her footing.

Light from a flaming torch shone on her. Two strangers in dirty clothes stood in front of her.

The tall man in front eyed her from head to toe. She peeked at him from the corner of her eyes. He appeared only a few summers older than her. Even covered in shadows, she could see he held himself erect like a warrior. But neither wore any insignia. Did they fight for her or King Dushyant?

"Are you hurt?" he asked, his tone gentle though he towered over her.

"Your light frightened my horse," she said as a sudden ache stabbed her. She clenched her fist, waiting for the agony to subside.

The tall man knelt beside her. "Where does it hurt?"

"Curse King Dushyant! My right ankle," she gasped as her eyes watered.

He froze briefly and then shifted her sari to expose her lower leg. A bluish bruise started to form around her ankle. He touched her lightly, and she nearly yelped.

"What are you doing here in the middle of a battle?" asked his companion, who stood a few feet away. An ugly scar marred his face, and he stood like a tiger, ready to pounce on its prey.

Lalitha was visiting her aunt to request her to attend the swayamvara her father had promised to host. Swayamvara allowed a girl to choose her husband. Lalitha knew her father's desire to allow her this choice was rare and spoke of his fondness for his daughter. Most royal women did not even meet their betrothed, let alone select them, before their wedding. Her father had agreed to invite all the eligible young unmarried noblemen from her kingdom to the event, and Lalitha could choose her future groom from among them. When she learned that King Dushyant had attacked her kingdom and that her dear father might be in danger, she left immediately to find him.

"My sister is about to give birth. I came to visit her," lied Lalitha boldly, reaching into the depth of her heart to find her courage. Raised in the warrior tradition, she would not betray her father by displaying fear.

"This place is overrun with men who have fought and killed. It is not safe to travel now," the tall man answered.

"My sister needs my help," she insisted.

"Still, the battlefield is no place for a girl." He sounded like a man used to command. Who was he?

"I heard there was only a skirmish here," she said, hoping for more details. She'd heard her father had only led a small army to confront that tyrant, Dushyant.

The men ignored her words. Instead, the tall man pressed her skin, and she grimaced in pain. "We will take you to our hut nearby. You can rest there tonight. Tomorrow, if you are able, I can escort you to your sister."

His eyes gazed at her intently, making her uncomfortable. She was no fool to grab what he offered so readily. She did not trust these men. She could not reveal her destination.

"Help me onto my horse, and I will find my way home," she muttered.

The tall man shook his head, and his large ears almost flapped like an elephant's. "Did you not hear what I said? You are in the middle of a battle. There are enemy soldiers all over. And you are not fit to fight or flee. You are coming with me," he said.

How dare he insult her. She pulled her knife out. "I can protect myself."

He lifted his brows and knocked the blade out of her hand.

She wanted to rip his face. Instead, she gritted her teeth, picked up the weapon, and tucked it back into her sari folds.

He placed his hands under her knees and waist and scooped her up like a child. Realizing the futility of arguing with him, she shut her eyes. He shifted to clasp her waist tightly, pressing the right side of her chest into his firm body. She sensed him move forward and opened her eyes a slit. His face appeared a mere foot from hers, and she flushed.

"Are you comfortable?" he asked, though his eyes appeared like a still ocean, conveying no emotions.

She nodded, a distinct unease spreading through her at their closeness.

His companion guided her mare to him, and the tall man placed her delicately in the saddle, her legs hanging on one side. Then, holding the reins, he walked the horse forward while his companion followed.

"The battle—do you know what happened to Prince Bhimasena," she whispered, afraid of finding out her father's fate. Did she imagine it, or did the tall man beside her stiffen?

"King Dushyant's men captured him," he said.

"Captured?" she asked, with hope rushing in like a flash flood.

"Yes," he answered, shifting slightly.

Her father was her only family since her mother abandoned her. Her mother, Princess Charulatha, had renounced her worldly ties and joined a Buddhist monastery a few years ago. The thought of also losing her father crushed Lalitha. Thankfully, he was alive. Lalitha pressed her right thumb into her left wrist, releasing the tense knot. She had to rescue him from the clutches of the tyrant king.

"Was he wounded?"

"He is a valuable prisoner. King Dushyant will treat him well."

Valuable? She nearly snorted. Her father would say a plate of rice had more value than him. Why hadn't her uncle, King Samrat, sent men to free him?

When a messenger arrived a week ago with the note that Dushyant's army marched toward Garthapuri, she wanted to return home immediately. After she'd unsuccessfully pleaded with her aunt to let her go, she slipped away.

She noticed the tall man glance at her frequently. Heat rose in her cheeks at his unwanted attention. Who did he think he was?

"Did you fight for Prince Bhimasena?" she asked.

"My cousin and I are ordinary men," he replied. She observed his pattern of not answering her question. The scars on his face and arms told her that he'd fought. But she had more important things on her mind than figuring out their names.

With her father captured and her uncle apparently oblivious to his fate, she wanted to slice King Dushyant to pieces. "Is King Dushyant here?" she asked.

The tall man appeared taken aback, and the tip of his ear turned red. She saw a glance pass between the two men. Then the tall man shook his head.

The king destroyed her father's army, and he was not even here to savor his victory. Rage coursed through her when she imagined the brave men who had died for her father. She would visit their families when she returned to Garthapuri to thank them. And she wanted King Dushyant to inflict no more harm on her kingdom. She had to chase the king away or bargain with him. But she had nothing to offer him. While her uncle sat on the throne, her father ruled Garthapuri. With her father detained, she had to return to the palace and plan a way to get him out. Her kingdom needed her.

Darkness descended around them, and the earth blended with the sky. A small hut loomed in front. The tall man halted the horse, and his eyes glinted in the moonlight. While his cousin held the door open, he carried her inside, heat from his palm spreading to her back. He lowered her to a mat.

She slid toward the mud wall and leaned against it. The tiny room held only the mat, a lighted oil wick lantern, and a pot of water.

He left her side and went outside to talk to his cousin. Though she could not hear them, she could sense from their arm gestures that they were arguing about something. After a while, his cousin departed with the flaming torch, and the tall man entered the hut.

"My cousin left to fetch you food and something to ease your pain."

"You don't need to stay here," she mumbled, feeling trapped by his presence.

"I cannot leave you alone," he said, dropping to the floor.

"Why? I am not going anywhere with my injured leg."

He gazed at her, tugging his ear. "To protect you. How long will you lie?" She stared at him with her stomach twisted in fear. "Princess Lalitha," he stated coldly.

2

DUSHYANT

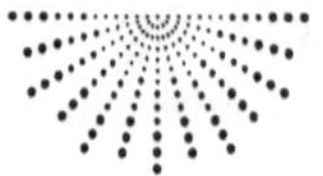

Dushyant regarded the princess on the floor. Princess Lalitha swallowed, her eyes fluttering like butterfly wings. To hide her identity, she would have to lie better. A maid's body would be hardened with labor, not soft like hers. And the thick silver anklets on her feet were likely filled with gemstones and typically worn only by noblewomen.

A transformation came over Lalitha, and she straightened. With fiery eyes that sparkled, she gazed at him with contempt. Her contempt would only grow if she knew he was King Dushyant.

"If I am Princess Lalitha, what do you intend to do? Hand me over to King Dushyant?" Dushyant saw no sign that she recognized him. She breathed fire with no trace of fear on her face. Despite himself, he admired her courage.

"If?" Dushyant had men who could make even a mute snake sing. A few days in a darkened solitary cell with only rats for her company would have her dance to his tune. Some in his council might suggest he twist her ankle, but he abhorred such acts.

He moved closer to her. Her nostrils flared with each breath. Dushyant could sense she was as stubborn as her father. Prince

8

Bhimasena refused to aid him. Dushyant could throw her in a cell across from the prince to loosen her father's tongue. Then, another thought crept in like smoke entering a room through gaps in a door. He could attempt to win her trust without revealing his identity. And use her to achieve his desire of vanquishing Garthapuri. "I only care for your safety," he lied.

She arched her brows. Winning her trust would not be easy. "I know nothing about you. How do you expect me to trust you?"

"What do you want to know?"

"Let us start with your name," she said. A few strands of her dark hair framed her face.

Name? He could not reveal his real name. She considered King Dushyant an enemy. "Puru," he replied with the name of his grandfather. She mouthed it soundlessly while her eyes regarded him.

"What are you doing on the battlefield?"

"My cousin and I repair weapons." *Another lie.* After his father's untimely death, he was the new king of Vidarpur, while Ayobahu, who was no cousin of his, served as his general.

Her eyes swept his shoulders with a frown.

Before she could ask him more questions, General Ayobahu arrived with two packets of food wrapped in dried lotus leaves. Ayobahu handed them to him, and Dushyant opened one of them. Ayobahu had the sense to bring them day-old tamarind rice instead of what likely awaited Dushyant at his royal tent—a rich dish dripping with ghee. Dushyant handed the other parcel to her. She sniffed her food and held it back to him. "Give me yours."

He raised his eyebrows. Did Lalitha think he would poison her? Earning her trust would require delicate skill on his part. "I am not an assassin. Even if I was, why would I poison a commoner?" he replied, giving her his untouched food. Did she forget she pretended to be an ordinary maid?

Lalitha colored deeply. She picked up a few morsels of rice and put them in her mouth.

Ayobahu handed him a banana leaf wrap. "For her leg," he said.

Dushyant took the leaf and looked at her. "Do you want me to wait till you finish eating?"

She nodded with her mouthful. Dushyant set it aside and picked up his rice.

"Are you not joining us?" she asked Ayobahu.

"No, I am leaving," said Ayobahu, glancing at him. Dushyant knew his general wanted him to treat her as a hostage, but he had no intention of listening. So he merely inclined his head. After Ayobahu departed, they ate the food in silence.

Her simple gold earrings cast a web of light on her cheeks. Dushyant took a deep breath and turned back to his food. The sour and spicy rice awakened his senses, and he polished it off quickly.

After they finished eating, she handed him her empty leaf like a princess. And he was a fool to play her servant. Cursing quietly, he collected the leaves and left them outside. Washing his hand in the water from the pot, he wet a clean cotton rag and offered it to her. She wiped her hands thoroughly.

He grabbed the banana leaf wrap and approached her. "May I?"

She dipped her head and moved her sari to reveal her swollen ankle. Her anklet pressed against her flesh.

"Can you remove your anklet?"

She bent her knee and winced in pain. Did she tear some tissue as well?

"Allow me," he said and sat near her feet. Slowly, he unscrewed her jewel. He held the ornament in his palm and shook it gently. Filled with pearls? He handed it to her. Then, he wrapped the banana leaf packed with boiled turmeric root around her ankle and tied a thin strip of cotton cloth around it.

Sweat erupted on her forehead, and her breathing came more rapidly, but she sat still.

"Thank you," she said after he finished. In the light of the lantern, her face glowed like the moon.

She continued to look at him with her big brown eyes, twisting her fingers.

He waited for her to say something. "I need to visit the fields," she mumbled with a blush spreading across her cheeks. Of course. She needed to relieve herself. What a mess he got himself into! Should he bring a maid to serve her? No. That would increase her suspicion.

"I will carry you outside," he said, and she reddened.

He placed one hand on her bare mid-back and another under her knee and heaved her up. She froze in his arms and glanced away from him. Her discomfort brought a smile to his lips, but he suppressed it. Dushyant despised feelings, especially any that would make him forget his mission. He wanted to use her to subdue Garthapuri. She was no more than a tool.

He walked toward a cluster of bushes behind the hut. In the dark, he stumbled over a small piece of rock, and she slipped from his arms. Hastily, he pulled her close to him. A faint scent of sandalwood floated from her.

"Hold my neck," he said.

She refused to look at him while she clasped her arms around his neck. That action caused her sari to slip and reveal the knotted band she wore around her chest. With difficulty, he tore his eyes away. Still, he could feel her heart beating against his.

In the glow of the full moon, he set her down carefully. Her face still contorted in pain as her leg touched the ground. For some strange reason, that twisted his heart. Dushyant chased his concern away. He could not give in to weakness.

"Yell when you are ready," he said with an unusual awkwardness and walked away. A small cluster of trees stood on the other side of the hut, and he wandered toward them. The moonlight filtered down through the branches forming a web on the ground.

"My Majesty," a voice whispered from above his head.

Dushyant scanned the trees. A man parted the branches to reveal his face. "Jayanth!" Head of his guard. "Any news from the battle?"

"The few Garthapuri men still alive have retreated to their fort. Our physicians are helping our wounded."

"Send word to Upananda to gather the war council. I will join them." Upananda had served King Lambhodara, his father, as his advisor for many years and continued his duties under Dushyant.

"My Majesty, what do you intend to do with her?" he whispered.

"Be you for one night."

"Stand guard outside the tent while the princess sleeps inside?"

Dushyant chuckled. "No, I will sleep outside and let you guard us both."

Jayanth grinned, and his white teeth shone brightly in the dim light. "Honored to do my duty. But is this wise, my king? Our men are waiting for my sign to come and imprison her. She will be a valuable hostage in our negotiations with her uncle."

"Instead of sending a messenger, she felt compelled to return home. If I arrest her, she will clamp up like her father. If I win her trust while hiding my identity, I could use her to capture the traitor who betrayed my father." And kill the traitor.

Jayanth twisted his thick mustache with a smirk. "King Dushyant, many men have fallen for eyes less fine than Princess Lalitha's. You are both unmarried. I am not sure—"

Dushyant interrupted him. "Watch your words, Jayanth. You are questioning my honor." He did not even consider her beautiful. His guard had lost his mind. Why would Dushyant care about the niece of his enemy when kings lined up outside his door to offer their daughters in marriage? Dushyant intended to keep his heart untouched no matter whom he wed.

"Apologies, my Majesty. What happens tomorrow?" asked Jayanth.

Unusual for him, Dushyant had not thought about that. He rubbed his chin. "I will escort her back to her palace."

Jayanth shook his head. "It is not safe for you to travel through Garthapuri, my Majesty. Not while we are at war. My advice would be to bid her farewell tomorrow and walk away. I will find men to escort her."

That would be wise. But Dushyant shook his head. "I might learn something from the princess. If I befriend her, it might come in handy in my quest to find Kanva, the man who betrayed his oath. I will travel with her tomorrow. And it will allow me to mingle with her people without revealing my identity." He could sense Jayanth's unease with his proposal, but his guard did not press his view.

"Do you have your dagger?" Jayanth asked.

Dushyant touched the blade hidden in the sash tied around his waist.

"Allow me one suggestion, my king. Take your guards with you. We can remain hidden from her but will still protect you."

He imagined his guards hiding in treetops while he tried to engage Princess Lalitha in a conversation. His lips curled up. "Wise counsel. Follow me discreetly. Don't bow when you see me."

Jayanth rolled his eyes. "If you hear the sound of an owl, you know we are near. Princess Lalitha is coming back," he said and let go of the branches. The leaves covered him again. Dushyant walked back hurriedly.

He could see her silhouette against the deep blue sky. That foolish girl hopped on her good leg, grimacing with each step.

As she tripped, he bounded to her, trying to catch her. Instead, she fell against him, causing them both to tumble to the ground.

As they sped to the earth, he tried to shield her from the impact of their fall. He succeeded by landing on his back with her sprawled on top of him. Her face hovered inches from his, and her lips parted tantalizingly. For a moment, he imagined kissing her. She drove his imprudent thoughts away by pounding his chest with her fist. Curse her. She was a spirited princess. He tightened his grip on her.

Surprising him, in one graceful motion, she drew her knife. Pressing the cold blade against his throat, she hissed, "Let me go."

Before he could react, his head guard, Jayanth, materialized out of thin air and held her wrist.

3

LALITHA

That donkey-brained idiot touched her like she belonged to him. Her helplessness had grated her, so she had tried to reach the hut on her own. But Puru dashed to her like an excited dog causing her to lose her balance. Why didn't he let her fall? He'd tried to fly to her like the monkey god, Hanuman. And failed. Now, she rested on top of him with no space between them. She could feel his heart beating rapidly, and his breath mingled with hers. She wanted to scream. Instead, she punched his chest. The fool pulled her in close like he desired to absorb her.

Fortunately, she managed to grip her knife handle. Shifting her hip, she held the weapon to his neck. "Let me go."

While she struggled against Puru's grip, a stranger dressed in Vidarpur garments crouched in front of her. Though of medium height, he moved nimbly like a ferocious tiger. A gold chain glittered around his neck. He must be more than a foot soldier for that tyrant, King Dushyant.

"Drop the knife," the stranger growled, rocking on his heels. Without waiting for her compliance, he grasped her wrist with his calloused palm and twisted her arm. Shrieking in pain, she dropped the blade, and he caught it deftly. The stranger stood to inspect the ornate ivory handle as it glinted in the moon. It was a gift from her father. She cursed her foolishness in bringing that weapon.

Puru pushed her off and jumped up to his feet with a scowl. She rolled on her back to sit and watched the two men.

Puru approached the stranger with a frown. "To what do we owe the pleasure of your visit, Commander?" he asked in a cold tone. Commander? Did Puru know him?

The man addressed as the commander stroked his mustache and ignored his question. "How are you two related?"

Puru placed his hands on his hips, and his face turned into a mask. How did he stand so calmly? Seeing he had no intention of answering the question, she said, "He is my intended."

Puru spun and stared at her. She flushed. Why didn't she say he was her brother?

"Why were you fighting then?" the commander smirked.

"A family matter," Puru answered. His tone would have put out a fire.

"There is a rumor that Princess Lalitha is en route to King Samrat. My men are scouting the place for her. Have you seen her?" The commander's eyes darted toward her when he uttered his question.

Lalitha held her breath as an eerie cold wrapped her skin. Would Puru reveal his suspicions to Dushyant's man?

Puru snorted. "Is King Dushyant afraid of a mere girl to send his men after her?"

A fleeting smile appeared on the commander's face, but it vanished quickly. "Watch your words. I can throw you in our dungeon for disrespecting our king."

"Commander, your action of assaulting ordinary folks traveling these lands is more of a disrespect than any words uttered by me."

She stood astonished at Puru's defiance. Before the situation could escalate, she hobbled to a stand and bowed deeply to the commander. "Puru and I saw no princess."

"Puru?" asked the commander with raised eyebrows.

"That is my name," Puru muttered with the slightest hint of annoyance. "If there are no more questions, we will be on our way," said Puru and looped his elbow through hers.

"With him by your side, you will not need this," the commander said and tucked the blade into the sash around his waist. Then, he waved them on.

After a few feet of nearly dragging her, Puru whispered, "It will be easier if I carry you."

"No, I don't want you touching me," Lalitha spat the words out at Puru.

"I am touching you now. How is it any different? Do you want your ankle to heal?"

To prove she could walk on her own, she placed her right leg on the ground and winced. Without waiting for her permission, Puru scooped her up like a child and strolled to the hut without even breathing harder. Curse the man and her weak leg.

"Let me go, brute. Why did you confront the commander? He could have thrown us both in prison," she spewed in quick succession. Though she called him names, he'd treated her with respect so far. Except for his insistence on carrying her around. Her chest rose and fell rapidly.

He jutted his chin. "Any foolishness lies on your side. Do you always act so rashly? You drew your knife and alerted him to your presence," he said curtly.

Lalitha bristled at his insult. She could hear his heart pound like a drum and feel his warm breath on her. Puru smelled of horses and rain. His eyes glinted like deep pools in the moonlight.

He kicked the door open and entered the hut. The lantern light illuminated his large ear. Lalitha worried he would drop her on the floor, but he lowered her gently onto the mat.

"You will be safe here tonight. I will be outside," said Puru. A strand of her hair had come loose from her braid, and he reached his hand to push it behind her ear.

"Do you know the man we met outside?"

Puru remained silent and turned down the lantern light. Then he shut the door behind him, leaving Lalitha alone in the tiny room. Curse him. She decided not to waste any time on him.

She closed her eyes and thought about her father rotting in prison. What happened to his loyal soldiers? Did any survive? She had to reach the castle soon.

The tiredness from her long journey crept in, and sleep claimed her.

She dreamt of a pair of hardy arms engulfing her. The man lifted her chin and leaned in to kiss her.

Suddenly, she woke and sensed something crawl past her injured leg. She opened her eyes and heard a loud hiss. She glanced toward the noise, and her heart jumped into her throat. A few feet away on the ground, a cobra raised its hood. Her legs were within striking distance of its venomous fangs. An unuttered scream vibrated within her and burned her throat. She clenched her fist as fear twisted her entrails. Fear embodied in the shape of a hooded beast with sharp fangs.

4

DUSHYANT

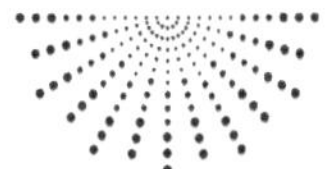

ushyant leaned against the closed door and gazed at the stars that glittered in the sky. The night was dark and windy. The crowns of the trees rustled like a melodious flute.

He could still feel her warmth in his arms and never wanted to let go. He shook his head. He could not let a mere girl hamper his efforts to bring Kanva to justice. His soldiers had spilled their blood for him. He'd have to finish this war to avenge his father.

He straightened with a fierce determination. Lalitha's mare tied to a tree trunk snorted. As he glanced at the horse, a light caught his attention. A signal from one of his men. Dushyant marched toward him.

The man holding the lantern had a new scar that ran along the base of his neck. A scar he earned while fighting for him. "The council is ready for you, my king."

"Watch the hut," Dushyant ordered. The man nodded and handed the lantern to his king. Dushyant walked toward his tent. Two shadows joined him shortly, his guards sworn to protect him with their lives.

19

Dushyant could hear the grasses sway in the light wind as he approached the large tent. The chattering he heard from the outside subsided when he entered. Uniformly, his council stood and bowed to him. They all wore silk robes and gold jewelry while he stood in front of them in his dirty rags. They judged him as young and inexperienced already. Foolishly, he'd given them another reason to doubt him.

"All this mud. Do you want to change first?" Upananda whispered in his ear as he took the seat next to him. His advisor gazed at him with concern.

Dushyant shook his head and cleared his throat. "Did Prince Bhimasena reveal anything?"

"He has remained silent, my Majesty. But we have not tried our severe methods on him yet," said General Ayobahu.

"No," Dushyant uttered. He imagined Princess Lalitha finding her father with broken bones and bruises. *Curse her.* And curse himself for letting her affect him.

"Not yet," amended Dushyant. His men eyed him curiously at this sudden hesitation. Except for his advisor. Upananda, who had also served his father, had a knowing look on his face, like he could sense the reason for Dushyant's reluctance. But the man had no knowledge of the princess in his care.

"Wise decision, my Majesty. Prince Bhimasena will hold his tongue under torture. Earning his trust is the path to loosening it," said Upananda.

Dushyant inclined his head, gratitude surging in him for the support of his advisor. Earning the trust of the other men would not be so easy. "General, any news from King Samrat?"

"According to our spies, King Samrat has locked up Kanva," said Ayobahu.

"I heard King Samrat is an invalid with no interest in his duties. His brother, Prince Bhimasena, ruled the kingdom. With him captured, it is likely Queen Padmavati rules in her husband's name," said Upananda.

Whether the king or the queen held power mattered little to him. Garthapuri refused to release the man who killed King Lambhodara. Dushyant had promised to avenge his father when he'd lit his pyre. "How long can they withstand a siege?"

"They are better prepared to withstand a siege than we are prepared to engage in one," remarked Advisor Upananda.

General Ayobahu gave him a withering glance. "Words of a coward. Samrat has a smaller army than ours. We should invade him now. If we wait longer, then victory will elude us."

Dushyant glanced at the men around the table. Many had counseled his father before him, but he'd yet to learn where their loyalties stood. Briefly, he wished for the company of his father, who knew these men better than him. Then, he remembered how his father had let grief ruin his life. His father was not interested in his children, and though Dushyant would never state it aloud, he was relieved at his father's death. Dushyant would avenge King Lambhodara because it was his duty as the new king. Not because he loved his father. "What is the advice of this council?"

"Send a messenger to Samrat," Upananda answered.

Ayobahu, who had led from the front in many battles, leaned back with a scowl. "King Samrat has ignored the first three we sent. Why do we think the fourth one would be different?"

Dushyant stared at the men who bickered. They had failed to protect his father and now acted like children. "Enough," he said quietly. "How long do we need to prepare for a siege?"

"About two months. We need to recruit more men and collect supplies."

Ayobahu snorted. "A month should be plenty."

"Prepare for a siege," Dushyant ordered. A month or two gave him time to see things firsthand. Dushyant could change his plans once he knew more.

His servant, who had waited patiently, approached him after

the men emptied the tent. "My Majesty, I can draw you a bath," he said, observing his grimy appearance.

Dushyant remembered the princess stretched on top of him. Her scent lingered on him, and he was in no hurry to get rid of it. "I will find a river to bathe in," he assured the man and departed.

Ayobahu stood outside and fell in step with him. "Don't reveal anything about the princess," Dushyant warned his general.

Ayobahu dipped his head. "Do you still intend to accompany the princess?"

Dushyant nodded.

"There is an easy way to win the war. Make her yours."

Dushyant looked at the man with a pale scar stretching from his ear to his throat. He regretted spending so much time away from Vidarpur. He did not know these men who served him now. "Make her mine?"

"Dushyant," Ayobahu said his name to assert a friendliness that did not yet exist between them. "You are a king. While your first marriage is crucial to gain support for your rule, you can marry several women. Express your desire to marry her and claim her body. It will force her—"

"You are advising me to violate her," Dushyant stated calmly. He had no intention of revealing his loathing for such an act.

"You are in a war. Nobility will get you nowhere in defending your father's honor." Ayobahu grinned at him, and the scar made him menacing. What Ayobahu suggested would besmirch Dushyant's virtue.

"I will keep your words in mind," Dushyant answered, keeping his voice neutral.

His general bowed and turned back.

With Ayobahu's words ringing in his ears, he made his way back slowly. The man guarding the hut approached him. "All well?"

"Yes, my Majesty."

"I will sleep outside," said Dushyant. The sky lightened at the horizon. It would be dawn before he caught any sleep. While he watched the departing man, a loud owl hoot startled him. His guards were in place. At the hut, he pressed his ear to the door, hoping to hear stillness. Instead, he heard a loud hiss.

He touched his waist to feel his dagger. Then, he pushed the door open quietly. Still, it creaked faintly. From the threshold, the faint light from the solitary lamp illuminated a serpent ready to strike Princess Lalitha. She'd risen on her elbows. Except for her chest expanding and contracting, she appeared like a statue. Her eyes met his. He could sense the swelling panic in her.

Dushyant strode inside in one fluid motion, like a dancer moving on stage. His heart thudded as he watched the snake turn to him. *Come to me.*

The man and the beast glanced at each other. The snake darted from him to her, ready to strike. Dushyant could sense Lalitha watching him, but he kept his gaze on the snake.

He leaned in front, with his arm stretched toward the snake. Threatened by his action, the serpent hissed again. As the cobra brought its fangs down, Dushyant pulled his hand in and leaped to the other side. Before the snake could spin, he grabbed it right under its head. Lalitha watched him with her mouth open.

He marched outside and headed behind the hut. The sound of birds chased away the early morning darkness. Jayanth materialized next to him.

"My Majesty, was it wise for you to handle the snake?"

"There was no time to call for help." He could not risk her life.

The tail slashed wildly as the serpent tried to slip out. Jayanth frowned at him while gripping the other end of the cobra. Dushyant took a deep breath. Then nodding at Jayanth, he walked a few paces away. The beast slid its tongue out frantically.

"Now," said Dushyant and let go of the head of the snake. Hissing loudly, the cobra raised its hood to strike him. He hopped back while Jayanth swung the animal from its tail and tossed the cobra into the bushes. The serpent slithered away rapidly into the undergrowth.

Jayanth cursed while Dushyant touched his shoulder. Shaking his head, Dushyant grinned at him. But Jayanth did not seem amused.

Another guard joined them and inspected their arms. "No bite marks," the young guard whispered to his commander. Jayanth dismissed him.

"This mission is getting dangerous, my king," Jayanth said in his ears.

"I trust you to keep me alive." These guards had been by his side since his father had crowned him as his heir two years ago.

Jayanth shook his head. "Protecting you on the battlefield is an honor. This game of hide and seek is perilous."

"Just one more day," said Dushyant. Will that be enough to earn her trust?

"You are entering a viper's nest. Deadlier than this one snake." Jayanth stared at him like he was a child throwing a tantrum.

"I understand the danger," Dushyant said. Jayanth opened his mouth to say something but then shut it.

Dushyant watched him vanish and then returned to the hut.

Lalitha sighed on seeing him. "I heard noises outside, and I was worried."

"I struggled with the serpent for a few moments," he said, strangely pleased by her concern.

"Come closer, so I can check you," she ordered.

He banished the smile that erupted at her command and

stepped toward her. She scanned his skin. Then she looked at him with misty eyes.

"I owe you an apology," she mumbled, twisting her thick braid that fell below her waist. Dushyant viewed her intently. Her eyes darted to the ground as she blushed under his scrutiny.

"None needed, my lady. I would not have forgiven myself if you had perished to a snake bite."

She glanced up, and he bathed in the warmth emanating from her. Dushyant was in danger. Not from the serpent but from her.

"Puru, you saved my life twice. And I hid the truth from you. The time for my reveal has come. I am Princess Lalitha." A turbulent storm swept through Dushyant. He, too, hid his true identity from her. What will she say when she finds out?

"Help me reach the Garthapuri palace so I can save my kingdom from King Dushyant's invasion." A trace of bitterness rose in his throat. He was King Dushyant, and he intended to use her to conquer her kingdom.

"Please help me rescue my father," she pleaded. Dushyant could snap his fingers and release her father. But he would not. Prince Bhimasena would remain his prisoner while her uncle sheltered the man who had murdered his father.

5
LALITHA

*P*uru stood like a frozen statue as if he'd not heard a word she uttered. She'd hoped he would aid her. Did she make a mistake by trusting him with her name?

With trembling lips, she added, "I can pay you."

Puru came to life and knitted his brows. "Pay me?"

"For escorting me to safety."

He pressed his lips into a thin line. "Payment?" He paused for a long moment, and her stomach rose into her throat. What if he revealed her identity to her enemy? "A jewel from the princess would be sufficient."

She nodded, but her mistrust swept back in.

"Rest, my lady. I will return with some food."

He shut the door behind him, and she laid back on the mat. Sleep eluded her, and she worried about trusting this stranger. What choice did she have in her current state? If he betrayed her to that tyrant, at least she would join her father in the dungeon. Then she remembered her people who had perished under King Dushyant's attack. She owed it to them to defeat the king.

Light crept into the room, and she grew tired of waiting for him. She rolled to her side and stood on one leg. Hopping slowly, she reached the door and opened it.

Along with the creak of the door, she heard a muffled sound outside. Her heart pounding, she peeked through the opening. The corner of her eye caught a shadow, and she swiveled her head to the right. Nothing. Leaning on the door, she caught her breath. Her injury caused her to see a ghost in every shadow. Then, slowly, she pushed the door open and stumbled outside.

No sight of Puru. She scanned the surroundings and found more than one faint footprint on the ground in front. Puru and his cousin? Or was someone else spying on her? What if Puru had left to fetch the man he called commander? She did not want to meet the one who had confiscated her blade. She had to set off now. She hopped forward and searched for her horse and could not spot her. Curse the man. Did he steal her mare?

Just then, Lalitha heard a faint trot and saw Puru emerge from a distance mounted on her ride.

As he came closer, she saw water drops glisten on his bare chest. He halted and jumped off gracefully. With his wet hair sticking to his forehead, Puru appeared young and vulnerable.

"I borrowed your horse to ride to the river," he said. A river bath. She noticed the dhoti draped around his waist was old but clean.

"Is the river far?" she asked, longing to wash some dirt off her.

"No," he said, his face a mask. What did he hide behind that façade?

"Help me up on the horse and show me the way. I will go for a ride."

Puru raised his eyebrows. "How do you plan to dismount when you get there?"

Lalitha had not thought about that. She would risk harming her leg if she jumped.

"Allow me to ride with you," he said, his expression flat.

Lalitha twined her fingers, hoping to see another way. None appeared, so she inclined her head.

With a deep scowl etched on his forehead, he lifted her onto the saddle. Then he climbed behind her, taking care to leave some space between them. Yesterday, he seemed to have no problem touching her. Today, he acted as if she were a smoldering coal piece. Did her revelation affect him? Now that he knew her identity, he might be worried about offending her. That seemed a good thing. She did not want him to get too comfortable with her.

He tugged the reins, and her mare took off, eager to stretch her legs. Fields of rice flashed by, untouched by the war. She gazed at them, surprised Dushyant had not ordered his men to burn them. Invaders routinely burned crops to starve the locals.

The horse slid to a stop at the river bank, and Dushyant lowered her gently, holding her away from his chest like she reeked of a strange odor.

He handed her a new wrap for her injured leg.

"I will be behind the trees," he said and walked away swiftly. Lalitha sniffed her body. She smelled of herbs from her foot wrap. If that bothered him, that was his problem. She sat on the shore with her uninjured foot dangling in the water. A school of silverfish swam to her and then darted away. She scooped the cold water in her palm and washed the grime off her face and neck. She repeated the action a few times, feeling almost normal again. She untied the old swathe and washed her hurt leg carefully. The swelling had reduced since yesterday, and the touch of the cool stream restored her. She tied the new banana leaf around it.

Though Lalitha longed to linger, she called his name. He appeared with two small clay pots. The sour smell of fermented rice assaulted her.

He held one of the pots to her. "Rice with buttermilk."

She wrinkled her nose. Ignoring her, Puru sat a few feet away and started eating.

"Do you expect me to eat this?" she asked.

"Up to you," he said. "I am not sure when we will find food again," he added. Did his lips curl up for a brief instance? He seemed to mock her.

She cursed him silently and looked inside. She took a bite of the salted mango pickle and ate a mouthful of rice. The combination tasted surprisingly good. Before long, she cleaned the pot. She washed it in the river and filled it with fresh water. As she drank the liquid, she glanced at him. He stood and tossed his pot on the shore, breaking it into pieces. Then he wiped his mouth with the back of his hand, his arm muscles stretching taut. She looked away when he caught her watching him.

Her thoughts turned to her father's words before she left for her aunt's. Her father had promised to invite all the eligible noblemen in Garthapuri and hold a swayamvara for her to choose her groom. Though, she did not plan to invite kings or princes. Neither her uncle nor her father had any male heirs. They had raised her to rule as Garthapuri's queen. A marriage of equals was not what she sought. She needed a husband who would obey her when she wore the crown.

Puru's shadow fell on her, and she regarded him. She needed to marry an inferior who was still acceptable to the lords of her court.

"Are you ready?" Puru asked, his face blank. The man seemed impervious to emotions. Would that make him a good husband?

When she did not answer, he cleared his throat.

She nearly jumped.

"Do you need to return to the hut, or can we depart from here?" he asked as if he were addressing a child.

"Are we traveling by the same horse?" she asked stupidly. Suddenly, she did not relish riding with Puru.

"I see no other way, my lady," he said. His face contorted briefly as if the mere thought of accompanying her agonized him.

"My leg is healing, so I will not be a burden for long," she said, hurt by his expression.

His mask went up. "It is my honor to serve you," he mumbled, still looking like one led to a torture chamber. Why did he despise her company?

"Your cousin is not joining us?" Lalitha asked.

"He is a wiser man than I," he replied, gazing at her.

She opened her mouth as if to say something and then shut it. For his troubles, she would pay Puru well when she reached the safety of her castle.

They made their way north silently. The wind rippled through the fields, rustling the rice stalks. Clouds sped across the sky as Puru spurred her horse. She keenly sensed all the parts of her touching him—her thigh, shoulder, and hip. He smelled of fresh rain with a hint of the earth. The scent that arose when the first drizzle touched the ground.

To distract herself from these thoughts, she started talking to him.

"I was surprised to see the fields unharmed. Why do you think King Dushyant hasn't burned them?"

She could sense him stiffening and turned to look at him. A muscle twitched in his firm jaw.

"The king's war is not with the common people," said Puru slowly.

"What a strange notion," she said. "Most kings would claim all was fair in war and lay the land to waste."

"Those kings would be fools then," he said stiffly.

She peeked at him, surprised he voiced that view. Fortunately, he regarded the horizon, and her gaze lingered on his profile. He looked nearly handsome except for his large ears that protruded from his face like a fan. A luxurious mustache adorned his upper lip. A strange urge to tug it took hold of her, and she clenched her fist firmly and turned away.

Their slower pace gave her plenty of opportunity to enjoy the scenery. The sparse trees surrounding them allowed the light to cascade in, illuminating their path. Tiny white flowers spread on the ground like a carpet, dispersing their fragrances into the air.

"Wait here," he whispered suddenly. Lalitha nodded without turning to look at him. He jumped off and strode toward a clump of trees. The five trees clustered together appeared ordinary except for the anthill next to them. He knelt on the earth between the anthill and the trees and moved the leaves covering the ground. It appeared like he felt around for something. Then he peeled back a jute cloth and uncovered something. She watched with mounting interest as he reached in and pulled out a bag. Without looking inside, he slung the bag over his shoulder. Then he stood up and scanned the area. An owl hooted loudly, frightening her. She searched the tree branches for the bird. Only seeing some crows, she wondered if she had mistaken the sound.

He walked back and halted a yard away. He peeked inside his bag and pulled out something dark.

Puru shook the ugly nest out and then placed it around his chin. False beard! He wore a disguise to escort her. Why did he hide it in the dirt? He threaded the ends into his hair and tied a knot. The long, crooked beard on his youthful face caused her to snicker.

"What?"

"You need to fix it."

"Why? What is wrong?"

Puru turned sideways to inspect himself, and she laughed at the sight.

"I am glad to be a source of amusement, my lady," he said, a rare smile erupting on his face. His eyes crinkled in the corners, and she gulped her glee.

"The hair on your head does not match the beard," she said, looking away.

"I know," he said. Curious, Lalitha glanced at him as he pulled out a wig. That looked worse than what covered his chin. He placed it on his head and spun for her.

"How do I look?"

She howled, tears streaming down her cheeks. His eyes twinkled. Tying his bag, Puru climbed behind her.

As he reached to hold the reins, his hand grazed her waist. Her skin burst into flame. What foolishness, she scolded herself. He was a nobody. Not worthy of her. But a man like Puru might heed her wishes, whereas even a vassal might seize control of her throne. Immediately, she scolded herself. She knew nothing about this stranger. She could not be contemplating a lifelong union with him.

She sat straight. "Why does a bladesmith need a disguise?"

"Because kidnapping a princess is a dangerous business."

"Kidnapping?" she asked and glanced at him.

A teasing smile played on his lips and caused a flutter in her stomach. "Are you traveling willingly with a strange man?"

Heat rushed into her face, and she tore her eyes away from his idiotic grin.

"Do you know what the punishment is for abducting a princess?" she asked sharply.

"Hence the disguise, my lady," he said lightly. "Though I believe you would never accuse me of a false crime."

His words confused her. "N-No," she stammered.

A delicate fragrance floated in the air, and she noticed a Champa tree up ahead, laden with buds and flowers.

"My sisters love these flowers," said Puru and reached up to pluck a flower in the color of an elephant's tusk. He held the bloom to her in his palm. A dusting of tiny yellow pollen coated his skin.

Lalitha picked up the bloom and brought it to her nose. The scent reminded her of spring and laughter. She tried to tuck the flower into her hair but nearly slid off the horse.

Puru grasped her waist and pushed her back, sending a strange tingling sensation all over her body. "Allow me," he said, taking the Champa bloom from her hand. His fingers were long and lean but hardy. They brushed hers like the wings of a butterfly, causing her heart to race. He tucked the flower into her hair, his touch like a whisper in her ear, reverberating through her body and making her tremble. "Beautiful," he muttered, and she gazed at him. His eyes caressed her face, and heat rushed into her cheeks.

"Your sisters?" Lalitha asked, looking at the trees.

Puru did not answer for a while. "I have two sisters," he said after a long pause.

"Younger than you?"

He grunted a yes.

"I wish I had a sister or a brother," said Lalitha. She was close to her friend, Agamathi. But, the company of a sibling would have helped her handle her estranged parents better.

"Mine are living with my aunt. I have not seen them in more than a month." She heard faint notes of longing in his voice. Puru said no more, and Lalitha did not press him.

They left the forest behind and entered a village. The sun had started its descent in the west and painted everything orange. She felt safe riding with Puru and strangely content. Near the village square, sweet music rose to the accompaniment of a mellow drum. Young maidens wearing flower ornaments danced to the beat while men wearing Asoka leaf wreaths threw turmeric and vermillion powder on them. The spilled dust caused the women's saris to appear like molten gold.

"It is the Vasantotsava festival," said Puru in a strange tone.

Her people celebrated the festival of spring to honor the rebirth of the god of love, Kama. In the past, Lalitha had only watched the festivities from her palace balcony. Today, she stood amid the hum of the people's merriment.

She'd expected distress among her people. Instead, joy flowed around her like a rising river. "I cannot believe King Dushyant is allowing these celebrations," she whispered.

Puru shifted in the saddle but did not say anything.

An older woman beckoned them to join the festivities. He dismounted and held the reins, and the rejoicing crowd pulled Puru and her forward.

A young man scattered the fragrant powder, tinted yellow by saffron dust, on her. A woman moved sensuously toward them and presented a twig of mango blossoms to her.

"Strike your lover with it," she said laughingly. Lalitha flushed as she realized the blossoms formed part of the god of love's arrow.

"Is he your brother?" the woman asked, pointing toward Puru.

"No," Lalitha whispered.

"You will be joined in marriage with your lover if you touch him with the mango blossom on this day when Kama was reborn," she said.

"Same is true for you if you throw this red powder on the girl of your heart," she added, pressing vermillion powder into Puru's hand.

Lalitha woke to her senses as Puru gazed at her. His eyes seemed to seek nothing save her. Yet, they remained clouded like a misty river hiding its reeds. Any feelings presumed were on her end, for he remained unaffected like water on a lotus leaf. She imagined her father chained to the wall of a dark dungeon. Though her uncle was king, her father had ruled Garthapuri. Without her father, Garthapuri was leaderless. Lalitha knew marriage was never about love. Her parents' separation had provided ample proof for that. Lalitha wanted two things from a union: sons to wear the crown and a husband who would let her govern Garthapuri till her firstborn son came of age. The fate of Garthapuri rested with her, and she would not squander her kingdom's future. Her marriage was always her sacrifice for her land.

She tossed the mango twig on the floor, reddened by the drops of powder from the boisterous dancers.

"I have no need for Kama's blessing," said Lalitha defiantly. A boy chased a girl in front of her, and the girl laughing rapturously, nearly collided with her mare. The young couple spun on their heels with hasty apologies and ran in a different direction. A yearning surged through her, and she suppressed it vehemently, took hold of the reins, and rode away from the village and the festivity. She had no time for merrymaking.

6

DUSHYANT

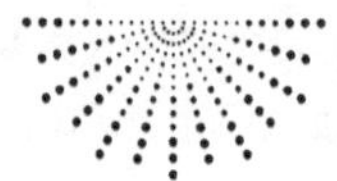

As the people around him celebrated the Vasantotsava festival, Dushyant regarded Princess Lalitha, unable to tear his eyes away. Under the golden light, her thick dark hair glistened like the deep blue night sky. Her back straight, Lalitha moved swiftly, creating a dust cloud of saffron behind her. Kama, the god of love, would gladly wed this princess with no blemish.

He opened his fingers and let the vermillion spill to the ground. But a light breeze picked it up and created a swirl around his ankles, mirroring the agitation in his mind. He'd hoped to gain Lalitha's trust and use her to defeat her uncle. Instead, he was in danger of becoming entangled with her. He abhorred attachments since he'd seen how they made his father weak. He remembered the day his mother had died a decade ago. Holding the hands of his little sisters, Ambika and Kanika, ten-year-old Dushyant approached his father's chambers. As Dushyant stood by the door, he heard the servant announce them. His father denied them entry. His father's words still echoed in Dushyant's head. With her gone, his father had stated, he could not bear to look at her children. *Her children!* Tugging his sisters along, Dushyant had walked back to his chambers, tears streaming down his chin. That was the last time Dushyant had wept. Four-year-old Ambika had cried for their mother incessantly, not understanding she would never return. Six-year-old Kanika had huddled close to him and refused to leave his side. He'd held Ambika in his arms and rocked her to sleep, humming a song his mother sang to them. His father had remained a shell ever since, and Dushyant had vowed to keep his heart closed to love. Such attachment only resulted in pain and suffering.

"King Dushyant sanctioned the festivities. He said his men would hold off any attacks during this time," said a man walking past him, bringing Dushyant back to the present. He'd granted the villages around the fort permission to celebrate. If he sieged the fort, he needed these villages to aid his conquest and knew simple acts like these helped overcome any resistance.

Lalitha halted her horse at the edge of the village. He strolled toward her before she changed her mind and fled.

She glared at him so severely he expected his body to burst into flames. "Don't get any ideas about me," she spat out her words. He sympathized with her. Like him, her duties to her kingdom preceded any demands of the god of love.

"What ideas would that be, my lady?" he asked, feigning humility.

She tossed her head like an angry mare, causing her braid to swing side to side. "I am hungry. Find me some food," she ordered, her tone dismissive. But her pale knuckles betrayed her emotions. Puru, an ordinary swordsmith, was not her peer in stature or wealth. Did she worry about developing feelings for him? Could he exploit her weakness? That would not be honorable. He wanted her trust, not her adoration.

His eyes swept the area, and he spotted a temple. "Stay here, my lady. I will bring us something to eat." She ignored him and stared straight ahead.

Mingling with the crowd, he heard the conversations as he strolled through the narrow street.

"King Samrat ordered our granary to be emptied and sent to the palace. I pleaded with the village elders to share some of our harvests back with us so we don't starve," said a thin man to another. Samrat was stockpiling for a siege.

He joined the devotees who had gathered for the twilight *pooja* and entered the temple courtyard. The brick wall had crumbled in places and looked in need of repair. The black granite idol wore no jewels. Simple flowers adorned the god.

"Let me be your vessel for good," Dushyant said his usual prayer silently and approached the priest handing out the prasad. He received one ripe banana. During the festival, wealthy families typically donated food to be shared with the devotees. He suspected that people were hoarding their grains. Princess Lalitha would not be pleased with a single banana, especially if she had to share it with him. He smiled at that thought.

He walked around the small courtyard, observing the crowd. Turmeric, vermillion, or saffron dust coated the skin of many young people, evidence of their participation in the spring festival. For a moment, envy stabbed his heart.

"Did you lose the girl of your heart?" a woman with greying hair and wrinkled skin asked.

With his eyes narrowed, Dushyant quickened his pace without responding to her.

"You would be a fool to let her go," she said to his receding back. He was a fool to let her affect him.

On the way back, someone bumped into him. He nearly grabbed the wrist of the older man with a long grey beard. The eyes twinkled at him. Jayanth!

Jayanth inclined his head toward a small alley, and Dushyant followed him. "The beard suits you," Dushyant teased him when they were alone. The one he wore irritated his skin, and he'd been fighting the urge to scratch his chin.

"At least I am not wearing a sari," Jayanth grimaced, gesturing toward a slender girl in a blue sari holding a basket of flower garlands. Dushyant recognized his young guard in the alert eyes that swept the street. The closer they approached the Garthapuri castle, the more risk his men had to take to defend him. He felt like a thorn pricked his finger.

"Jayanth, keep them safe," he urged the head of his guard.

Jayanth eyed him intently. "Being part of your guard is the most coveted job for our soldiers. So these are the best of our men, well-trained and loyal. They understand the risk." Dushyant knew each of his guards would use their body as a shield to protect him. The knowledge only increased his guilt. He tugged his ear as if that would ease his discomfort.

Jayanth dropped a banana leaf into his palm. It contained still-warm rice cooked with jaggery and ghee. The faint smell of cardamom floated from it.

"I was worried I would have to face the wrath of the princess when I handed her a single banana," Dushyant grinned.

"She is attracting attention," Jayanth whispered.

"From Samrat's men?" Lalitha wore no concealment. Dushyant did not know if the Garthapuri men knew her by sight.

"Our men," said Jayanth, surprising him. "A lady traveling alone by horse is garnering the attention of our spies sprinkled among the crowd. If they inspect closely, they will recognize you. That would jeopardize your plan."

He'd to abandon the horse, but Lalitha could not walk for long. "Find a cart with a covered wagon and bring it along," said Dushyant, sharing his plan.

Jayanth left to carry out his orders while Dushyant returned to Lalitha.

"Did you eat yours?" Lalitha asked when he handed her the rice.

Dushyant showed her the banana. "That's all the rice I found." Why didn't Jayanth get him more? He did not lack coins.

She frowned at the food. "We will split it," she declared while staring at the food as if it would magically expand. Her words tugged his heart. She wanted to share the food with an ordinary man, a near stranger.

"There is just enough rice for one person," he started, but she interrupted him.

"Help me off the mare," she ordered. Her face turned pale as if his touch repulsed her. Dushyant feared it, too, because he wanted to hold her closer.

With one arm under her knees and the other around her mid-back, he lowered her to the ground. She gazed at him with those brown eyes of hers. In the setting sun, they turned golden. He wanted to fall into them and never leave. She let out a long breath when he moved away. Using her right hand, she separated the rice into two halves.

"I will eat this half and give you the rest," she said, pointing to the shorter mound. She picked up a small portion of the rice with three fingers and blew on it before putting it in her mouth. Dushyant watched it travel down her slender neck and turned away. It would be foolish to let his heart rule his mind.

A sudden commotion caught his eye. Two drunk men held the reins of her horse. He recognized his men.

"This is a pretty donkey. Our father would be proud if we bring it home." They started untying the rope.

"Hey," he yelled at them.

Lalitha shook her head at him to be quiet. She did not want to create a scene as he'd hoped. He stood still, letting them *steal* the horse.

When they moved away, he stomped his feet, pretending to be frustrated. "What now? How will we get to our destination?"

She handed him the remaining food. "My silver anklet. Can you find us another horse by selling it?"

Another thorn pricked his heart, but he ignored it. He nodded, not trusting his voice. "Eat," she commanded and dug into her waist pouch for the jewel. She pulled the anklet he'd helped remove from her leg and offered it to him.

Dushyant threw the empty leaf wrapping and wiped his ghee-coated fingers on his shawl. He approached Lalitha and held out his palm. She placed the faintly gleaming jewel on it. Using his index finger, he rolled it, admiring the intricate craftsmanship. He put it in his pouch, vowing to return it to her when Garthapuri became his.

"Please stay here, my lady. I will find us a transport," said Dushyant and departed. He met Jayanth shortly after. His guard rode a bullock cart with a cloth-covered wagon.

"Are you ready for me?" Jayanth asked.

Dushyant nodded. "Is there space in the back?" he asked and walked around the cart.

Sacks of some kind filled the back, leaving hardly any room for them.

"How do you expect the two of us to fit in the back?" he asked, trying hard to be patient.

"Poor folks travel with goods," Jayanth answered. He was right. It would be rare for carts just to transport people. "You can sit right next to me while the lady can sit in the back."

Dushyant sighed and hopped on next to him. The bull flicked his tail and hit his lower leg. He grimaced.

"Wait till he drops his dung," said Jayanth, grinning at him. Dushyant rolled his eyes. This was his idea, so he refrained from complaining.

When they reached the princess, she looked up at him. He jumped down and walked to her.

"This is the best you could find?" she asked, wrinkling her nose.

"Yes," he said and lifted her in his arms. She pinched her brows and studied him like she wanted to find his darkest secrets. He arranged his face so it betrayed no emotions though he longed to press his lips to the corner of her mouth that turned up. When he walked toward the back, she said, "No, to the front."

He halted. "The bulls smell like dung," he mumbled. Would Lalitha recognize Jayanth if she sat next to him?

"Then you should sit next to me," she grinned for a moment. Just as suddenly, her smile vanished like she remembered something terrible.

He placed her gently next to Jayanth.

"Puru, do you know how to drive this wagon?" she asked.

He sensed a smile erupting on Jayanth's face and cursed him silently. "I can manage," he muttered.

"I will take a nap in the back," said Jayanth and hobbled off the cart.

Dushyant took his spot and tugged the reins. The two bulls moved slowly.

"What is in the sacks?" Lalitha asked.

"Coconuts," Jayanth answered and leaned on them. He shut his eyes, pretending to go to sleep.

"Can he hear us?" asked Lalitha, leaning in to whisper in his ear. Faint notes of saffron still clung to her.

"The old man likely has ears like a bat," said Dushyant, resisting the urge to pull her against him. "I am new to these parts. Which path should we take to your castle?"

She arched her brows and looked at him like he'd grown wings. "I am surprised you are asking me for directions when you pointedly ignored my counsel earlier."

A smile threatened to erupt on his face, and Dushyant barely suppressed it. "Those earlier times you wanted to jeopardize your well-being. Now, it feels prudent to ask you for the way to your palace."

Her face brightened like the moon peeking from behind clouds. "Prudent says the man who picked a fight with an enemy commander."

Dushyant allowed his lips to curl up.

Lalitha smiled. "We can travel through the forest and then take the king's road once we get to the river. Be careful in the woods. A group of bandits has been spotted there from time to time, and they are known to terrorize the travelers along that route."

Dushyant nodded. Any bandits trying to attack them would meet a swift end at the hands of the guards following him. The wagon lumbered along as flies swarmed the cart. The bulls swished their tails to swat them away. He crossed his legs under him to avoid being hit by the hairy tails.

She remained silent for some time in the gathering darkness. "I was expecting disaster and ruin when I heard Dushyant was marching his army," she whispered, gazing at the trees swaying in the light breeze. "Instead, people are celebrating. I don't know what to make of the king."

Dushyant knew Jayanth had heard every word. Instead of answering her, he asked her a question. "Why did you choose to come unaccompanied?"

She glanced at him with fire in her eyes. "I heard my father had led a small army to face King Dushyant. And then, no news of him reached me. I could not wait. Why did that vile king attack us unprovoked?"

"Unprovoked?" he asked, keeping a tight leash on his emotions. "Do you not know what happened?"

She looked at him with her eyes wide open. In another life, he would have wanted to swim in their warmth. "Tell me what you know," she whispered.

Dushyant breathed in deeply. "I don't know the complete story. King Lambhodara had gone hunting. Kanva, one of the commanders in his army, pierced him with an arrow. Instead of waiting to save his king, he fled to Garthapuri." The truth about why Kanva committed treason remained concealed from him, and Dushyant worried he could not face the answer. "King Samrat gave Kanva shelter in his castle and has refused to meet the messengers from Dushyant."

"And Dushyant wants to avenge his father's death," she finished the story for him, her fingers twined tightly in her lap.

7

LALITHA

She shivered in the cold, alone in the dark. Suddenly, someone wrapped her in a soft blanket. She felt warm and safe. The gentle motion of the cart rocked her back to sleep.

She heard the tinkle of bells. And then stillness. Her head swayed from side to side and then halted. A light wind rustled her hair, and her eyes opened. She spotted the deep blue sky dotted with stars. As she followed their path, her sight landed on a pair of eyes glinting like an ocean. Puru?

The bells rang again as the bulls shook their heads. Lalitha turned to look at them and spotted a cotton dhoti. Did her head rest on his lap? She bolted up and hit his chin.

His face contorted in pain. She reached out to touch him and then dropped her hand. Puru blinked his eyes and looked at her.

"You fell asleep," he said, his voice devoid of emotions. A shadow covered his face, and her toes curled in embarrassment. How could she have let sleep claim her in the presence of a stranger? Puru reached out to her, and she shrank from him. His eyes still as a waveless pond, he tucked her hair behind her ears with tenderness. Then, she noticed the cotton cloth that covered her. Did he fetch the sheet for her? Her heart beat faster, imagining him taking care of her.

Confused by her emotions, she asked a more mundane question. "Why did we stop?"

He pointed his finger, and she followed it to see her castle appear like a dark hill. Then the clouds parted, and the moon peeked out. In its silvery glow, the palace towers gleamed. A flag fluttered in the wind. Though she could not see it, she knew a pink lotus adorned the flag.

"We part here. I cannot accompany you any further," said Puru as he stepped down from the cart.

She turned toward him, and he appeared like a sculpted statue while she ached all over, like a part of her was ripped. She wanted him to stay. *Forever. Be hers.* Why did he seem unaffected while her insides churned at their separation? With determination, she squashed the turmoil brewing in her head. She could not fall for a man with no titles or land. However, if she wanted to rule Garthapuri, a strong man like Puru might be a better partner than one of her lieges.

"Here is your knife," he said, and she was confused by his possession of it. He held out the weapon. She took it from him, their fingers touching, tingling her skin. He was silent for a moment while she felt dizzy with his closeness. "This path should lead you back home," he said. "Leave now, and you will reach the castle as the sun rises."

"How did you get this?" she asked, rubbing the handle.

He shrugged his shoulders. "I confiscated it from the man with the mustache."

At the mention of the Commander, Lalitha remembered Puru had agreed to escort her for payment. Lalitha bent to unscrew her remaining anklet. "I only have this jewel to pay you."

Puru stepped closer, pulled her hand away from her leg, and covered it with both of his, heat spreading from his fingers down her arms. She wanted to stay there, touching him. "There is no need. I still have the other anklet."

His skin set hers on fire, and her heart thudded faster. Ignoring it, she asked, "Did you not use it to pay for the cart?" She spun around to look at the back of the wagon. Empty except for the coconuts. "Where did the other man go?"

"Lalitha," he said, using her name for the first time. Lalitha glanced at him as the warmth from his hands found its way into her heart.

"If you are in danger," he paused here. A flicker of emotions crossed his face like a fleeting lightning bolt. She waited for him to continue. "If you are in danger, send me a message." He continued to hold her hand, and she let him.

"Send you a message? How?" she asked as if she contemplated sending him a letter. She was a princess. If someone threatened her, what could an ordinary man do?

He gazed at her as if trying to read her mind. "At the Goddess Durga temple, a neem tree leans on the courtyard wall. It has a small hole in the back of the trunk. Leave a message in the hollow, and it will find its way to me."

Her eyes darted to their clasped hands. "What if you need to reach me?" she asked and then wished she could take her words back. She did not want him to contact her. *A lie.* She wanted him in her life.

He let go of her hand and lifted her chin. His eyes stirred her stomach. "If I need you, I will show up at your door." He dropped his hand. "Farewell, my lady." With that, he walked away, leaving her seated on the empty cart. Watching his back, she understood she'd lost something but did not know where to begin looking for it.

8

DUSHYANT

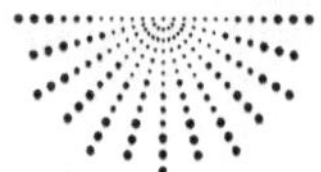

*L*alitha had fallen asleep on his lap. He was acutely aware of all the parts of her that touched him. And he kept gazing at her, feeling a tug in his heart unlike any he'd experienced before. Her face was serene and wiped clean of all the demons troubling her. She even murmured his name. No, not his name. She despised King Dushyant. She murmured the name of the ghost he'd created: Puru, the man who did not exist.

His horse snorted and brought him back to the present. Another horse appeared alongside him, Jayanth's.

"Did the princess reach her castle?" asked Dushyant.

"Yes, I saw her cart ride into the fort."

"I told her about the hole in the neem tree."

Jayanth spun in his seat and stared at him. Dushyant looked straight ahead, trying to avoid revealing what he did not want to examine himself.

"So she can reach you?"

"Yes, if she is in danger." Or if she needed him or wanted to see him.

"Love makes us fools," Jayanth muttered.

"Love?" Dushyant scoffed, denying the warmth uncoiling in

his stomach when he imagined her in his arms. "Would you be able to sneak me into the castle? Once I am in, with her help, I can capture Kanva." He could put to rest the ghost of his father haunting him.

Jayanth shook his head. "I can breach their security and slip you in. But leaving the castle will not be easy. If Gartha-puri men catch you, your life will be in danger." Jayanth did not add that Lalitha could betray him, but Dushyant knew that possibility existed. She would betray him if she learned his identity.

They rode back to his men camped on a meadow and arrived as the sun descended.

"Jayanth, get some rest. We can discuss the matter tomor-row." Since the hunt for Kanva started, he'd barely slept.

He bathed in a nearby stream, ate all the food his servant brought him without tasting anything and fell asleep as soon as his head touched the simple wooden cot.

Princess Lalitha approached him with a smile. He hid behind his wooden mask, watching her hips sway.

"Let me see your face," she said and pulled his mask. A toe-curling scream erupted from her, banishing the smile that slowly bloomed on his face.

"My Majesty," a hand shook his shoulder. He opened his eyes to gaze at his guard. Jayanth stood at the foot of his bed. "A messenger arrived from the minister this morning."

Dushyant wiped his eyes roughly and swung his legs down.

Jayanth handed him a palm scroll.

Dushyant perused the message. *"Several village elders have gathered outside the palace requesting to speak with the king about the additional levies. It would be prudent for the king to return to the capital to meet with them."*

"What new levies have we imposed?" he whispered, his voice measured.

Jayanth shrugged his shoulders.

He heard voices outside, and Advisor Upananda entered the tent, followed by one of his guards.

"He wanted to see you immediately and did not want to wait," the guard apologized.

"Treat him like an intruder," said Jayanth, twisting his mustache.

"What? There is no need for that. I am here on urgent royal business."

Another guard entered, and the two men held Upananda's thin shoulders to drag him out.

"My Majesty," Upananda howled.

Dushyant kept a straight face. "Jayanth will throw me in a cell if that will keep me safe. Follow his orders."

Upananda shook both men off and bowed deeply. "Apologies for my mistake," he said with the corners of his lips drawn and then left the tent.

Jayanth grinned at Dushyant. "That man thinks he runs this place."

Dushyant let his lips curl up. "He was my father's advisor. Go easy on him."

A guard peeked in. "Upananda is here to see you, my Majesty."

He waved him in.

Upananda bowed from his waist again. "Forgive my intrusion earlier."

"Upananda, I have a message from Minister Panini about village elders protesting new tariffs. Why did we levy them?"

"We needed funds for this invasion," said Upananda, rubbing his forehead.

"What happened to the crown funds?"

"King Lambhodara had spent most of our funds. The minister and I tried to prevent the complete collapse of the kingdom, but we had to obey him." Upananda rubbed his thigh. "A wise ruler can restore us to glory," he said and gazed at

Dushyant. Wise? He was his father's son. Could he succeed where his father had failed?

Dushyant's servant entered the room with his morning meal. After they broke their morning fast on finger-length bananas and lightly seasoned boiled rice, he said, "Upananda, stay here and help General Ayobahu prepare for the siege. I will set things in order in Vidarpur and return to lead the battle."

"My Majesty, this is a trivial matter that I can sort out. Allow me to ride to the capital and settle this."

Dushyant wanted to stay and follow Lalitha into her castle. He suppressed that longing. Since his father's death a moon month ago, he'd been chasing Kanva and left the actual ruling to his minister. He did not know about his kingdom's affairs, and it could not continue that way. "Upananda, I have to start governing this land. I will entrust the war efforts to you and return to our capital."

Dushyant started his journey soon after. Instead of dashing past the first village, he halted in it. Surprised to see their king, the folks arranged for feasts and dances. Seated on the floor, he asked after their welfare over the meal served on a banana leaf.

"How was the rice harvest?"

"With god's grace, even with our paltry rains, we had a good harvest. This village sent fifty bags of grain to the palace," one of the elders stated.

"Asking for more—" a young man began, but their headman silenced him with a piercing look.

Dushyant surveyed the men who sat around him. They sat stoically with tiredness etched on their faces. "Let him speak," he said softly.

"My Majesty, we just received a summons for more grains. Our families would starve if we sent more." An older man wiped his eyes while others bowed their heads, staring at their hands.

His heart twisted at their plight. "The man who killed our king is hiding, and I need coins to wage this war," Dushyant stated, keeping his struggles to himself. As he saw their resigned faces, he added, "No need to send more grains yet. I will send another message for them."

In the next village, he approached a young cowherd reclining under a tree. While his cows grazed the tall grass, he rested on his back, staring at the sky. Dushyant followed his gaze to watch a few clouds shift their shapes.

"Bow to your king," one of his guards said.

Startled, the boy jumped up and stared at him. Then he prostrated on the ground, his forehead touching the soil.

"Rise," Dushyant ordered, and the boy stood scratching his elbow. "What do you get paid for watching these cows?"

"Last year, I got enough milk for my brothers and me. And butter for my mother and a bag of rice. Sometimes, I would get bananas too. Now, I only get watered-down milk."

Dushyant looked at his patched dhoti and thin face. He took out a silver coin from his pouch and held it out. The cowherd took it from him and gazed at it with interest. "Give it to your mother," said Dushyant and rode off.

Village after village, similar tales unfolded. The narrow streets leading through them offered glimpses of torn clothes, broken carts, and leaky roofs. The dull eyes staring at him expressed more than any uttered words.

As Dushyant neared the city, he passed foundries with huge furnaces that made copper and silver. Thin wispy smoke oozed from them and cast a gray gloom over the sky. The mines were to the east of them. Once, statues, weapons, coins, and jewels manufacturing thrived in this region. But, in the last decade, like in many other areas, the mines were neglected by his father. He should visit them soon and sanction the needed repairs.

On a cloudy morning, he arrived on the king's road and gazed at the Vidarpur city carved out of the basalt cliffs in the Nandri hills. The dark rock surface gleamed in the light. The construction that began during his great-great-grandfather's reign was completed during his grandfathers'. He rode the short distance uphill and entered the castle with a heavy burden pressing down on him.

"My Majesty," Minister Panini greeted him warmly. His eyes gazed at Dushyant kindly from beneath his gray eyebrows.

"I can grant an audience to the village elders today," said Dushyant.

Panini stared at him with his mouth wide open. Collecting himself, he said, "I will arrange for it, my king." Then he handed Dushyant a scroll. "A message arrived from your sisters."

His face brightened in anticipation as Dushyant grasped the palm leaf. His sisters, Kanika and Ambika, had remained with his aunt in Jaisalpur, and he missed their merry presence.

Dear Brother,

Your last letter was too brief but still gave us much joy. We pray you catch the murderer who killed our father soon.

Today is a day of fasting and prayer. You know how strict our aunt is about those. Still, Ambika and I have managed to eat some ripe bananas dipped in honey to keep hunger at bay.

We are continuing to study our history and poetry. Do you know how many poems there are about swords? Too many. Don't the poets know any idiot can brandish a sword?

Ambika wants me to write about a giant peacock that tried to attack her. She dodged it by somersaulting, much to our aunt's chagrin.

Your battle adventure worries and troubles us very much. May Goddess Durga's blessing stay with you.

Brother, you promised to send a word so we can come and live with you in Vidarpur. We are eagerly awaiting your letter though we lack nothing in our aunt's place except you.

Your Sisters, Kanika and Ambika

He smiled as he read Kanika's words. The letter brought forth a longing to see his sisters. Dushyant desired to fetch them, but till he apprehended his father's assassin, there was a bleakness about the palace. He wanted to clear out the cobwebs that his father had allowed to accumulate before bringing his sisters. He would sit down and write a response to them today. For an instant, he wondered if his sisters would approve of Lalitha. He burst that thought as soon as it emerged. He had no room for Lalitha in his life. Like a farmer weeding his land, he needed to remove her image from his mind. But she clung to him like his breath, and he cursed himself for his weakness.

Dushyant entered his chambers and walked through the first room that held no hint of him. He'd never lived long enough in Vidarpur to add personal touches, and the bare room screamed at him. The next space housed a round table and chairs carved from the rocks. The table meant for family meals had seen only his company. He glanced at the lone painting adorning the wall. His sisters sat on the laps of his smiling parents while he stood between them. A vision of his mother and sisters plucking flowers in the garden erupted in his mind, along with their laughter. All the joy in the castle had vanished with his mother. Only an eerie stillness remained in its place. He entered his bedroom and let his servant help him out of his clothes. After washing the dirt off his body, he dressed in fine silk. Images of the patched garments worn by his subjects flashed in his mind. He dispelled them while vowing to bring back prosperity to his kingdom. His servant brought his crown on a silver platter. As he held the gold crown crusted with sapphires, he remembered trying it on as a young boy. Then, the headdress had slipped to his nose. Now, it sat snugly on his forehead.

Dushyant strode to the throne room and paused. The ghost of his father sat on the silver throne, combing his beard with his fingers. Dushyant blinked, and the mirage vanished. He climbed the three steps to the chair, aware of the eyes on his back. He sat on the edge of his seat and scanned the room. In front of him stood Minister Panini and other members of his council.

Above him, the balcony that his mother had used remained

empty. Though she'd died a decade ago in childbirth when he was only ten, he felt her presence within these walls. When he did something wrong as a child, she never admonished him. Instead, she would tug his ear in affection and ask him if he knew how he'd erred. He reached to touch his ear lobe, wishing for her wisdom to guide him.

Smoke from the mounted torches created a haze, and the many carved pillars hid most of the corners from his sight.

Minister Panini cleared his throat. "Can I fetch the village elders, my Majesty?"

Dushyant inclined his head. Minister Panini clapped his hands, and six men entered the room. Their bodies worn by hard work and faces darkened by the sun, they bowed to him in unison.

"I heard you had a petition for me," Dushyant stated.

"My Majesty, we thank you for seeing us today. We pray to God Vishnu that the kingdom will prosper under your rule. For the past few years, the crown has asked us to provide more and more of our harvest, leaving little for seed grains or our children." As he regarded their thin frames, he could imagine them rationing their meals.

Another man with a missing finger stepped forward. "This latest order would starve us. Instead, we can spare our boys to fight in the army."

Dushyant heard their stories patiently. He did not want to shed the blood of farmers on his fields. "Come see me tomorrow. I will have an answer for you," he said and dismissed them.

Later that day, he regarded the council members who had gathered there. "Where did the coins go?" he asked.

"King Lambhodara was fond of feasts and horses," said one.

"He invited dancers from all over to Vidarpur and showered them with gifts," said another.

Dushyant rubbed his forehead. Hidden in their words were stories about his father they did not want to reveal.

"Find ways to cut our expenses. We will meet again tonight to go over it," Dushyant ordered and dismissed them.

Dushyant sat with his head in his palm. He had been away at his aunt's for too long, and it appeared his father had abandoned his duties.

"My Majesty," Minister Panini whispered.

He looked up to see the man lingering at the door.

"There is someone I would like you to meet."

"Who?"

"Kanva's daughter," said the minister. The daughter of his father's murderer?

9

LALITHA

"Give me a hand," Lalitha yelled to a maid. Leaning on her, Lalitha hopped up the palace stairs wishing for the sturdy arms of Puru to steady her.

"Is the king in his chambers?" she asked, dragging herself to her uncle's room. Foolish question. Her uncle rarely left his room.

"He is in his chambers, my lady," said the woman, slowing down to match her stride.

Lalitha arrived in front of King Samrat's door out of breath. "Open the d-door," she stammered, gulping in air.

The two men standing sentinel at the door crossed their spears in front of her, not recognizing her.

But a voice commanded them to part. "Let the princess through," ordered Minister Kapila, standing a few steps behind her in the hall. A friend of her father's, he viewed her with a frown.

Lalitha glanced at her soiled clothes and shrugged her shoulders.

The guards opened the sturdy teak door with a creak, and Lalitha hopped in on one foot. In the dim light, she scanned the sitting room. The round mango wood table held scrolls and quills. She peered into the bedroom.

"Kapila," a feeble voice called.

"My Majesty," the minister answered. "Come, child," he beckoned her and walked into the bedroom.

She followed him and paused at the threshold. One of the guards opened the curtains, and the morning light streamed in, illuminating the faint dust clouds hanging in the air. Her uncle squinted at her from the bed.

"Lalli?"

"Uncle Samrat," she said and hobbled to the foot of the bed. Holding his ankle, she bowed and placed her forehead on his feet.

"My child, you are here. My heart gladdens on seeing you. May the goddess shower you with long life," said her uncle, raising on his elbows to gaze at her. She rose and walked to his side. Dropping beside him, she held his hand and gazed into his cloudy eyes. "Your father went to fight against my wishes and now languishes in a prison cell."

She noticed his frail frame and the new scabs and lesions that covered his arms. Several years ago, her uncle had fallen off his horse and broken his back. Since the incident, he'd been paralyzed from his waist down. "Uncle, how are you?" she asked, worries swirling in her stomach.

Uncle Samrat's face contorted briefly. He let out his breath slowly. "Some days are better than others." He paused and tugged the sheet covering his chest.

She could sense his hurt from being confined to this room for many years. Tears glistened in her eyes for both of them.

"Lalli," said her uncle softly, "do not worry about me. I don't have long to live—"

"Uncle," she admonished him.

"Don't interrupt me. If you want to worry, think about what will happen to us if Dushyant sieges us. With your father rotting in a dungeon, we have no one to lead our armies. I have sent a message to Prince Giridhar of Nidhapur with a marriage proposal."

"Marriage?" she asked, her voice sounding like it came from the depths of a well.

"Yours," answered a melodious voice, and Queen Padmavati, wife of King Samrat, entered the room. Dressed in a green silk sari, she'd bundled her gray hair into a bun at the top of her head. With a silver bowl in her hand, she approached them.

"My brother-in-law insists on treating you like a child. You are seventeen and should have been married a year ago. My nephew, Giridhar, is a second son and will be your ideal partner in marriage and ruling this land. I have invited Giridhar to come to Garthapuri and expect him anytime now," she said. Lalitha doubted a prince would be a suitable ally in governing her kingdom. Giridhar would likely take the reins from her and relegate her to raising children and throwing feasts. She stood up to approach her aunt and touched her feet. "May you bring glory to Garthapuri," said Queen Padmavati, placing her hand on her head.

"I received a message from your mother's sister, Chitra, this morning. She said you left without her blessing. I was about to mount a search for you. Callous on your part to let your aunt worry for these many days."

Padmavati did not raise her voice, but Lalitha felt the scale of her disappointment. Ashamed, she vowed to send a message to Aunt Chitra. Her own mother had abandoned her with no regrets. She never sent letters, nor did she attempt to visit her daughter. But Aunt Chitra, her mother's sister, had showered her with motherly love and indulged her wishes to make up for her mother's lack of attachment. While Queen Padmavati was not known to pamper her, she'd raised Lalitha to be a queen. Lalitha owed a lot to her two aunts.

Queen Padmavati continued to stare at Lalitha, her eyes

widening. "Where have you been? Look at you. Your sari is torn, and your hair is matted. You are not fit for any company. Go and wash," she ordered.

Lalitha moved forward reluctantly. While she longed to be out of her dirty clothes, she wanted to stay and protest this marriage scheme. Her father had promised to hold a swayamvara for her to choose her groom.

Queen Padmavati occupied the spot she vacated and attempted to feed her uncle.

"Get something to eat, my child," said her uncle after he swallowed a spoonful of gruel. Hearing the dismissal in his voice, she hopped to the door.

"What is wrong with your foot?" Queen Padmavati asked.

"I twisted it," Lalitha answered.

Queen Padmavati stared at her like she'd rolled in the mud. Glancing at her clothes, Lalitha realized she looked like she had.

"Sit in that chair," Queen Padmavati ordered, pointing to a wooden chair. "Guards, carry the chair to the princess' room."

At her chamber, her maid gulped on seeing her. "I need help," the servant whispered and ran out. Soon she had two men haul in several pots of hot water.

Behind a curtain, Lalitha stripped her clothes and wrapped a towel around her chest. Then she sat in the middle of the tub. Like scrubbing a tarnished silver lamp, her maid rubbed a paste of sandalwood and turmeric on her, intent on making her skin glow. Her vigorous action drove any residual fatigue away. Then, she poured water from a pot of lukewarm water, washing Lalitha clean.

Lalitha wore the yellow sari her maid had picked for her. Agamathi, the minister's daughter and her friend, strolled in with a wide smile on her face. "Princess Lalitha, my father mentioned you are back."

Lalitha clasped her friend's hand. "Tell me everything that happened since I left nearly two months ago."

They sat side by side on a wooden bench. "Nothing of significance happened for the first few days. In your absence, time crawled to a stop, and I even listened to my father's boring speeches," Agamathi started.

"Did you not fall into Nambi's hands to relieve your boredom?" Agamathi favored one of the city guard commanders. Knowing her interest, Lalitha sought him to accompany them on their expeditions.

Agamathi blushed. "Without you, it has been rather hard to find time alone with him."

"Well, I have to remedy that. Tell me when Kanva arrived in the city."

"About a month ago, he arrived seeking shelter from King Dushyant. The king granted him an audience. After hearing his story, our king ordered our men to detain him."

"Prison?" said Lalitha and bolted up.

"Yes, he is still there."

"Let us go see him."

"In the dungeon? That would not be wise."

Lalitha snorted. "We have hardly any prisoners, so if my uncle threw him there, I want to hear his story." And she did not want to return to the king's chambers yet. The conversation would be about her marriage.

"My lady," the royal physician called from her door. "The queen sent me to inspect your foot."

Lalitha sat down with all the patience of a five-year-old child. The healer inspected her leg. "It is healing well," he said, wrapping it up with a cloth dipped in herbs. "Please do not put weight on this foot. I will send my apprentice with an underarm crutch."

Armed with the crutch, Lalitha set out with Agamathi. The stairs down to the dungeon posed a challenge. Imagining Puru carrying her in his arms, she hopped down slowly. In her gleaming silk sari, the folks Lalitha encountered recognized her and bowed. With no one stopping her, she reached the giant double doors that led to the dungeon.

"My lady," the head guard approached her.

"I want to talk to Kanva," said Lalitha. He regarded her for a moment and then nodded to someone in the shadows. An enormous man moved nimbly on his feet and opened the iron lock. Two men swung open the doors.

"Princess," muttered Agamathi, tilting her head to peer inside the dungeon. Her chest rose and fell rapidly.

Sensing her reluctance, Lalitha said, "You stay here."

As Lalitha took a step forward, Agamathi stammered, "Don't leave me alone. I w-would rather accompany you."

Soon, they walked through the dark halls lit by flaming torches mounted on the wall. After a few empty cells, they arrived at one where a man sat cross-legged on the floor, clasping his head in his palms.

"Princess Lalitha is here to talk to you."

His head jolted up, and he gazed at her with eyes crusted with salt.

"Princess?"

She nodded. "I am Prince Bhimasena's daughter."

He fell to the floor. "Protect my daughter. She is carrying King Lambhodara's child," he cried. The dead king's child? Lalitha's head spun.

10

DUSHYANT

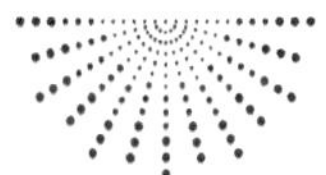

The tiny windowless room had a sole oil lantern. The dim light illuminated a woman a few years older than Dushyant. She had a pleasant face but looked at him like a deer caught in a hunter's net.

"This is King Dushyant. Tell him your story," said Minister Panini, shutting the door. The small space grew smaller with them crowded in it.

"Are you King Lambhodara's son?" she asked.

Dushyant dipped his head. "What is your name?"

"Sundari," she murmured.

Dushyant wanted to ask Sundari why her father had killed his father. But he waited for her to tell her story.

She twisted the end of the sari around her index finger. "I am carrying King Lambhodara's child," she said and looked at him with misty eyes.

His eyes traveled to her stomach, and he noticed the tiny bump. Her words did not make sense. "My father married you?" he asked stupidly.

She shook her head, a lone tear spilling down her cheek. Why would his father desecrate her honor? And his honor.

63

"Are you married?" he asked. Did his father covet another's wife?

"No," she whispered.

Confused by his father's actions, Dushyant tugged his ear. "Tell me what happened," he said softly, though he did not relish hearing the details of his father's errant ways.

"There was a dance at the palace, and I had come to watch it. A man said the king wanted to see me," she said and paused. She twisted her hands with her eyes cast down.

Dushyant remained frozen, suppressing the fury unraveling in his heart. "More than a month ago, I revealed the story to my father. He approached the king, who denied it all. That is when my father killed—" She broke into a sob.

Dushyant felt helpless watching her, and the tightness in his chest grew. "Move her to a better room and keep her safe," he ordered and strode out of the room. Searching for fresh air, he reached the palace garden set in a valley among the cliffs. A bee caught in a spider web drew his attention. The insect struggled to free itself from the web, mirroring his fight. He walked to a bench under an Asoka tree and dropped down.

"I can comprehend the act of Kanva, a father angered by the violation of his daughter. I cannot make sense of my father's." There was no dishonor in his father marrying Sundari. But to deny it when she carried his child appeared monstrous. What happened to the man who had wept endlessly when his mother had died? Dushyant remembered the months after his mother had perished giving birth to a child. His unnamed brother had joined her a few days later. His father had sobbed uncontrollably at the mere sight of his children. The burden of remaining calm fell on the ten-year-old boy. Dushyant had buried his emotions and taken care of his two younger sisters. When his mother's sister had come for a visit a year later, she'd found him withdrawn and distant. Announcing that Dushyant needed the company of boys his age, she took him and his sisters to her home in Jaisalpur. Dushyant had spent the last decade away from Vidarpur except for the occasional visits to see his father. Before he understood what marriage meant, Dushyant had decided he would never let his heart be affected similarly. Each visit to his home only strengthened his resolve.

Jayanth stood behind him like a tree stump, not intruding into his thoughts. "Jayanth, what happened to my father's guards? If he visited Sundari, they would know." The buzz of insects circulating the flowers that warm morning sounded like the notions coursing in his head.

Jayanth cleared his throat. "My Majesty, we swear an oath to protect our king with our lives."

Dushyant's chest tightened. "They failed that pledge."

Jayanth remained silent for a few moments. "Punishment for that blunder is death. They took their own lives."

"If I die, don't k-kill yourself," Dushyant stammered.

"King Dushyant, if someone got past me to threaten you, I am likely already dead," said Jayanth in a clear voice. No tremors in his conviction. Was Dushyant worth protecting with their lives? He'd done nothing notable to gain that eminence.

Dushyant stared at the ground beneath a mango tree. Birds pecked at the immature fruits littering the soil. Many flowers blossom every spring, but only some ripen into golden mangoes. His rule reminded him of the frailty of the tiny green fruit. A strong wind could end it.

"There might be one person to question," Jayanth interrupted his musings. "A young boy had joined the king's guard just before the incident."

Dushyant jumped to his feet. "Where is he?"

"I released him to join our army. I saw him fighting with our men at the Garthapuri border. I can send someone to question—"

"No, I want to talk to him myself." The father, who had

broken into pieces when his mother had died, floated into his memory. Did that kind man die with her?

Dushyant marched back to the palace with Jayanth at his heels. As his servant packed his trunk for the journey, Minister Panini arrived in his chambers. "Withdraw the additional levies we imposed. Then join me on my travel. I want to start fixing our problems," Dushyant ordered. He no longer wanted to wage war to capture Kanva. Whether he won or lost this battle, he would sacrifice the lives he'd vowed to protect. He could not justify the slaughter of thousands of lives to seek a man avenging his daughter.

"I will make arrangements to accompany you." Minister Panini glanced around. "My Majesty, the king's chambers have been closed for the past month. It is customary for the new king to move into his quarters after the coronation. During our absence, I can ask the servants to—"

Dushyant had avoided going into his father's rooms. The thought of making them his own turned his stomach. "Not now," he stated.

"My Majesty, I hoped to talk to you about your marriage. Before you head to battle, it would be wise to wed," said Minister Panini.

Images of Lalitha drifted into his mind. "I promise to marry soon." First, he had to solve the mystery of his father's death.

11

LALITHA

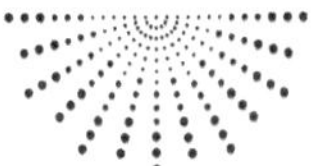

With the wind of fury at her back, she limped into her uncle's chambers.

"Why did you imprison Kanva? The man committed no crime," she cried. The vision of her father rotting in prison wafted into her mind.

"My niece," her uncle called, holding out his hand. She grasped it and sank beside him. A faint smell of turmeric rose from him.

"I heard his story. That is why I refused to hand him over to Dushyant."

"He should not languish in a dungeon," Lalitha argued, her mind tossed like a boat caught in a storm.

"Lalli, just hearing his side of the story is not enough. I am duty bound to seek the truth." He let go of her hand and wiped his forehead.

"I don't think Kanva is lying. I cannot imagine a father tarnishing his daughter's virtue."

Her uncle held her gaze. "You sound like your father. Ready to believe the good in others because of the good in you. Bhimasena was supposed to dig into this matter. Instead, he is languishing in a dungeon. I have spies in Vidarpur investigating this tale." Her uncle dismissed her and leaned back into his pillows.

Letting him rest, Lalitha made her way back. Her stomach grumbled loudly, reminding her she had not eaten any food yet. Knowing she made rash decisions on an empty stomach, she ordered her maid to fetch her some food. After a meal of sesame rice and long bean stew, she collapsed into a chair. She could not let two innocent men rot in captivity. She needed to unmask the horror committed by King Lambhodara and confront his son. But how?

Words uttered by Puru drifted in. On her journey here, he was resourceful in keeping her safe. He would be a valuable ally to go places she could not visit and hear things folks kept hidden from their rulers. She decided to send him a message and immediately leaped up and shuffled to her table. Grabbing a palm leaf, she sat to write to him. *"Talked to the man sought by the tyrant. Need your help to find answers."* She trusted the man who buried his disguises would understand her cryptic message. Her inner voice whispered that she wanted to see Puru again for more reasons than to solve the mystery of Kanva, but she blew that thought away.

With the letter tucked into her sari, Lalitha ordered two men to carry her chair. "Take me to the queen," she said. They carried her to the queen's chambers.

"She is in the kitchen, my lady," a maid answered while wiping the furniture.

As she neared the kitchen, the smell of browned ghee reached her. She remembered sneaking in here with Agamathi to grab sweet lentil balls made for feasts. She found her aunt talking to the cook. Past her, she could see steam floating from huge pots. In the corner, a woman pounded rice on a circular stone in a rhythmic style. Lalitha waited impatiently, shifting restlessly in her chair.

An old servant approached her and placed a freshly made burfi in Lalitha's palm. Lalitha noticed a dusting of flour on the maid's hands. Inhaling the delicate hint of cardamom, Lalitha ate the decadent sweet in two bites. Made with evaporated milk, ghee, and sugar, the cube melted in her mouth.

"Lalli," her aunt called, and she thanked the maid, and the men carrying her hurried after Queen Padmavati.

"Aunt Padmavati, I want to visit the Goddess Durga temple tonight to pray for my father," she said.

Her aunt squeezed her arm. "No harm will come to your father." Then she sighed. "I will join you. I am not sure the goddess hears my prayers, but I am not ready to give up either."

"Uncle will live a long life," said Lalitha, terrified of thinking otherwise. But her aunt joining her posed a problem with her plan to drop a message for Puru. Lalitha needed to find a moment to be alone to complete the deed.

Nestled among houses on either side, guards and soldiers frequented the small temple for the warrior goddess. That evening, as the sun set, Lalitha, Agamathi, and her aunt arrived in an open chariot. Two men carried her in a wooden plank with handles while her aunt walked beside her. Vendors selling flowers and coconuts hailed them.

"I will buy the entire basket," her aunt smiled and pointed to the stringed flower garlands. A guard paid the woman who bowed several times to the queen, thanking her profusely. In the courtyard, the priest rushed to her aunt and welcomed her.

While the crowd followed the queen, Lalitha commanded the men to take her to the back.

"What are we doing here?" Agamathi asked as she ran to keep up with Lalitha.

Lalitha asked the men to halt near the tree. Dismounting from her seat, she asked them to step away.

"I heard unmarried girls will be blessed with the man of their choice if they circle the neem tree and tie a red cloth on a tree branch. I brought two pieces for us," Lalitha whispered. The tree rustled melodiously while its limbs creaked in the wind. She noticed many bits of fabric tied to the trees in the temple courtyard. She wondered how many of these wishes remained unfulfilled. "You can tie one for Nambi," teased Lalitha.

Agamathi blushed and stuttered. "Forget about m-me. I heard Prince Giridhar is on his way to the castle." Lalitha grimaced. She will have to face that trial soon.

As they completed one round around the trunk, Lalitha searched for the hole Puru mentioned. She found it in the back, just as he said. "There is a nice branch in the back. I will fasten my piece there," said Lalitha. She deposited the palm leaf in the hole and hoped it would reach Puru.

"Think of the man you want to marry," Agamathi called, and a vision of Puru wafted into Lalitha's mind. Annoyed, Lalitha pushed the image away. She tied the cloth hurriedly and rushed back into the temple before her aunt sent someone to look for her.

In the temple's main sanctum, a young girl beckoned her. When Lalitha neared her, the child touched her elbow. "Are you lost? What you seek, you will find if you open your heart to all your senses," she said, her eyes blank like she was in a trance.

Disoriented by her words, Lalitha nearly ran away from the girl and into the inner sanctum. What did those words mean? She sought to free her father. She sought strength to rule Garthapuri. How about her desires, ones she refused to acknowledge, even to herself? Puru drifted into her vision. When the deity came into view, Lalitha stood still while her heart continued to race. As the priest prayed, Lalitha decided she'd misheard the child. She bowed her head and beseeched the Goddess to liberate her father.

At the palace, as they dismounted, Lalitha noticed a bullock cart stop a few yards behind the chariot. A young man jumped out. He removed the turban covering his head and tousled his long curly hair.

"Giridhar!" her aunt exclaimed. Prince Giridhar? Though they shared an aunt, he was no blood relation of Lalitha's. She regarded the man in simple clothes with curiosity and apprehension.

"Aunt Padmavati," he greeted her. He approached them to touch his aunt's feet.

Her aunt beamed at him. "No trouble in your travels?"

"Not as a sari merchant. I brought some fine silk saris for you," he said and waved to his cart with a grin.

"Princess Lalitha, meet my nephew." The young man dipped his head while observing her with keen eyes. "Your soon-to-be betrothed," her aunt added.

12

DUSHYANT

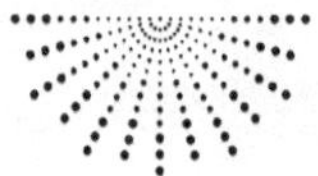

*D*ushyant paced the tent waiting for Jayanth to fetch the young guard. Why would his father refuse to marry Sundari if he was the father of her child? A sense of revulsion rose in him as he imagined King Lambhodara stooping so low.

On hearing footsteps, Dushyant raised his head. Jayanth entered the room alone, sweat glistening on his face.

"The boy is missing," stated Jayanth with a frown.

"Missing?"

"No one has seen him since yesterday," said Jayanth, clenching the hilt of his sword.

"Did you reveal what I intended to ask him?" Dushyant asked.

Jayanth shook his head. "I did not divulge any of our conversations. But I told his commander that you wanted to talk to him."

"This feels like capturing a ghost. Even my father's motives are beyond my grasp."

Jayanth glanced at him. "There is one reason for King Lambhodara to deny the relationship," he whispered.

Dushyant looked at him with narrowed eyes.

"Someone could use the new prince to usurp the crown. That would put your life in danger."

"My life? How could a baby hurt me?"

"He would be a pawn in someone's quest to conquer the throne. With you out of the way, they could shape a young child to follow their course."

Dushyant imagined an arrow aimed at his back. "Jayanth, tighten the guards around Sundari. Tell her it is for her safety. Watch her. I want to know whom she meets and whom she writes to." If she gave birth to a boy, he would raise his brother himself.

A gentle wind ruffled the cloth tent. Dushyant resumed pacing, his mind mired in a storm. A rival prince seemed strange. His next male heirs were cousins. Jayanth moved swiftly to the entrance just as a guard called his name. "King Dushyant." Dushyant could see the silhouette of a man outside his tent.

Dushyant waved his hand, and Jayanth allowed the guard to enter.

The sturdy man bowed to Dushyant. "My Majesty, I have a message for Commander Jayanth."

Dushyant glanced at Jayanth.

"What is it? The king can hear my messages," said Jayanth with impatience.

"We found the soldier you were looking for." Dushyant leaned forward. "His body, at least. He'd drowned in the stream."

"Drowned?" Dushyant asked.

The guard shifted to face him. "Yes, my Majesty. A man who went swimming found the corpse. We pulled the dead body out to the shore. Though the face had bloated, we could recognize him."

Jayanth dismissed the guard. A horse snorted outside as a stable boy walked the animal. In the distance, he heard the clatter of blades against shields as his men trained. Inside the tent, a stillness prevailed as Dushyant considered the information.

"My Majesty, all the king's guards are trained to swim. I cannot imagine one of them drowning in that knee-deep water."

"Do you suspect foul play?"

Jayanth dipped his head. "Someone did not want us to talk to him."

Dushyant rubbed his chin. "Someone did not want me to find the truth. But they made a mistake. I now know there is a secret concealed from me. Find out whom the young soldier met in the last two days."

"My Majesty, your life is in peril. We have to be cautious—"

"They would not risk it till Sundari gives birth," said Dushyant.

Jayanth shook his head. "It is best for you to wed a princess soon."

An image of Lalitha wearing a red silk sari wafted into his head. That headstrong princess would refuse to see him if she knew his real name. Still, a yearning spread in his limbs.

"Enough talk of my marriage," said Dushyant, swallowing his longing. "Let us find the culprit behind the drowning."

Jayanth nodded and departed to carry out his instructions.

Dushyant walked to meet with his small council. On the way, the leaves on a large banyan tree whispered to him, and a goat tethered to one of its roots bleated. He entered the large tent, and men seated around a round table stood up and bowed stiffly.

He waved them to sit and took his place. Dushyant ran his eyes over those assembled. "On my travels, I found poverty and despair among our people. Our farmers toil at the field night and day and yet are unable to feed their families."

Like waking up from a dream, the assembly stirred to life. "While there may be suffering among some small peasants, most large landowners are hiding their grains from us. We can enforce obedience through a whip," General Ayobahu remarked, his eyes narrowing imperceptibly.

"We are choking our people with our taxes," said Advisor Upananda.

"Our coffers are empty," thundered Ayobahu. "Do you want our soldiers to starve?"

"No, I will take care of men who have pledged their loyalty to me. Cut our other expenses. No more lavish feasts. No more silks and gold jewels," said Dushyant, keeping his voice calm though a mild irritation flared in him.

"Your father had ordered some expensive tapestry," said Upananda with a scowl.

A sudden fear struck him as he glanced at the eyes staring at him. They judged him, and he failed in many measures. His youth and inexperience washed over him. Curse his father for not grooming him to rule. Like everything else, he'd to learn this on his own. And he had plenty of practice doing that. As it arrived, the fear vanished.

"Halt those purchases and any new furnishings. Stick to the necessities," said Dushyant coldly. A murmur arose from the men gathered, and they discussed at length what repairs to continue and what funds to divert.

Dushyant returned to his tent and massaged his neck. As he sat down, Jayanth reentered the tent.

"My Majesty," said Jayanth, hurrying toward him. "I only attended part of the council meeting, but that was sufficient for me to form an opinion. You commanded their respect today. I can picture you uniting us into a tightly knit country, prosperous—"

Dushyant grinned. "Stop the praises. My journey is just starting."

"You are on the right road, my Majesty. Our spy in Garthapuri brought this," he said, handing Dushyant a scroll. "Princess Lalitha left this for you."

"*Talked to the man sought by the tyrant. Need your help to find answers.*" Tyrant? Who? Did she call him a tyrant? Who did he seek? Kanva!

"She talked to Kanva," said Dushyant, looking up. "I need to go to her."

"My Majesty, that would not be wise. You will only find trouble. I will send men to talk to her."

"She will not talk to strangers. But she will talk to Puru." She'd sought his help. A warm glow spread in his chest.

"This could be a trap. Prince Giridhar of Nidhapur slipped into the palace to marry Princess Lalitha."

"Marry Lalitha?" Dushyant asked sharply, crossing his arms.

Jayanth gazed at him intently. "Garthapuri aligned with Nidhapur would be a powerful enemy. My king, let us return to Vidarpur and strengthen our alliances through your marriage." The words did not reach Dushyant. His heart pounded rapidly at the thought of losing Lalitha. What foolishness. She was never his for him to lose her. Yet, he wanted to see her again.

"Jayanth, we are sneaking into the Garthapuri palace," Dushyant commanded.

13

LALITHA

"Come, Agamathi. We cannot keep the young man waiting," Lalitha urged as her friend slipped on some bangles.

"How do I look?" asked Agamathi. Clad in a pale blue sari, she had a pleasant face, except for the ugly bump shaped like a leaf on her right cheek. The blemish of a childhood fire, Lalitha rarely noticed it these days.

"After one look at you, Nambi might desire to seek your father's permission to ask for your hand." Nambi saw beyond her friend's flaw. In a small corner of her mind, Lalitha was jealous of Agamathi.

Color rose on her friend's face. "I am grateful for your help. Without your encouragement, I would have never found the courage to share my feelings with him."

Lalitha smiled. "You are giving me too much credit. You chose a good man who recognized your worth. My only role is in arranging your meetings. Don't reveal that to your father. I don't want to incur the minister's wrath."

"Hardly. You can never do any wrong in my father's eyes. My lady, do you think my father will agree to the match?"

"Why not? Nambi is a commander with good prospects. He will be loyal and faithful. I can whisper my approval in the minister's ear too."

In the garden, Nambi bowed deeply when he saw them approach. Then his eyes darted to Agamathi, his lips curling up. Agamathi kept her gaze on a flowering shrub, stealing glances at him slyly. They stood on either side of the bush, with Agamathi plucking leaves and Nambi rubbing his palms. Neither said anything, and their silence spoke volumes.

"Agamathi, stay here. I see a butterfly that I want to get close to," said Lalitha and wandered away with a brimming heart, leaving the young couple alone.

She found Prince Giridhar lying under a tree staring at the cloudless blue sky. A black crow cawed incessantly from a top branch and then took flight, its wings beating rapidly. As Lalitha approached him, Giridhar turned toward her, curly hair framing his face. In the patch of light and shadow, he almost appeared handsome.

"My lady," he said and sat up, crisscrossing his legs. A pleasant smile played on his face and reflected on hers.

"I did not mean to interrupt your musings," she said.

"The interruption is welcome, my lady. I was idling my time dreaming about a play I had watched." He picked a black feather from the ground and twirled it in his fingers.

"What was the play about?" she asked. She'd found plays about kings and their battles dull. Men in masks prancing about the stage to the beat of the pounding drums and clanging their swords bored her.

"A beautiful ballad of love by Kalidasa. A king meets a young woman on his travels, and their love grows like a forest fire. Upon return to his kingdom, he forgets her due to a curse. The woman pines for his company. Have you seen this play? If you have not, I will not reveal the ending," he said with his lips curling up.

She dropped down beside him and hugged her knees. "Whether it ends in tragedy or not, such fantasy tales have no connection to my life. These fanciful stories invented by poets and filled with destiny and love to make them more touching are just figments of their imagination to give us hope. There is only determination and sacrifices ahead for me," she said as her lips quivered. Afterward, she worried that she'd revealed too much to him.

"Sacrifice? Does your marriage fall under that category?" Giridhar whispered, leaning toward her.

She swallowed and nodded. "Isn't that the biggest sacrifice of all? To commit to spending a lifetime with a stranger and agreeing to share in their joys and trials? My kingdom is facing difficult and dangerous times. I must do all in my power to protect this land. The man I wed needs to be willing to shed his blood for this land." And obey her commands, she thought. While Giridhar would be willing to do the former, unlikely he would consider the latter.

Two yellow butterflies danced on a flowering shrub in front of them. Giridhar remained silent for a long while. "Strangers can become friends," he said softly, gazing at her.

A vision of Puru drifted into her memory. A childish dream that she clung to instead of squashing it like a bug. A man with no titles could not claim her hand. Or her heart, she told herself vainly. Like a stubborn weed, he'd taken root in her mind. A man with no lands would stay in Garthapuri, which argued in his favor. He might heed her. But the noblemen of her kingdom would oppose such a union. They would want her to marry a lesser lord rather than a stranger.

"A union with a friend would be a miracle. What about you? Is there a woman who has claimed your heart and mind? Unlike me, you can marry many women," she said without bitterness.

He regarded the feather in his hand and tossed it to the ground. "My brother is the king of Nidhapur, and I am bound to obey his commands. Including in matters of matrimony." He rose abruptly. "Come, my lady. Let us not wallow in pity. We are still young. While poets may not sing about our lives, it need not be a burden. For either of us."

She glanced at the man in front of her. Why could her heart not fall in love with this prince? He seemed kind and honorable. She stood up slowly. Up close, his eyes stayed clouded. Like he did not believe his own words. She sensed sorrow in his pinched lips. She decided not to probe his wound. Neither had the luxury of following their heart, and she hoped time would heal his scar.

She walked the halls of the castle mired in her thoughts when a voice reached her. She turned her head from side to side, trying to identify the source. The sound appeared to come from behind the tapestry depicting Goddess Parvati stringing a flower garland for God Shiva. "Come to the stables just before dawn to meet Puru." Stunned, she halted. Puru! He'd received her message. Her back tickled at the thought of seeing him again. Puru had taken his leave eleven days ago, though it felt like an eternity. She ran her eyes over the tapestry and sensed no movement behind it. With quick steps, she reached and pulled the cloth aside. Empty. For a moment, she wondered if her imagination had conjured the voice.

She slept poorly that night, tossing and turning on her bed. Would she see Puru, or had she been tricked? In the pre-dawn hours, she threw off her blanket and rose. She grabbed her knife and tucked it into the sari folds around her waist. Throwing a shawl over her shoulders, she crept stealthily along the corridors. The light from the torches stuck in iron mounts on the walls flickered, and she could dimly see her shadow moving alongside. Outside, a heavy mist hung in the air. Before she reached the stables, she heard the sound of hooves. She paused and peered around. An enormous shape emerged from the darkness. Horse? A cloth covered the face of the lone rider revealing only his eyes. His horse tossed its head. The man stretched his hand, and she noticed it held a scroll. As she grabbed it, the man and the horse vanished into the mist.

In the faint light, she read the message. *"Meet me under the large banyan tree adjacent to the orchard."* Her heart thudded like the temple bells in anticipation of seeing him. What if this was a ruse to get her alone? Would she risk her life for a chance to see him? Yes, echoed her heart.

Lalitha went into the stables to fetch her mare. Her horse nuzzled her neck. Distracted, Lalitha rubbed the horse's nose and saddled her. A sharp wind greeted them outside. The horse rode into the darkness confidently while Lalitha considered her foolishness in meeting this man unescorted. Puru had never harmed her before. And she wanted to see him alone.

She tied her horse to a tamarind tree and walked the last few yards. In the faint light of the stars, she searched under the banyan tree—no sign of Puru. Coming to a halt, she held one of the roots and waited. A light thud sounded behind her. She turned and gazed at a tall man with gray hair and a long gray beard. But the big batlike ears gave him away.

"Puru," she rushed to him and stopped in front of him. She felt relieved. Happiness bubbled up inside her. "You came. Is this because of my message?" Lalitha felt like she floated on a cloud of bliss. Why should his arrival surprise her? She was a princess and was known to pay well. He might need the gold. Her feet touched solid ground again.

"You asked for my help." He gazed at her strangely. "I could not refuse your call."

He stepped closer to her, and Lalitha yearned to feel his arms around her. Overcome by a sudden shyness, she lowered her eyes and blurted out words that shielded her thoughts. "You are in a new disguise."

"It was either this or come dressed as a lady. I decided I was too tall for a sari," he said.

"You have the waist for it," she teased him. A smile erupted on his face like a lightning strike and vanished quickly. She wished she could read his mind. Did he care for her as much as she did? "Take the beard off, so I can see your face," she muttered.

"Are the rumors true, my lady?" he asked, his fingers fumbling with the strings that attached the beard to his head.

"What rumors?"

"That you and Prince Giridhar are betrothed," he said with a tightness around his mouth.

"I a-am," she stammered and then glanced into his eyes. For a moment, the mask he hid behind slipped, and she witnessed a sudden vulnerability. Was he jealous? But he rearranged his features quickly. Why was he so cold? She wanted to lie, but the truth came out. "I am not engaged. While my aunt wants me to wed her nephew, I hope to free my father. He'd promised to hold a swayamvara for me so I could choose my destiny." His eyes lingered on her face as turmoil whipped in her stomach. With her parents separated, she did not think about what marriage meant. Naively, she assumed a man who would heed her commands would be the perfect husband. Could she share her marriage bed with a stranger? Should she have feelings for him before she wed him? What use is having the choice to select a groom if she did not choose wisely?

"Help me take this beard off," he said in an even tone.

Lalitha had to stand on her toes to reach the string that secured it. "Bend down," she ordered, and Puru obeyed readily. With shaking hands, she undid the knots. Puru dropped the artificial hair to the ground, and she could gaze at his face. Puru was here with her. And he smelled of horses and emanated a warmth that she craved. Could he hear her heart beating against her chest? Why didn't he fold her into his arms?

Puru's eyes darted to her feet, and his head heaved up. "You walked here. Your leg has healed since I saw you twelve days ago." *Twelve days!* Did he keep track of their time apart? Like her?

She lifted her sari a few inches to reveal her ankle. It looked normal, with all signs of swelling gone. "You don't have to carry me around anymore."

"A pity. I had imagined my arms around you," said Puru and sidled close to Lalitha. Her skin tingled. Did he care for her after all?

The fire in his eyes ignited a spark in her stomach. This time he did not try to hide his emotions. Did he cherish her? An acute longing shot up her chest, and she leaned toward him. "I need not be an invalid for your arms to wrap around me," she whispered. Puru, an ordinary man, might not be a sound partner in ruling Garthapuri. But her heart thundered, ignoring reason.

"Lalitha," he said her name gently and held her chin up. She gazed at him with her lips parted. His fingers traveled to her mouth, tracing the outline. A shiver ran through her, and he pulled her against his frame. The slide of his warm palm against hers caused her to shudder. She could hear the rapid beating of his heart. "May I kiss you?" he asked, already leaning in. In response, she stood on her toes, put her arms around his shoulders, and pressed her lips to his. A shock reverberated through her body as the kiss deepened. After an eternity, his mouth traveled down, and he kissed her throat, causing sparks to ignite on her skin. Fleeting light touches traveled to her ear. Shrouded in darkness and mist, she wrapped her arms around his neck and tugged him closer. Her body melded into his, and their breath mingled. Their lips met again in a blaze of passion. Her body erupted like a log bursting under intense fire.

A rooster crowed to welcome the pending dawn. She parted reluctantly from his embrace, like a night-blooming water lily closing its petals to the sun. All thoughts emptied from her head, and she could only remember his warmth. A heat she craved. He twined his fingers in hers, and she leaned her head on his shoulder. She felt safe in his arms. She decided to invite Puru to her swayamvara. She imagined putting the garland she held around his neck and smiled against his chest.

Neither moved away. Still holding Lalitha tightly, Puru asked, "Tell me what you learned from Kanva."

She straightened and faced him. "His daughter is carrying the old king's child," she said with a touch of anger.

He squeezed her hand. "And he killed the father of his grandchild?"

She moved away and crossed her arms. "The king denied any relationship. Kanva had acted in rage, out of his love for his offspring." She remembered the two fathers, Kanva and her own, rotting in prison. Lalitha approached Puru and took both his hands in hers. "Help me free them both."

"Both?" he asked.

"My uncle has imprisoned Kanva. And my father is held in that king's prison. Will you aid me?" she asked, lifting her chin to gaze into his eyes.

He pulled one hand out of her grasp and tugged his ear. Her hand moved up to cover it. "You are nervous," she said.

"What?" he asked, his tone mild.

"You are tugging your ear. You only do that when you are upset."

Puru regarded her intently. A gentle wind rustled her hair, and he pushed it out of her face. "How well you know me. I was thinking about freeing these men. Even if Kanva is telling the truth, Dushyant will punish him for treason. But there may be a way to save his life. Can I talk to him?"

"I don't see how. My uncle has him locked in our cells."

"I can come disguised as your guard," said Puru, and he pressed her hand against his chest. She could feel his heart rising and falling with each breath. For a few moments, she lost all thought of Kanva and floated like an eagle in the current.

"You asked for my help," continued Puru, bringing her back to the ground.

She shook her head. "It is too dangerous, Puru. If the guards catch you, they will put you in chains. Even I cannot free you then."

He put his arm around her mid-back and drew her to him. In the mellow light of the dawn, his handsome face caused a flutter in her stomach. "Don't worry about me. If I can ask him some questions, I can clear up some things." Picking up his beard, he shook it to remove debris and reattached it to his face.

She still did not consider this wise, but she wanted to spend more time with him. "Come with me to the stables. I will fetch you some clothes to change into, and then we can devise a plan."

They walked side by side, Lalitha aware of his every step. A stranger who stood a few feet from her horse bowed to her. "Princess Lalitha."

With a worried glance at Puru, she nodded and hurried on. The stranger followed them with his eyes. She noticed a dark mole on his left cheek. "King Dushyant, is that you?"

Dushyant? Why would he travel to Garthapuri in disguise? "You are mistaken. This is my friend, Puru." She glanced at Puru. He tugged his ear, and the color drained from his face.

"Even in disguise, I can spot those ears. You are in danger from this man, my lady. Let me fetch our guards."

The man started shouting. Panic swirled in her chest. "Enough," she yelled at the stranger. Dushyant? That made no sense. "Go. Take my horse and escape," she said, pushing Puru away.

Puru glanced at her once and ran to the screaming man. He put his elbow around the stranger's throat and choked him. The man with the mole kicked vehemently. Half a dozen men loitered on the street. While two were engrossed in a conversation, the others started to look in their direction. One even started walking toward her.

"Puru! Go. Now," she cried. The stranger's face had turned red, and his eyes popped.

Puru released the man, and the stranger collapsed to the ground, coughing violently. Puru ran to her horse. Jumping on it, he drew a dagger out. As he galloped away, he leaned in. "I am Dushyant," he whispered in her ear. Lalitha stared after the disappearing horse and rider as terror gripped her.

14

DUSHYANT

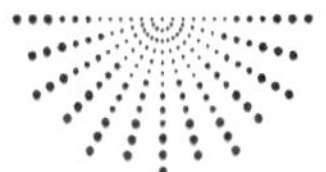

ushyant noticed the revulsion flashing across Lalitha's face as he uttered his name. She'd reason to despise him. He wanted to take her in his arms and explain everything that had happened since his father's death. But he had no time. The men around them pointed at him and whispered. He had to flee Garthapuri before an arrow embedded in his back. The man who revealed his identity started to rise. Dushyant kicked him hard and trotted away.

The shouts and Lalitha's voice faded out. They would be after him soon. He needed to find shelter. His eyes swept the surroundings while he nudged the horse with his thighs. The mare recognized his scent and responded to his touch. Galloping through the morning mist, he heard his fake name. "Puru." He halted and scanned the area. In a dark alley, he spotted two figures. The woman dressed in a cotton sari gestured for him to come near—Jayanth without his mustache. Dushyant guided the horse toward them and dismounted.

"Quick, my Majesty. Please remove your disguise and give it to Amudhan," said Jayanth, pointing to the young man beside him. Amudhan, his youngest guard, nearly matched his height.

"He will wear it and lead the hunters away while you and I escape on foot."

A thorn pricked Dushyant's heart for putting Amudhan's life at risk. One reason why he did not like learning the names of his guards. It was harder to feel remorseful for an anonymous soldier. "Surrender to them if needed."

"Bah," the man bleated and bowed his head. When Jayanth recruited Amudhan to his guard, Dushyant had doubts about his abilities because of his lack of speech. But, Amudhan had served him well with his keen sense of sight and intuition. Amudhan sensed danger before it manifested and saved his life more than once.

"He is a good climber. He can scale the fort wall. He will find his way back to us."

Hurriedly, Dushyant took off the false wig and beard and his shawl. The young guard wore them and leaped onto the horse. He tore through the streets. Without waiting to watch him, Jayanth untied a pouch.

"Please use this vermillion powder and place red dots on your face, neck, and arms. I will tell people you have contagious pox to keep them from inspecting you closely." Dushyant followed his direction and soon covered his exposed skin with red blemishes. Jayanth placed a woven basket on his head and walked down the alley. Dushyant followed him with hunched shoulders. Light chased the darkness away, and Dushyant heard yelling. "There he is. You!" someone shouted wildly.

Jayanth and Dushyant pressed their backs against the wall. Jayanth drew his short sword, still hiding the weapon in his sari folds. Hooves pounded the cobbled road, and horses raced down the street, leaving behind a trail of dust.

"I am his king. I cannot let him take the fall," said Dushyant and moved toward the main street.

Jayanth stretched his arm across Dushyant's chest, halting him. "If he were any ordinary subject, I would agree. But

Amudhan is part of your king's guard, sworn to protect you. He is doing his duty. Let me do mine." Dushyant gazed at his guard. "What will happen to our kingdom without you? Do you want those distant cousins of yours to wear the crown? Come, my king. Let us keep you alive so you can see the princess again."

Dushyant followed Jayanth through the meandering path. Lalitha may never want to see him again. Dushyant would not blame her for such feelings. The fault rested with him for lying to her.

"What is wrong with the boy?" a woman with grey hair asked with narrowed eyes. She stood a few feet away, facing them.

"My son has the pox. Don't come too close," advised Jayanth in a high-pitched squeaky voice.

She blanched. "Bathe him in neem water," she urged, walking away.

They picked their way through the alleys bounded by palace walls that rose on either side and met high above him. It grew warmer, and sweat gathered on his neck and trickled down his back. Soon, the red powder would melt and drip from his chin. Jayanth and he marched toward the forest, and dry branches broke under their feet. They stepped over fallen tree trunks and skipped over puddles.

"How do we leave?" asked Dushyant, hoping for a breeze to cool him.

"We have to wait till the dark. There is a hidden door on the fort wall, but one or two men guard the spot. If I distract the men watching it, you can escape through this exit."

"Isn't there a river flowing on the other side?"

"Around the fort, it is no more than a shallow stream. You can cross it without difficulty."

"What about you?" Dushyant did not like abandoning his men. This was his foolish plan, and they seemed to be paying for it.

Jayanth cleared his throat. "If I perish, I will make sure I take as many of their men with me as possible."

"Don't give me that idiocy. I want you to find a way to live," said Dushyant quietly while looking at his guard.

A sheepish expression appeared on Jayanth's face, and his hand reached to twist the non-existent mustache. "I will," promised Jayanth, dropping his hand. "For now, let us shelter in that hut," he said, pointing to a dilapidated structure with crumbling brick walls.

They walked toward it, and Dushyant heard branches grating. Leaves rustled as he looked up. The piercing sun nearly blinded him, and he shut his eyes. At that moment, something flashed by in the trees and landed on his back with a smack. A man wrapped his arms around Dushyant's neck, and Dushyant struggled to push him off. Jayanth uttered a quiet cry that had more despair in it than fury and rushed toward them. Dushyant managed to loosen his grip and shoved the stranger. The whistle of a blade. As he turned to face his attacker, something cold touched his back. For an instant, everything slowed down. Then Dushyant felt like someone stuck a lighted torch on his back. Dushyant groaned and executed a half-turn, pulling out his dagger. The man who had unmasked him earlier grinned at him, but his mole appeared menacing. Dushyant hacked at the man wildly, missing him. Losing his balance, Dushyant collapsed and hit the ground. Everything darkened.

"Puru is hurt," said a muffled voice. Puru never existed. He lied to her. Anger coursed through her veins as Lalitha remembered his arms around her. She'd let him deceive her though there were several signs of his treachery—he kept the dagger stolen from her and never sold her anklet to pay for the cart. Curse him. Lalitha looked around for the source of the voice. A rather stout woman swept the floor briskly, eyes cast down. There appeared something odd about her appearance. But what did the woman mean by hurt? Lalitha shuddered, imagining Puru harmed. Queen Padmavati's voice floated out from the mansion of a famed painter. Her aunt conversed with the son of the artist, who followed in his father's footsteps.

Glancing around, Lalitha crept to the corner of the large yard. Bees hovered around a jasmine shrub covered with wilting flowers that had bloomed last night. A faint scent rose from them. The woman with dark rings under her eyes followed with her broom. "Please help him," she whispered in an odd voice. Her face seemed familiar.

One shout and Lalitha could have the guards capture the

woman. But something held her back. "Hurt?" asked Lalitha, hiding the tremors she felt.

"Stabbed by that traitor," muttered the woman with her face darkening.

"Who are you?" asked Lalitha.

After a brief hesitation, the woman said, "Jayanthi."

"How is h-he?" stammered Lalitha while her fingers crushed a leaf. Why did Lalitha care about that treacherous man who had used her?

"He is bleeding and needs care that is beyond me." Jayanthi clasped the broom handle tightly.

Puru, no Dushyant, kept his identity concealed from her. "He betrayed me," said Lalitha. He'd deceived her. Heat rushed to her face as she realized how easily she'd fallen into his trap.

"Only about his name," Jayanthi whispered. Her eyes pleaded with Lalitha.

"A crucial part of him," answered Lalitha coldly. Dushyant had imprisoned her father. But Puru had saved her life and had come to Garthapuri, risking his own on receiving her message. If Puru was wounded, Lalitha at least owed him care. "Where is he?" Lalitha asked.

Jayanthi regarded her intently and then whispered the location. "Stay with him. I will send help."

"Lalitha," called her aunt. Lalitha rushed to her. On the way back to the palace, her aunt described the painting she'd viewed. "The young artist showed me a miniature painting on a palm leaf depicting Goddess Saraswati seated on a white lotus. He'd captured her divine beauty with sensitivity. He will paint a large-scale mural of the same picture on our temple wall." Lalitha made appropriate responses while her mind centered on Dushyant. She wanted to hate him, but a strange longing filled her stomach.

"Aunt Padmavati, someone spotted a few golden birds near our forest. I want to take Agamathi and see them."

Her aunt nodded absently. Shortly after, Lalitha climbed into a palanquin with Agamathi. She pulled aside the curtain to greet passers-by and to watch for the worn-down hut. When she spotted it about ten yards away, she asked her men to halt. The four men placed the palanquin on the ground gently. Agamathi and Lalitha descended and adjusted their saris. Nambi, the only guard accompanying them, dismounted from his horse.

"I am looking for the golden oriole bird. They have a distinctive song. Split into pairs and search. If you see one, come and find me. Agamathi, go with one of them. Nambi, you stay with me," Lalitha pointed away from the hut, and the four of them dispersed into the woods. Agamathi stalled, glancing at Nambi. "Nambi will be here when you return," hissed Lalitha, giving her friend a nudge. Agamathi left reluctantly. Lalitha hoped the orioles would stay hidden today.

When she could no longer see the searchers, she whispered to her trusted guard. "Nambi, check the hut. I thought I heard a noise from there." Lalitha did not trust the woman with the broom.

Nambi approached the hut carefully with his knife drawn. He peered through the open door and then pushed in. Lalitha twisted her fingers, scanning the area.

"My lady," Nambi called from the door. A deep scowl appeared on his face.

"What did you find?" Lalitha asked, a slight tremor in her voice.

"There is a wounded man in the hut."

With unsure steps, she reached him and peeked in. At first, she saw only darkness. Then her eyes adjusted to the light seeping in through the holes in the thatched roof. She heard a faint moan. With her stomach tightening into a knot, she followed the sound and found him on the floor. She recognized Puru though his eyes stayed closed. She wanted to rush to his side, but she resisted the urge. She could not forget he was a foe.

Lalitha heard the crunch of branches and shifted to face the entry. Nambi moved outside and said, "Show yourself."

Jayanthi appeared by the hut. She glanced at Lalitha and then at Dushyant. "He needs care," she said in a voice laden with grief.

"Do you know him?" asked Nambi, his hand clasping the hilt of his sword.

Jayanthi nodded. "He is my son," she said. *Another lie.* But Jayanthi's eyes misted as she gazed at the wounded man.

Lalitha knew what she had to do. "Carry him and place him inside the palanquin. We will take him to the physician," she replied. She owed him that because Dushyant had saved her life from the snake. Nothing more.

Nambi staggered out with Dushyant. Jayanthi rushed to support his shoulders. Dushyant muttered as they laid him down.

"Thank you for helping him," Jayanthi whispered in a husky voice. Before Lalitha could respond, another voice interrupted her.

"My lady," Agamathi called, and Lalitha swiveled toward her. Agamathi stood 20 yards away near some trees, with the servant behind her. They viewed the strange woman with narrowed eyes. Lalitha felt a prickle on her skin. Agamathi could not travel back with them. Not with Dushyant accompanying them. Though Lalitha trusted her friend, she was not ready to answer the many questions that would arise. Not when she did not know her own heart.

"No sign of the birds, my lady," said Agamathi with a frown on her face. Lalitha pondered how to send Agamathi away. Suddenly, an idea erupted in her mind.

"Agamathi, forget the bird. Escort this woman to our physician's house. She is looking for an herb for her son. Walk with her." Even before Lalitha finished talking, she noticed Jayanthi walking toward Agamathi. "Arrive after me," whispered Lalitha to Jayanthi's retreating back. Jayanthi dipped her head in acknowledgment. Lalitha saw Jayanthi exchange a few words with Agamathi, and then they departed.

"Fetch the others. We will leave now." The servant left to get the other three men.

Per their traditions, Lalitha should not be sharing the same litter as Dushyant, but she desired time alone with him. She turned to Nambi. "Take us to the healer's house." He dipped his head in understanding. Lalitha climbed into the palanquin. With the curtains drawn, she sat beside Dushyant. Her stomach roiled when she looked at him. Dushyant had fooled her with his kindness while using her to obtain knowledge about her kingdom. She remembered his kiss earlier that day, and she used the back of her hand to wipe her lips of any traces of him. Anger at her naivete coursed through her. She wanted to shake his shoulders and demand the truth from him. Dushyant murmured something. Lalitha placed her ears next to his lips. "Lalitha," he mumbled her name with his eyes closed, and her heart beat like a temple bell. The anger seeped out, and another feeling filled its place, a feeling that accompanied a hot stew on a cold rainy day. She waited for his eyes to open and the world to begin. With her fingers, Lalitha combed the hair off of his forehead. Dushyant's feverish skin burned her fingers. The lips she had kissed earlier now seemed parched. She wished she'd carried some water to quench his thirst. Whether he called himself Puru or Dushyant, she cared for the man. Lalitha remembered his arms encircling her waist. Her heart whispered a secret, but she did not want to listen because guilt tore her. Dushyant had waged a war against her kingdom, and her father languished in his prison. Why did her heart betray her?

Lalitha sensed her men lift the palanquin. It swung side to side as they carried her on their shoulders.

"I found some sacks in the hut that I placed in the palanquin following the princess's order," said Nambi. What sack? Then it dawned on her. He was explaining the extra weight of Dushyant.

Dushyant moaned softly.

"What was that noise?" asked one of the palanquin bearers. Lalitha's chest rose into her throat.

"That was me clearing my throat," said Nambi, and he broke into a song about the king's valor. Lalitha let out the breath she held.

The litter slowed down, and she parted the curtain with her index finger. Twilight had descended around her and cast a mellow light on the surroundings. Her men placed the wooden structure on the ground. Nambi moved the men away from her, and she climbed out slowly, taking care to conceal Dushyant.

Lalitha glanced around. She saw no sign of Jayanthi and Agamathi. Jayanthi had succeeded in delaying them. "Nambi, send two men to find Agamathi and escort her here. I will talk to the physician," said Lalitha and moved toward the door. She heard Nambi execute her order while she climbed the few steps and stood in front of the entrance. Lalitha wanted to conceal the impropriety of her accompanying Dushyant. She walked down the stairs and called, "Nambi." Her guard rushed to her side. "Carry him out when no one is around. Tell the healer he is the son of the woman who left with Agamathi," she whispered. Nambi dipped his head. Satisfied, Lalitha ascended the entry again and pushed open the door.

The physician looked up from the floor when she entered the large room. Seated cross-legged on the ground, he held some palm scrolls in his hand, and more were scattered in front of him. "My lady, I would have come to see you if you had sent for me," he said, rising to his feet.

Lalitha glanced around the room. "We are alone, my lady. My wife has gone to the temple."

"I met a woman looking for medicines to heal her son," said Lalitha. With eyes narrowed, he tilted his head, waiting for her to explain why she disturbed him at his home. Right then, they heard noises from the outside. "That must be her," said Lalitha.

"Allow me, my lady," said the healer and opened the door. Agamathi stood with Jayanthi. Her guards stood behind them.

Jayanthi took a step forward and bowed from her waist. "My son fell while climbing a tree. He landed on an ax that stabbed his back. Please help him," said Jayanthi covering her mouth with the end of her sari.

Nambi staggered with Dushyant leaning on his shoulder. "This is her son."

Jayanthi and the physician rushed to his side and helped carry Dushyant inside. Lalitha paced the floor of the front room while Agamathi wrinkled her nose. "There is something odd about Jayanthi." Like a lightning flash, the answer revealed itself to Lalitha, who had sensed the same thing. Jayanthi was a man. Likely one of Dushyant's guards. That would explain the voice. But she did not reveal her thoughts to Agamathi. "She is a mother worried for her son," said Lalitha and shrugged.

Agamathi looked at her with her keen eyes. "I get the sense that her son is no stranger to you," she muttered in a low voice. Her childhood friend knew her well.

The physician came out of the room, and Lalitha shushed her friend. "I will share the story with you later." Once she understood her mind better.

Then, Lalitha gazed at the healer with fear cloaking her. "My lady, thankfully, the ax did not pierce any vital organs. I have patched him. He lost blood, but because of his youth, he will recover." Only then Lalitha realized she'd held her breath.

"Can I see the mother and son?"

The physician escorted her to a small windowless room with a single wooden cot. Light from an oil lantern did little to disperse the darkness.

Jayanthi looked up at her. "Thank you for saving his life." Lalitha approached the bed. Dushyant rested on a thin sheet that appeared devoid of color, like his face. "Healer, I can help you make the herbal drink," said Jayanthi and departed with the physician.

Left alone with Dushyant, her feelings threatened to overwhelm Lalitha. Like a cloud parting to reveal the moon, Dushyant opened his eyes. Dazed, his eyes darted across the room, landing on her face.

"Lalitha," he croaked, and she leaned closer. "Is it really you, or am I dreaming?"

Emotions choked her. "It is me," she said, hiding the swell crashing in her stomach.

"When I see you, I cannot tell if I am awake or asleep because you linger in my thoughts," he said, gazing at her face with hunger. "Forgive me for lying to you."

Dushyant looked oddly vulnerable, but Lalitha remembered his deception. "My father is still in your prison," she said, heat coating her words. A serious war between their kingdoms would result in ruined villages on both sides filled with widows and orphaned children.

Dushyant looked at the ceiling, his pale face gleaming with sweat. Then, he caught her eyes. "Help me bring my father's murderer to justice. I will release your father."

Before she could answer, Jayanthi arrived with the potion. Slowly lifting Dushyant's head, she held the cup to his mouth. Lalitha noticed Jayanthi's large calloused palm and the scars on her forearm. How did Lalitha miss these signs earlier?

"My lady, his life is in danger. We need a safe passage home," said Jayanthi, lowering her arms defenselessly.

"You ask too much of me," snapped Lalitha angrily, spinning on her heels. She stood still for a moment. Aiding him would betray her kingdom. But what about the alternative? What would happen to him if her aunt captured him? Her father would continue to languish in prison. "Stay here tonight. I will bring a boat in the morning by the stream that runs behind this house."

That evening, Lalitha arrived at the castle, irritable and restless. She joined her aunt and Prince Giridhar for the evening meal as the wind howled along the walls. They talked about the approaching summer while Lalitha yawned.

"What is wrong, child? You seem unwell," her aunt remarked, watching Lalitha push the food around her plate.

"Nothing is wrong," said Lalitha. *Except her world had turned upside down.*

"Maybe, the rumor that Dushyant was spotted in the city is troubling the princess," said Giridhar, staring at her.

Tamping down her fear, Lalitha asked, "Did they find him?"

"Someone insisted he saw Dushyant and hailed the city guards. But our soldiers found no sign of him. Why would Dushyant come to our city?" asked Queen Padmavati.

"He might be looking for a way to capture Kanva, the man you hold captive," mused Giridhar.

Lalitha lost what little appetite she had. "Aunt Padmavati, my head is throbbing. Please excuse me," she pleaded and left the room.

She found Agamathi waiting for her in her chamber. "Let us go for a walk," said Lalitha. They strolled quietly through the palace halls, greeting the maids scurrying past them. In the garden, Lalitha led Agamathi to their secluded bench surrounded by neem trees and flowering shrubs. Seated, Lalitha gazed at her clasped fingers and narrated the story of how she met Puru. When she reached the part of King Dushyant deceiving her, emotions choked her voice. After she finished the tale, Agamathi remained silent. She could hear the humming of insects around the lights.

"Be careful, my lady. King Dushyant appears to be a thief as well as a liar. He stole our princess's heart," said Agamathi, with her lips turned up.

"No, you are wrong. I did like him once when he was Puru. I hate Dushyant," Lalitha roared in anger.

Agamathi smirked. "Are you going to tell the queen about him then? He will be thrown into our dungeon and rot there for the rest of his life."

"No," blurted Lalitha. Heat spread to her cheeks. "I don't want his men to harm my father, so I will help him escape."

"If he came to Garthapuri risking his life, he is under your spell too, my lady."

That night sleep abandoned her. She stared at the ceiling, worrying about Dushyant and her father alternatively. Was Agamathi right in her assessment? It did not matter because Lalitha was not marrying a king. Dushyant would annex Garthapuri to Vidarpur, a fate she wanted to avoid. Finally, before dawn, she discarded the blankets and dressed hurriedly. Nambi arrived at her door as he'd promised. Silently, they crept through the dark halls and entered the garden.

"I found your horse, my lady. I brought the mare back to the stables," whispered Nambi.

Lalitha thanked him quietly. She did not want anyone to connect her to yesterday's incident. She quelled the voice in her head that mocked her for the risk of her present actions. She owed that maddening king her life, and Lalitha would repay her debt.

The main river flowed outside the city, but a smaller tributary flowed through the palace garden. She stepped into a boat, and Nambi rowed swiftly while Lalitha gazed at the outline of buildings that loomed through the morning mist. Soon they arrived near the physician's house. Clean and wet garments hung out to dry, fluttered in the wind. Jayanthi waited for them beside a neem tree. Lalitha scanned the area for Dushyant and found him wrapped in sheets beside Jayanthi. As the craft glided in, Jayanthi lifted Dushyant in her arms and waded into the water. Nambi frowned at her bulging arms but remained silent.

Lalitha moved aside to make space for Dushyant, and Jayanthi settled him down gently. Nambi picked up the oars again and rowed nimbly. The sky lightened in the east, and a gentle wind caused tiny waves across the water. The sound of birds waking up filled the air.

As they approached the palace, Lalitha ordered, "Cover him."

Jayanthi stood up and concealed Dushyant with a light-weight cotton sheet. Then she sat beside Lalitha on the thin plank, with Dushyant's head between them. Dushyant moaned in pain, and Lalitha grimaced, wanting to comfort him. Curse the man for affecting her. Green bushes grew on the edges of the silver water. A deer drinking water lifted its head to view them, its ears pricked and neck strained. At the sound of the oar splashing against the water, it disappeared into the woods, flashing its rump as it skipped away. A large rock stood on the damp sand. The face of an elephant chiseled out of the stone stared at her, worn out by the running stream.

As they reached the palace, guards approached the shore to scrutinize the boat. Nambi slowed down as Lalitha waved at them. Seeing her, they waved back and dispersed. The sun rose and turned the water golden. As they pulled away from the castle, Jayanthi tugged down the cloth covering Dushyant's face. Lalitha was startled to see his eyes open. He stared at her for a moment as if he was etching her in his memory. Then slowly, he gazed toward his foot. Nambi returned his glance and then shifted to view the water. They reached a small bend in the river path hidden by trees. Nambi rowed the boat skillfully into the canal, and darkness descended around them. The stream washed the roots of many trees. Slowly, Nambi halted the vessel next to a gravel shore.

Lalitha pointed to a compact overturned craft on the land. "Jayanthi, take that and follow the river. When you reach the city wall, you have to leave the boat and swim through the canal that flows under the wall," said Lalitha, guilt and anxiety coating her throat. Letting Dushyant escape instead of capturing him represented a treasonous act. It made sense to seize him to force the release of her father. But Dushyant had said he would free her father, and her treacherous heart trusted him.

Nambi and Jayanthi hopped out to fetch the boat. Alone in the boat, Dushyant looked at her. The blankets cocooning him sparkled with the morning dew. "Farewell, my lady," he whispered.

To harden her heart, she shifted away from him. "Free my father," said Lalitha, staring at a duck diving in to catch a fish.

"Lalitha," he said, and she turned to look at him, holding her breath in anticipation. His eyes beseeched her, but his silence lasted a long time. "I regret deceiving you," he said finally. "Will you forgive me?"

A part of her wanted to embrace him tightly, never letting go. A part that mortified her. "Get well, Puru," she whispered.

Soon, Jayanthi and Nambi hauled him out and placed him on the smaller boat. Jayanthi bowed to her deeply before climbing in. Without a backward glance, Jayanthi rowed away swiftly. Lalitha watched Dushyant's disappearing craft for a few moments. Her boat rattled as Nambi stepped in and picked up his oars. He placed them on his thighs, waiting for her. "Take me back," she said as the other vessel vanished from sight.

When they returned to the palace gardens, Queen Padmavati stood on the steps that descended into the river, surrounded by city guards. Surprised, Lalitha regarded her aunt. Her thin lips caused a tremor in Lalitha. As the boat reached the bottom step, one of the guards held it and helped her out.

Her aunt motioned for her to follow. Out of earshot of the men, she asked, "Tell me where you have been this early in the morning."

Worried for Dushyant's safety, Lalitha muttered, "I could not sleep, so I asked Nambi to—"

Her aunt interrupted her, a stern expression on her face.

"You are the princess of this land. I cannot have you wandering the city unchaperoned. From today, you are not to leave the palace unless I accompany you." Shocked at her loss of freedom, Lalitha bit her lip and decided protesting was unwise lest her aunt discovered her true betrayal. Lalitha was a traitor. She'd helped their enemy escape. Then the ax fell. "I had put off your wedding for your father's return. No more. On the next auspicious day, you will marry Giridhar."

16
DUSHYANT

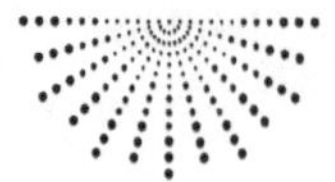

*D*ushyant did not fear his enemies as much as he feared the emotions swirling in him. Like waves pounding a beach, they crashed into his heart, leaving him drenched in his feelings. He had kept passion at bay and built a wall around his heart. But Lalitha crumbled his defense and swept away his indifference. As he rested on a wooden cot in his large tent, staring at the white cotton ceiling, his strengthening emotional ties worried him. Princess Lalitha was unlike any girl he'd met. He admired her bold rescue actions that befit a king. With no hesitation, she'd helped him escape Garthapuri. Dushyant tugged his ear. He did not want to turn into his father, a man who exercised no control over his affections. After his mother's death, his father lost himself in grief. He forgot his duty to his children and his kingdom. Dushyant dreaded following in his father's footsteps. No, he had to put Lalitha out of his mind. An impossible task when she never left his thoughts.

The physician arrived to inspect the wound on his back. "You are healing well, my Majesty," he said, unraveling the wrap around his midsection.

"I am going out of my mind with all this rest. Can I start training?" asked Dushyant, trying hard not to grimace. He needed a sword in his hand to vanquish the demons in his head.

The physician gauged his injury and frowned. "My Majesty, you can start slowly."

Lunge, attack, dodge! Dushyant trained with Jayanth. Rather, Jayanth parried his attacks, barely moving his feet, while Dushyant exhausted himself.

"Are you tired, my Majesty? We can take a break."

"I can go on longer. I am not that weak."

"No, you are not. And you are definitely not panting like a dying dog," teased Jayanth. Still, it felt good to wield the blade.

"I have not thanked you properly for saving my life," said Dushyant, wiping the sweat on his forehead. New growth of hair sprouted above Jayanth's lips. He'd shaved his facial hair to disguise himself as a woman. And had worn a sari for him. How would he ever repay him?

"My young king, do you remember the day I met you four years ago when you were a mere boy of sixteen?"

Dushyant recalled that day vividly. He was visiting his father with his sisters. King Lambhodara, still drowning in his sorrow nearly six years after his mother's death, had found solace in toddy. He barely acknowledged his three children and his slurred speeches made no sense when he spoke. Once, he mistook his twelve-year-old daughter for his wife. Frightened, his sisters had huddled close to him. Dushyant had pledged then not to subject them to the tumultuous behavior of his drunken father. On the day of their departure from Vidarpur, Dushyant climbed the cliffs to view the sprawling kingdom spread around his feet. The rage he'd suppressed in front of his sisters coursed through him and matched the stormy weather outside. He'd hated his father that day for forsaking his duties. Dushyant had borne the heavy burden of caring for his little sisters. While kicking a rock in anger, he found Jayanth gazing at the same scenery, standing too close to the edge. The vacant look on the man's face had frightened Dushyant. Without hesitation, Dushyant jumped on his back and pushed him to the ground.

"You had knocked me to the ground and sat on my chest. As I raised my fist to pound your face, I recognized you. Prince Dushyant. You asked me if I had lost someone. Surprised at your questioning, I replied yes. Then, like a mind reader, you said you understood my pain. Showing wisdom beyond your years, you said taking my life was not the answer. What was the answer I asked you," said Jayanth, staring at him with misty eyes.

"Why kill yourself when you can serve others," said Dushyant, remembering the howling wind as they had stood against the cliff that day in the past.

"I had lost my wife the day before. She'd bled to death giving birth to my stillborn son. I was contemplating ending my life by jumping off the rocks. Then you arrived and saved my life by giving me a new purpose. When you became crown prince two years later, I volunteered to be part of your guard."

Dushyant swallowed, realizing he'd given Jayanth the advice he wished his father had followed. Meeting Jayanth had strengthened his resolve never to allow a woman to pierce his heart. Yet, he'd succumbed to the same temptations. He'd risked his life to see Lalitha and become more entangled with her. They both walked back to Dushyant's tent, mired in their memories. Guilt simmered in Dushyant's mind. Like his father, he allowed a woman to distract him from his duties. He knew he had to forget her.

"Any news from Garthapuri?" Dushyant asked, convincing himself the question was entirely appropriate for a king. He had a duty to know what was happening around him.

"Apparently, a date has been set for Princess Lalitha's wedding," said Jayanth, watching him closely.

"Wedding?" asked Dushyant, like he had trouble with the concept.

Jayanth nodded. "In a fortnight."

"With Prince Giridhar?" Dushyant asked though he knew the answer. Jayanth inclined his head.

All his previous resolve to evade distractions in the form of women fled him. Dushyant wanted to help Lalitha avoid an unwanted marriage. She'd hoped for a swayamvara to choose her groom. She might never choose him, but she deserved the choice. Dushyant knew what he had to do.

"Jayanth, bring Advisor Upananda and General Ayobahu to my tent," ordered Dushyant. The two men arrived with Jayanth while Dushyant read some messages. He waved at them to approach him and continued reading the scroll from his minister. With the frugal measures Dushyant had recommended, they had averted a need to raise tariffs on his subjects. Pleased with the outcome, Dushyant gazed at his three trusted men.

"I want to release Prince Bhimasena," said Dushyant without preamble.

Jayanth's lips curled up as if he had anticipated this action. Upananda inclined his head. Ayobahu's face immediately darkened. "Speak your mind," encouraged Dushyant.

"My Majesty, Prince Bhimasena is a valuable pawn in our quest to bring King Lambhodara's killer to justice. What do we gain by freeing him?"

Dushyant had promised Lalitha he would set her father free. He also hoped her father would stop the impending wedding. Dushyant did not want her to wed Giridhar. Beyond that, it terrified him to examine his sentiments. He did not share these views with his men. Instead, he stated what he should have said in the beginning. "This will be an exchange of prisoners, Prince Bhimasena for Kanva." Dushyant had no desire to conquer Garthapuri.

Ayobahu stared at him. "I will send a message to King Samrat about the prisoner swap. If he refuses?"

Dushyant tugged his ear. "Prince Bhimasena will remain in our custody. Ayobahu, stay here to receive the message from King Samrat. Upananda, you can join me on my journey to Vidarpur."

While alone, Jayanth said, "My king, you are not ready for the long ride—"

"I can rest in a chariot," said Dushyant hurriedly, a fire kindled in his heart. A fortnight was too short. Would he be able to save her?

Wishing he had wings, Dushyant pushed himself that first day on the road. Beaded with sweat, he rode his stallion for several hours, disregarding the pain raging in his body. Dushyant had less than a fortnight and no time to waste. He needed to free Bhimasena, so her father could halt Lalitha's wedding. He did not want to examine why that mattered to him. Upananda kept glancing at him discreetly but stayed quiet. The road they traveled was busy. They passed loaded wagons carrying supplies to his garrison stationed outside Garthapuri. His troop kicked up a cloud of dust in the hot air as they crossed small settlements.

Something itched unpleasantly on his back, between his shoulder blades. He wanted to rub his skin against a tree trunk but suppressed his urge to scratch.

The sun had begun its descent when Jayanth rode closer to him. "My Majesty, with your permission, we want to break for the day," said Jayanth, saving Dushyant from collapsing in fatigue. Dushyant slid down slowly. It took an effort to hold his head high and walk around, chatting with the men. A warm breeze brushed against his skin. A man handed Dushyant a small pot filled with water. Dushyant drank deeply, letting the water slide down his chin.

The supply wagons arrived slowly to the sound of neighs

and formed a circle on the open meadow. After removing their harnesses, the stable boys led the horses to a small pond nestled among some trees. The cook's help brought dry wood and started a fire. Soon, the cook stirred a large pot of rice with vegetables. As his helper added more logs, the flame shot up, bursting into a golden brightness. Behind him, his men erected his cloth tent. Soon, the Vidarpur flag fluttered from the top of the pole. The gentle wind rustled the majestic eagle portrayed on the flag, giving the bird wings. While most of his men would sleep under the stars, Dushyant desired nothing more than his wooden cot at the moment.

"My Majesty," called Jayanth. With his head held high, Dushyant strode to the tent. Opening the flap, he stepped in. Just five more steps, Dushyant told himself, resisting the urge to hunch his shoulders. When his knees hit the bed, he sagged onto it. Within moments, all his energy leached out of him, and he drifted into a troubled sleep.

"Son, you never stayed to help me," said his father, tears streaming down his cheeks.

"Father, I was only ten. It was your duty to protect me," said Dushyant, turning away from the raw emotions reflected on his father's face.

"At ten, I did not expect you to aid me. But when you turned sixteen, I sent for you. But you never came," said his father, contorting his face.

"That is a lie. I came and stayed for a week. But you were too drunk to recognize your own son," screamed Dushyant. Drenched in sweat, he woke up. His heart hammered against his chest as he opened his eyes. Darkness swirled around him. Then he heard footsteps.

"Who is it?" Dushyant asked, his voice croaking.

"My Majesty," one of his young guards said as he approached Dushyant. "I heard noises outside and wanted to inspect."

Dushyant heard the shouts and clamor of feet. "Go find out," he ordered. With his sword drawn, the young man walked forward. Just then, the flap opened.

The guard halted and clasped the hilt of his blade, ready to attack. "It is me," called Jayanth as he peeked in. The guard inclined his head but did not lower the weapon.

Jayanth entered by himself. "A group of monkeys has descended on us."

"Monkeys?"

"Yes, my king. Someone left a heap of bananas out in the open, and the smell drew them in. Some of the bold ones climbed on the back of the horses to peel their food."

Dushyant laughed, imagining one riding his horse. Jayanth joined him. As Dushyant sat up, his stomach growled loudly. He remembered he'd gone to sleep on an empty stomach. Jayanth continued to smile. "I will have your servant fetch you some food."

His servant arrived with rice cooked with ghee and jaggery, finger-long bananas, and a pot of warm milk. Hungry, Dushyant peeled three bananas and stuffed them in his mouth. Chewing furiously, he drank the milk. Somewhat satiated, Dushyant wiped his mouth and pulled the bowl of sweet rice close to him. Usually, Dushyant paid no attention to the food he ate on the road. Today, the aroma of browned ghee reminded him of a joyful day as a child. During an outing with his parents, his mother had served him the same dish under the full moon. Sitting on a rug pressed next to his father, Dushyant had not a care in the world. He wanted to stay in that past and hold onto his rare memory of happiness as he savored his first bite.

"Advisor Upananda is here to see you," said his guard as Dushyant scraped the last morsel of the sticky rice.

"Send him in," said Dushyant, rising to wash his hands in a bowl of water.

"My Majesty," said Upananda. For a moment, Dushyant felt tempted to shield his eyes from the bright yellow dhoti and shawl his advisor wore. The silk draped around Upananda's thin frame gave him the appearance of a flag pole.

"Any news for me?"

Upananda shook his head. "Nothing new, my Majesty." His mostly black hair had a sprinkling of grey in it. Dushyant knew Upananda neared the fourth decade of his life.

"You must be glad to see your family in Vidarpur," said Dushyant, remembering his wife lived in the city.

"There is no one home. My wife and two unmarried daughters are visiting my married daughter and her child. My first grandchild," said Upananda with a grin. Then he grew solemn. "King Dushyant, your father's death has hung over your reign like dark stormy clouds. I applaud your decision to release Prince Bhimasena. Holding him prevents you from focusing on governing. It is time to usher in your rule."

His words created a spark in Dushyant. Then doubt rained on it. "I worry I am going to repeat my father's mistakes," said Dushyant, giving voice to what plagued him.

Upananda's gaze pierced him. "My Majesty, I have observed you closely this past month. You are not your father."

Dushyant slowly released the breath he held. "You were with him for more than a decade and watched his stumbles. Help me avoid his mistakes." Dushyant drew his reserve of courage to utter those words.

"Your father forgot I existed, and I sat humiliatingly idle for most of my time with him. It would be my honor to truly serve you," bowed Upananda. Dushyant was glad he confided in his advisor. He needed Upananda's aid to govern the land.

As days went by, Dushyant felt more at ease in the saddle. He rode from dawn to dusk, halting only briefly during the day. At night, the rest was more for the horses, but he welcomed the respite to get out of the saddle.

He arrived in Vidarpur while the sun hid behind dark

clouds. The wind rustled the trees that stood among the imposing rocks.

Dushyant rode through the road carved from the cliffs and soon saw the city. Surrounded by hills, the tall towers glistened in the light. He reined in his horse and breathed in the scent of the bustling city. His kingdom. He spurred his horse and rode down the road at a canter, passing many carts and people. The guards at the gate noticed him at once. They opened the large doors and bowed in respect as he entered his fort. Chaos greeted his eyes. Guards ran through the courtyard yelling, swearing, and issuing orders. The usually invisible servants hurried along the castle walls. Dushyant noticed a small commotion near the stables where men milled around, edgy and nervous. Horses neighed, and hooves clattered. Dushyant clasped his sword as his herald blew the horn. At once, they turned to glance at him. One of the commanders rushed to him. "My Majesty, our prisoner Prince Bhimasena has escaped."

17

LALITHA

Once Queen Padmavati decided to marry Lalitha to Giridhar, she wasted no time. Consulting with the royal astrologer, she'd set the wedding date a fortnight from today.

Garthapuri law barred women from succession to the throne. After her uncle's accident, it became clear he would never have children. The duty to carry their blood fell on her father. He'd married Charulatha, a woman he'd never met. She bore him Lalitha and miscarried twice after. The experience left her mother desolate, and she became a recluse. A few years ago, on a visit to her sister Chitra, Charulatha had found peace at a Buddhist monastery and had remained there. Her father had refused to remarry, and plans for a male heir fell through. Instead, her father had hoped Lalitha might rule beside her husband or as the mother of her son without subjugating herself to either. Her father had taught her history and took her along on his visits, grooming her to rule. The swayamvara would have allowed Lalitha to choose a man who respected her too much to oppose her in anything. Puru's face drifted into her mind. Now, all that had gone astray.

A king sat on the throne. Any power Lalitha exercised would come from her husband. Giridhar might be unwilling to share the governance with her and might bundle her off to join the other womenfolk. If she did not bear him a son, her position would be even more precarious.

Lalitha remembered her time on the road with King Dushyant. Instead of throwing her in a cell next to her father, he drove her to safety. With a wounded leg, she was defenseless, but he'd treated her with respect and honor. Why did her thoughts take her down this futile path? He was an enemy king who had captured her father. She had to put him out of her mind.

A cat that had been dozing under a tree lifted its head and purred. From her perch on a rope swing, Lalitha glanced up.

"There you are, my lady. The queen is looking for you."

Agamathi found her in a secluded corner of the palace garden among flowering vines.

Lalitha grimaced and touched her feet to the ground. "What does she want?"

"I heard her mentioning your betrothal to my father. I was not spying on her, but they had forgotten I was in the room."

"Betrothal? What is the need for it? It is not like Giridhar needs to be tied to me. He does not appear to have any choice in the matter either," said Lalitha, raising her voice in a torrent of words. Unlike a wedding, she could break an engagement, but she would bring shame to her family and ruin her chances of finding another match.

"Maybe it is you the queen is worried about," said Agamathi with a frown.

Lalitha knew she could not blame her aunt for her worries. Lalitha was looking for every opportunity to obstruct the wedding.

"What will you do?" asked Agamathi.

"I don't know, Agamathi. I am not sure my aunt will listen to any reason," sighed Lalitha.

"There is one thought that came into my mind," said Agamathi, biting her lower lip.

Lalitha hopped from the swing. "What is it?"

"You might request the presence of your mother at the betrothal and wedding. That is not unreasonable for a girl."

Her mother? Would she even attend? Nevertheless, it gave her a reason to delay the engagement. Before Agamathi could continue, Lalitha embraced her tightly. "Agamathi, you have given me a new life. I will plead with my aunt to invite my mother and Aunt Chitra to the wedding. A girl needs at least one parent to bless her. That will put off any plans for the betrothal before the wedding."

Agamathi smiled. "Please wait for the plan to succeed before we celebrate, my lady."

"With all the bad news I have received in the past month, I want to revel in any tiny thing that brings me glee."

Lalitha found her aunt conversing with Prince Giridhar, their heads nearly touching. The queen spoke in hushed tones, and he listened while drumming his fingers on the table. Lalitha jiggled her hand, and her gold bangles rattled. They both looked up and cast their glances at her. He might as well hear it. "Aunt Padmavati, a girl only gets married once. I wish at least one of my parents to be present. Since my father is in prison, can we fetch my mother?" As she uttered these words, Lalitha realized she was ambiguous about her mother attending the ceremony. As a child, she'd wished her mother was like other mothers, willing to sacrifice anything and everything for her only daughter. But as years went by and her mother never showed she cared for her daughter, Lalitha considered her mother dead. It created an armor around her feelings, a shell to protect herself from getting hurt.

Queen Padmavati looked at her fondly. "My child, do you

think I would neglect to invite your mother and aunt? I have sent them messages." She paused and reached to touch Lalitha's wrist. "I don't want you to be disappointed. Charulatha shredded all ties with her past life when she moved into the ashram. She might not come."

Sadness pierced Lalitha's heart, and she blinked rapidly. A mother's love, something most children take for granted, was beyond her reach. Her mother cared for her as she cared for any living thing. Nothing more. Even thinking about her mother reopened old wounds. Ones she assumed had healed. Lalitha had believed her heart hardened like a diamond, but the pain still hurt her. She had to accept the truth. Her mother would never visit her. Lalitha should continue to pretend her mother did not exist.

"Where my mother is concerned, I have long given up any hopes," Lalitha said brusquely. Her aunt sighed while Giridhar regarded her as if noticing her for the first time. She did not need his pity.

"Still, I would request we hold no ceremonies marking the union till my aunt arrives," said Lalitha, rubbing her cheek.

Giridhar stretched his legs in front as if he did not care about their nuptials. Her aunt nodded eagerly. "Lalli, your aunts will host a grand wedding for you that will be remembered for ages."

Lalitha did not care for any imposing celebrations. Nevertheless, she thanked her aunt profusely while Giridhar lifted his head and searched her face.

A moment later, a knock sounded on the door. "Come in," said her aunt.

Minister Kapila entered. "A messenger from King Dushyant, my lady."

A small but wiry man walked in. He cast keen glances at them and bowed. Lalitha worried that her aunt could hear her pounding heart.

"Speak," ordered the queen.

"King Dushyant wants to swap prisoners. Prince Bhimasena for Kanva." Lalitha's hands trembled, and she twined her fingers. Dushyant kept his promise. He would free her father. Something like joy erupted in her stomach.

18

DUSHYANT

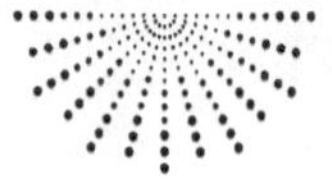

Dushyant swallowed the anger threatening to erupt in him like he buried most emotions. Feelings led one to make mistakes.

"How did my prisoner escape?" he asked coldly. His eyes swept the hastily summoned men around him. Light spilled through the large window, illuminating a trail of dust floating in the air. Commanders and veterans of many wars bowed before him, unable to meet his gaze. Men who had let Kanva kill his father.

The head of his city guard, Samudra, jingled a gold chain that dangled from his powerful neck. "This was planned, my Majesty. Prince Bhimasena was not housed with the other prisoners and enjoyed more liberties." He looked at Dushyant as if to accuse him of making these changes. And Dushyant did order these shifts after he returned from meeting Lalitha. Did he let the dreaded emotions cloud his judgment? Samudra continued, "During his brief outing into the sun, someone knocked his guards with arrows and dragged them out of sight. When the prisoner did not return for the mid-day meal, the other guards raised the alarm. They mounted a search and found the corpses." Murdered by arrows. Like his father. Since his ascension to the throne, he'd failed in his efforts colossally.

"Where did he flee? He could not have gone far on foot."

"The rocky path offered no clues, my Majesty. He is hiding somewhere in our city."

Dushyant gazed out the window to view the city carved out of the mountain. "He will find plenty of caves that offer him cover. We cannot search all of them. But we can inspect the horses and carts leaving our city. Post a checkpoint at all entries."

Lalitha's face as she arched her brows wafted into his head. If her father perished on his way to Garthapuri, he would fail her too. While his physical wounds continued to mend, his mistakes plagued his mind. "I want to capture the prisoner alive," growled Dushyant, surprising his audience. As they stared at his uncharacteristic outburst, he let out his breath. "I need him alive to trade him for my father's murderer," Dushyant said in a calmer tone. They nodded and dispersed to carry out his commands.

The next day, Dushyant paced the floor. His large room stood high on the cliffs and faced the gardens below. A rectangular mango wood table held neatly arranged parchments, scrolls, and feathers. Jayanth stood behind it and blended with the stone walls.

A knock sounded on his door. "Enter," Dushyant said without pausing. Minister Panini walked in first and came to a halt in the center of the chamber. Chief Guard Samudra strode in and glanced around. Seeing Jayanth, he came to stand next to him. Advisor Upananda followed in measured steps and hovered near the threshold. A guard closed the door.

Dushyant halted next to the table and stared at the three men.

"My Majesty," began Minister Panini.

"I hope you bring me news of Prince Bhimasena's recapture," interrupted Dushyant.

They avoided his eyes and looked at the wall. "We have ascertained Prince Bhimasena had help," said the minister. Dushyant viewed the men silently.

"With the backing of others, he killed his guards and escaped. Our guards are inspecting every vehicle leaving the city, but our intense search has not revealed his hiding place. He is either staying hidden at his location or has already fled the city."

"I was expecting more information since we last spoke," said Dushyant, keeping annoyance out of his tone.

"We hope to catch him soon," said Chief Guard Samudra.

"Soon is too late for me," said Dushyant. "Prince Bhimasena is an astute warrior. He is unlikely to do anything foolish. What do you propose we do?"

The men looked at each other. "We disagree on what to do next, my Majesty," said Upananda, taking two steps into the room.

"I am all ears. Reveal your plans to me," said Dushyant.

"I want to trace the spies who helped Bhimasena. If we find and question them in the traditional manner, they will reveal all," said Minister Panini stiffly.

"And also reveal what they did not know to satisfy the questioners," said Dushyant hiding any trace of sarcasm in his voice.

Samudra snorted. "What is your view, Chief Samudra?" asked Dushyant.

"I want to search door to door for the culprit. I don't think he has left our city." Samudra stood straight with his hand on the hilt of his sword.

"What about our numerous caves?" asked Upananda, fingering a large emerald ring on his little finger. "They stretch for miles in these cliffs."

Dushyant observed the ring, remembering his mother's

fondness for the gem.

"I think he has left the city, my Majesty. But his passage would be slow. I suggest we head back to Garthapuri on fast horses. We can arrive before him. With a fake prisoner, we can still exchange for Kanva," said Advisor Upananda.

"King Samrat is not going to release Kanva without confirmation that we have his brother," Minister Panini said.

"We don't need to swap the men. The prisoner exchange will take place outside the city. When Kanva appears, we just need to kill him," said Upananda. "They will never find out we don't have Prince Bhimasena."

"No," said Dushyant. He had to find out why Kanva killed his father. "I want Bhimasena and Kanva alive, not dead."

Chief Guard Samudra smirked, but Upananda ignored him. "Once Kanva is in our sight, we can capture him."

The one man in their custody had escaped. Dushyant had no confidence in their ability to snag Kanva. All their plans had holes as though a woodpecker had been pecking at them. "Jayanth, what do you think?"

Like a statue coming to life, Jayanth shifted. "Prince Bhimasena will head back to Garthapuri. Our garrison is stationed outside that city. Capturing him in the wide open meadows might be more fruitful than finding him in our caves."

A smile spread on Upananda's thin face while Samudra looked irritated at the man under his command. Jayanth glanced timidly at the Chief Guard but did not fool Dushyant. His guard was never afraid to share his views with his king.

Still, Dushyant felt like a pawn in someone's game. He had to take control of the game. "Minister Panini's plan is not without merit. Ask our spy chief to investigate who has been in touch with Prince Bhimasena." Minister Panini brightened at this and bowed.

"Chief Guard Samudra, with a small army, scour our city and caves methodically. Even if we don't find Prince Bhimasena, we will find whoever offered him shelter. That can lead us to the traitors." Samudra twisted his gold chain and nodded vigorously.

"Advisor Upananda, plan for our journey back. Let us leave immediately." Time for Dushyant to shatter the obstacles on his path. However, an unease spread through his limbs like he was blundering into a trap laid out for him.

"My Majesty," the minister began, and Dushyant brought his attention back. "I received a letter from the princesses—"

"My sisters?" asked Dushyant, narrowing his eyes.

Minister Panini nodded. "They are on their way to Vidarpur. The letter indicates this is at your behest."

"My order?" Dushyant asked stupidly. He did intend to bring them over once he settled the matter with Kanva, but he did not write this message.

Minister Panini inclined his head.

Dushyant did miss their familiar faces, and the danger of a war with Garthapuri had receded. "Chief Guard Samudra, send some of our best men to escort them to Vidarpur."

Panini and Samudra departed soon, but Upananda lingered.

"What is it?

"My Majesty, I ask your permission to speak my mind openly."

"You will always have my permission to speak the truth."

"My Majesty, your father was indecisive and inactive. He wasted his time on the throne. A king always takes action even if they cannot predict the outcome. History may judge them later, but a ruler cannot hesitate in the present. You demonstrated your courage today, and I am honored to serve you."

If his actions led to disaster, history would judge Dushyant harshly. That was a burden a king had to bear. "Thank you, Advisor," said Dushyant. Upananda departed, leaving Dushyant alone with his guard.

"Jayanth, there is something I don't understand here. If

Prince Bhimasena had spies, he knew I was coming to free him. Why did he stage a risky escape?"

Jayanth scratched his chin. "Maybe this was something he'd planned before the news arrived. And he may not have trusted the information, not knowing how deeply you have fallen for his daughter."

"You jest," smiled Dushyant.

"I am only trying to explain the situation, my king."

Dushyant tugged his ear. "What happened to the boy who drowned? Do you know who killed him?"

Jayanth shook his head. "Someone crafty. No strangers met him. Only the usual people."

These mysteries piling up frustrated Dushyant.

According to their plans, Advisor Upananda spread false tales about Prince Bhimasena's seizure and found a decoy of similar build and height.

Soon, they rode the familiar roads between Vidarpur and Garthapuri, passing fields and streams, and the decoy prisoner rode in a covered cart. Dushyant did not notice the wind gathering speed nor the flash of lightning that lit up the sky. His mind dwelled on Lalitha and her hand in his hair. He hoped to see her again and watch a smile spread on her face. But he was not bringing her father as he'd promised. Her brows would likely knit in anger at his debacle and deceit.

"My Majesty," said Jayanth, riding beside him. "A storm is approaching us. We need to seek shelter."

Dushyant woke up from his daze and scanned his surroundings. Dark clouds hovered overhead, and the wind grew stronger. A bolt of lightning pierced the clouds, and a moment later, it thundered. The trees tossed in the gale.

"A lightning like this without a little rain is dangerous, my king. It will strike a tree or a wagon, and we will have a fire on our hands."

Another lightning split the sky and illuminated an old

temple tower. His horse neighed and thudded its hooves. "Let us seek cover in that temple till the storm passes us," said Dushyant.

As they galloped toward it, drops of rain fell from the sky. The parched ground absorbed the water greedily. Dushyant heard the trembles of the thunder in the distance. They arrived in the temple courtyard, their wet clothes clinging to their backs. Dushyant dismounted and handed the reins to a stable boy. Taking shelter on the veranda, he leaned against the large stone pillar and watched the water stream down. He noticed Advisor Upananda standing next to a covered wagon, talking to a man holding a horsewhip. The shower soaked them, and their dhoti stuck to their bodies. But neither seemed aware of the deluge as they continued their conversation.

The thunder and rain reminded him of his father's shrieks and sobs after his mother's death. After his father beat his chest and cried over his mother's corpse, Dushyant thought he would have gotten over the grief. But his father never did, causing the young boy to avoid saying or doing anything that might open his wound.

Was his father ashamed of betraying his mother's memory? Was that why he never married Sundari? That seemed strange to Dushyant in a culture that permitted royal men to take on many wives. But why would someone drown a young soldier if he'd seen or heard of his father's disgraceful behavior? Apart from Dushyant, who else would care for his father's honor?

Dushyant felt like the lightning had struck him and set his body on fire. What if his father was not the one who had violated Sundari? Could Sundari be mistaken about the identity of the man who betrayed her? Did a lie provoke Kanva to kill his father? The real culprit might want the truth to remain hidden, and he appeared prepared to kill for it.

While the storm raging inside Dushyant intensified, the one outside abated, and the sun peaked out of the clouds.

19

LALITHA

"*L*alitha," called Giridhar as he followed her down the hall.

Lalitha halted, her back to him. A sharp sound startled her, and she searched the long narrow hall for the source of the noise. The fluttering of wings near the high ceiling caused her to look up. A sparrow circled above, chirping loudly. A row of windows lined the top of the wall, and another bird perched on the window sill cried back in answer. They chattered for a moment and then as a pair flew out into the sky, still tweeting incessantly. How did these birds decide they should build a nest together? Their chirps must communicate more than she could comprehend.

Giridhar arrived next to her. "My lady, I loathe to see you like this. You are facing our upcoming union with as much joy as a prisoner facing his execution. I am to blame for it. Tell me how I can rectify it." He gazed at her with concern.

Lalitha cast her eyes down, embarrassed by his intuition. He was right. She'd been trying to sabotage their wedding and did not hide her dislike. "Prince Giridhar, my apologies. With my father a prisoner, I have not been the best company."

"We just heard the good news about your father's release. I hope King Dushyant keeps his promise. But it is not just that, my lady. You rarely smile when you talk to me. It is as if I only remind you of unpleasant things." He leaned in closer. "I am not a monster, and I have no intention of making life miserable for you."

"No, I don't t-think you are a monster," stammered Lalitha. "It is not you, my lord. It is the thought of marriage. Neither my uncle and aunt nor my parents are good examples." Half-truths. She would have no trouble contemplating marriage to Puru, though not to King Dushyant. The man she became friends with was a mirage. Puru did not exist.

"Lalitha," he said, raising his hand as if to touch her elbow and then dropping it by his side. "If we respect and trust each other, we can build our life on top of it." He looked at her earnestly. "Will you give me a chance to earn your trust? I heard what you asked your aunt. I promise to defer any celebrations until one of your parents is here to witness it."

A lump rose in her throat. "Giridhar, you are a good man. I am not sure I deserve you."

"My lady, your modesty is another jewel in your crown," he said and dipped his head. She resumed her walk to her chambers with her mind in turmoil. Why couldn't she be content with marrying him? Her worry that he might usurp her power and push her into the background was unfounded. Dushyant's large ears floated into her mind. She remembered the feel of his lips, which stirred a deep yearning. She knew why she resented her union with Giridhar. He evoked none of the strong emotions she felt when she thought of Dushyant. What did it mean? She had to hate Dushyant for betraying her. But all she could think of was to escape her pending nuptials with Giridhar. How she could achieve this, she had no idea. Still, whatever her preferences, she needed to be careful around Giridhar and give him no reason to suspect her. A part of her chastised her for her deception, but she knew she had no other way. Her plans might fail, and she might marry Giridhar. She clenched her fist. If that happened, she could not give him cause to punish her.

Over the next few days, Lalitha made an effort to be pleasant to Giridhar. One crisp morning, he joined Lalitha and Agamathi on a walk by the palace garden. Agamathi fell a few feet behind as they wandered through the narrow path strewn with tiny branches and leaves. Lalitha knew her friend was casting her eyes around for Nambi.

"Reading poems does not seem like the appropriate pastime for a future king." Giridhar's love of poetry was fodder for her teasing.

He smiled. "My lady. The kingdom is yours. When the time comes, my title will be ceremonial while you rule the country. I am sure you will not begrudge a man the pleasure of some verses."

Lalitha's heart thundered as she looked at him. "Did you say you will let me—"

"Yes," interrupted Giridhar. "My aunt made that clear to me. Unlike a traditional bride, you will not come with me to Nidhapur after our wedding. Instead, I will remain here, and, one day, our son will rule this land."

"Do you not mind?" Lalitha asked, feeling like she floated on air.

"Why would I? I am the second son. I never expected to sit on the throne. I will only worry if you start treating me worse than my brother," he said, grinning.

Confusion reigned in her mind. "I will treat my husband with all the respect he deserves."

"My lady," Agamathi called as she ran toward them.

"What is it?" Lalitha asked, spinning to face her.

"Princess Charulatha and Princess Chitra are here." Mother? Her mother? Lalitha's stomach squeezed tightly. Taking Giridhar's leave, she rushed inside the palace. She found her mother and Aunt Chitra seated on Queen Padmavati's rosewood bench.

Lalitha gazed at her mother, blinking away the tears that threatened to spill. Lalitha wanted to scream at her for leaving her and clenched her fists tightly. Her nails dug into her palms. Waves of anger, disappointment, and hatred caused her to tremble. As always, her mother viewed her with serene eyes.

"Seek your mother's blessing," Aunt Chitra urged. Lalitha ignored that and instead sought her aunt's blessings by bending and touching her feet. Her aunt folded her into a tight hug. "You gave me a fright when you left without telling me, my child."

"I am sorry, Aunt Chitra. I was worried about my father and did not think properly."

Her aunt released her and held her at arm's length. Her kind gaze pierced Lalitha's armor. "Don't disappoint me again then," she said gently and nodded toward her mother.

Lalitha grudgingly approached her mother and touched her feet. Her mother placed her palm on her head. "May the divine light shine on you brightly."

Lalitha drifted back to Aunt Chitra's side. "Queen Padmavati mentioned that King Dushyant will free your father in exchange for a prisoner held here."

Lalitha nodded, hoping her trust in Dushyant was not misplaced.

Her mother seemed not to notice any of this. She stared out the window through which faint noises from the garden floated in: the sweep of a broom, the cawing of birds, and indistinguishable voices.

"Her father and I wanted to hold a swayamvara for Lalitha. While he is in prison, what is the rush to marry this boy?" she asked, still gazing at the clouds drifting in the sky. When did her father discuss the swayamvara with her mother?

Queen Padmavati looked at her mother with a trace of annoyance. "Garthapuri has no heir. Is that not reason enough?"

asked Queen Padmavati, speaking for the first time since Lalitha arrived in the room.

"That burden to produce an heir nearly killed me," her mother said in an even tone as if discussing a temple she visited. "I don't want to subject Lalitha to that, especially wedded to a man forced upon her." It felt strange to hear her mother come to her defense.

Queen Padmavati flushed in anger. "I don't need you to lecture me on Lalitha. You abandoned her while I have been raising her like my own. She understands her duties well, and my nephew, Giridhar, will be an able partner in ruling Garthapuri."

Lalitha's eyes darted between the queen and her mother; her stomach roiled between hope and anxiety.

Her mother folded her hands in her lap and ignored Queen Padmavati's taunts. "Lalitha can choose to garland Giridhar at her swayamvara if she desires. You cannot deny her that choice," she said firmly.

Lalitha's heart leaped to her throat as she watched Queen Padmavati press her lips together. "I am the queen of this land, and her marriage is my prerogative."

"You are mistaken, my lady. It is the king's prerogative. I can address this matter with him when I meet him later today." Her mother's blank face reminded her of Dushyant's. How neither of them displayed any emotions seemed beyond Lalitha's imagination.

"There is no need to disturb the king. I will consider this matter and make a decision tomorrow. Lalitha, take your mother to her chambers," the queen said, dismissing them.

DUSHYANT

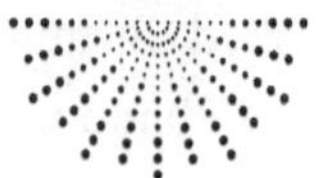

*D*ushyant rode into their garrison and slid off his horse in front of General Ayobahu and a small contingent of his men. A stable boy led the horse away while General Ayobahu bowed his head in greeting.

Leaving others behind, Ayobahu and Dushyant strode forward, discussing routine matters. In front of his tent, Dushyant halted.

"General, any news of Prince Bhimasena?" whispered Dushyant. They still pretended that the prince remained his captive and Dushyant was ready to exchange him for Kanva.

"I have several patrols along the road from Vidarpur to here. There has been no sighting of him. He seems to have disappeared into the air." Ayobahu's scar gave the impression of slicing his face.

Jayanth parted the cloth door and entered the tent, and they followed him. Jayanth walked around slowly, inspecting the meager furniture.

"How is that possible? Even if he traveled by foot, someone must have noticed a stranger. Do you have men in the neighboring villages looking for a visitor?" asked Dushyant, removing his silk shawl and throwing it on a bench.

Ayobahu nodded. "I have scouts in the nearby villages, my Majesty. No word of a newcomer." He rubbed his forehead. "Maybe, the prince is still hiding in Vidarpur." A light breeze rustled the cloth walls of his shelter.

Dushyant shook his head. "Chief Guard Samudra is searching door to door. Vidarpur is not a safe place for him." Prince Bhimasena would not risk remaining in Vidarpur. Where was he?

"Like smoking a snake out of its burrow, we may need a way to smoke him out. If we still held the princess, she would have come—"

"No," said Dushyant vehemently. Ayobahu's head snapped up to gaze at him intently. "Our men have been unable to capture Kanva, and now we have lost Bhimasena. No need to add to our failures," said Dushyant. Kidnapping Lalitha would allow him to spend more time with her. A deep yearning to see and hold her filled his entire being. Dushyant could not cope with the feelings he felt for Lalitha. He seemed doomed to repeat his father's mistakes as if he had a perverse need for suffering. He emptied his mind of these thoughts. Only one thing mattered at present. He would not put Lalitha's life at risk. She already resented him, and he suspected this would only add to their existing conflicts. "Continue the hunt for Prince Bhimasena. I want the prince captured alive. Jayanth, send for Advisor Upananda. I want to discuss our plan now that we have no prisoner to exchange."

People bustled outside, and their voices wafted inside. Soon, Upananda entered the room and bowed with respect.

"Prince Bhimasena still eludes us. Despite that, do we go ahead with the exchange using the decoy?" asked Dushyant, his eyes darting between the vigorous general and the thin advisor beside him.

Upananda cleared his throat. "That would be my recommendation, my Majesty. We entice Kanva out of the castle and seize him."

Ayobahu tore his eyes away from the advisor and turned to Dushyant. "What happens once they realize our deceit?" He scowled as he scratched his scar with his fingernail.

"Nothing," said Upananda, smiling slyly. "King Samrat is bedridden, and without his brother to command the army, he cannot mount any offense."

"Minister Kapila will advise them to mount archers on the fort towers. At a signal from the Queen, their arrows will pierce our bodies. It will be foolish on our part not to prepare for that outcome," argued Ayobahu, gesturing with his arms.

Jayanth, who had observed the proceeding silently, interjected. "Princess Lalitha might accompany the prisoner. Her presence will deter the archers from shooting down at us."

"You don't say?" said Dushyant, faking astonishment.

"It is common knowledge that the princess is fond—" Jayanth paused. Dushyant opened his eyes widely. He knew his guard would not betray his confidence, so he wondered what reason Jayanth would provide. "The princess is fond of her father and will want to escort him inside the castle," he explained. Dushyant let out his breath.

"Indeed," Upananda agreed. "There you go, General. With the princess beside us, no need to worry about piercing arrows," he said and smiled.

"If what you presume does not happen, and the princess does not join Kanva, I suggest we be on guard," said Ayobahu in a cold voice. "The king's protection lies in your hands, Head Guard Jayanth." Jayanth bowed his head. "My Majesty, I assume we will leave at sunrise tomorrow. I will take your leave to prepare for the encounter," said Ayobahu.

"Come and see me later today," said Dushyant, dismissing both.

They bowed again and departed, leaving Dushyant alone

with Jayanth. "There is something amiss here, Jayanth. Why have our men not found Prince Bhimasena yet?"

Before Jayanth could answer, Dushyant's servant arrived with his large trunk of clothes. As his servant helped Dushyant change out of his dirty clothes, Dushyant imagined what he would do in Prince Bhimasena's place. He would seek a safe haven first before plotting any revenge. Prince Bhimasena had orchestrated a meticulous plan to escape from his cell. He had help. What if they knew about Dushyant's scheme to use a decoy? Only a few members of his council knew the details. Did one of them reveal it to the prince? Or worse, did one of them aid in his efforts to break free? Dushyant regretted not spending time in Vidarpur to get to know his men. Now, he had no hint as to who might be the culprit. Dushyant decided to worry about the traitor later. First, he needed to figure out what the prince would do. The answer came to him slowly, like steam escaping a boiling pot through the gap between the lid and the vessel. When Dushyant presented the dummy as Prince Bhimasena, the real prince would make an entry to make a mockery of him and expose him as a sham.

The servant departed, and Dushyant paced the room, his mind buzzing with notions like bees around a flowering bush. "Yes," he whispered, " it is crazy enough that it might work." Jayanth tilted his head, looking at him. "I need your help to put this into action. Find Amudhan." He'd disguised himself as Dushyant once in Garthapuri.

* * *

Outwardly, Dushyant kept to the scheme he'd discussed with General Ayobahu and Advisor Upananda. The night before they arrived at Garthapuri, he dispatched a messenger to King Samrat, conveying their impending arrival with Prince Bhimasena. That night, sleep abandoned Dushyant, and he quit his tent to sleep on a blanket in the meadow. The stars twinkled overhead, oblivious to emotions churning in his stomach: a mixture of guilt and loss. Dawn arrived reluctantly, and Dushyant dressed carefully.

Strolling among his men, Dushyant made sure everyone saw his splendid gold crown embedded with sparkling blue sapphires and silk dhoti. In the sunlight, the gems cast a web of light on the face of his audience.

"Why are five wagons accompanying us?" Dushyant asked when he noticed them lined up side by side. The cotton covers on the wagons painted with ordinary village scenes fluttered in the light wind.

"To confuse any spies and scouts," whispered Upananda. "One of them hides our prisoner, and the others are coming to divert any attention." Satisfied with the explanation, Dushyant prepared for what came next.

When all gathered for their journey, Dushyant faced them, letting his eyes linger on those assembled. A moment later, he said resoundingly, "My forefathers ruled Vidarpur for generations with courage and generosity. My father's untimely death is a blemish in our history. Our mission today is to remedy that stain. We will return Prince Bhimasena to Garthapuri in exchange for the man who killed my father. Kanva in our custody will wipe our tarnish and usher in a new beginning, so I thank you all for joining me. Victory to Vidarpur."

As cries of victory to Vidarpur echoed, Dushyant marched away with Jayanth. In a dark corner of the makeshift stable, Dushyant took off his crown and gold chain and handed them to Amudhan. In their place, he wore a gray wig, beard, and a plain white cotton dhoti. His eyes caught a large brown spider hanging on a single thread, spinning its way down from the ceiling. He wished he felt more like that spider, sure of his path forward. A hazy mist seemed to cover his future. He tugged his ear and realized he still wore his large gold disc. He removed the earrings and held them to Amudhan. The boy shook his head.

"His ears are not pierced, my Majesty. I will find a goldsmith to take care of it after today," mumbled Jayanth. Dushyant placed the discs in a cloth pouch, and his fingers brushed the silver anklet of Lalitha. A sudden image of the princess as they rode together on her mare wafted into his memory. Every time her skin grazed his, her touch lit a trail of fire on his. Jayanth cleared his throat, and reluctantly Dushyant tucked the bag into his waist. "I have placed a trusted guard in the cart next to yours. In the event of a mishap, he will take you to safety."

"Keep Amudhan safe for me," said Dushyant. He worried about his guard taking any arrows intended for his back.

Jayanth and Amudhan dipped their heads, mounted their rides, and rode to the front of the column. After watching them, Dushyant hitched a sack containing his weapons on his shoulders and plodded to the covered carriage at the end. Depositing the bag beside him, he grabbed the reins while his eyes scanned the road in front. One of the two bulls pulling his wagon snorted loudly and swatted his leg with his tail. Dushyant drew his legs in. He then looked around for Jayanth's man. One wearing a wig that resembled a bird's nest caught his eyes. Recognizing him as one of the king's guards, Dushyant nodded subtly.

As he scoured the area, Dushyant could see the gems on the crown glimmer at the head of the line. Soon, he tugged the reins, and wheels creaked as the wagon moved forward. All appeared as it should. Nothing was out of place. Except for him. He heard someone cough rather violently, and he searched the wagons. One of the drivers bent at his waist as his chest spasmed in more coughing. Dushyant halted his cart to see if he needed aid. Before Dushyant could approach him, his neighboring carriage stopped to offer him water from a clay pot, and the cougher drank the water greedily.

"I choked on a nut," the man mumbled, wiping his mouth. Satisfied that he'd recovered, Dushyant rode on.

As they neared the city, ordinary folks going about their morning stopped and glanced at them. The eagle pictured on their flags indicated who they were. Dushyant brought up the rear, and he could see clusters of people along the road, talking among themselves while glancing at their procession.

The Garthapuri castle rose in front of him, and the river snaked past it. Dushyant spotted a few boats on the water. Their convoy came to a halt a few yards from the fort wall. A Vidarpur herald blew his horn and proclaimed the virtues of his forefathers before ending with, "King Dushyant, son of King Lambhodara, with mountain-like shoulders, rides leaping horses and chariots, commands an ocean-like army, and victorious on battlefields."

From his seat, Dushyant smirked. Somehow, he managed to squeeze his mountain-size shoulders to fit in the cart. Apart from being the son of Lambhodara, not one of the other words rang true. He'd barely fought in any battles apart from the skirmish with Prince Bhimasena. Dushyant vowed that he would give poets and heralds true acts to sing in his praise.

From the tower of the fort, a Garthapuri herald announced the many virtues of King Samrat. The large wooden doors with thick iron bars the size of his thigh nailed to them opened slowly, and a small retinue emerged with a lotus flag waving in the wind. Dushyant's eyes were drawn to the lady on the elephant with majestic tusks. She was too far for him to view the features of her face, yet he still knew her. Lalitha wore a green sari and appeared like a goddess who lived in a fragrant flowering grove. A fortnight ago, Lalitha had helped Dushyant escape her city on a boat. She'd protected him like a divine spirit even when she learned his identity. Everything he felt and could not voice surged in him. Glad of his disguise, Dushyant watched her move forward unobtrusively. A young man with a simple gold crown rode his mare beside her elephant. Behind them walked a man in chains. That must be Kanva, his father's killer.

Two horses peeled off from the front of his unit and approached the wagons. With his eyes still on the princess, Dushyant paid partial attention to what his men were doing.

"Open," muttered one of the riders, and the cart driver jumped down and untied the cloth cover. Dushyant took out a piece of mirror from his waist and held it discreetly so he could watch what happened behind him. The fake Prince Bhimasena emerged from the rear, his hands tied to his back. Another man, likely his escort, jumped out and stretched his arms overhead. Dushyant noticed the man's tall frame as he stood on his toes to stretch his legs. The two horses trotted forward, and the decoy prince followed them slowly, walking with a slight limp, his legs likely still numb from the cramped space. Where was the real prince? Dushyant scanned the area. If his hunch were correct, Lalitha's father would appear shortly to reveal his duplicity.

The two horses and the lone prisoner passed the wagons and continued toward the palace. Dushyant realized the tall man did not accompany them. He heard a rustle of cloth and picked up the mirror again. The missing escort approached the back of another wagon surreptitiously and undid the knots tying the cover to the cart.

"Get down," the tall escort hissed. A man with a long beard jumped out, and they both tugged an object in the carriage. Something crashed onto the ground. Before Dushyant could understand what was occurring behind him, a commotion erupted up front. He heard a shout and saw one of the horses turn around and head toward them. He recognized the man on the stallion. Jayanth! Why was Jayanth coming toward him? On seeing his commander, the king's guard wearing a wig that resembled a bird's nest, hopped down from his carriage and pulled out his dagger. What danger did they see that he failed to notice?

Dushyant raised his eyes and saw Lalitha and her elephant continue to move forward. Then, he noticed arrows flying. He grabbed his sack and undid the wrapping with nimble fingers. *Don't come forward, Lalitha. Death stands in your way.* Drawing his sword, Dushyant stood on his cart, ready to leap and run to her.

A movement behind him caught his eye. The tall escort and his companion hauled something upright. A man? The tall man held a blade in one hand. In the blink of an eye, Dushyant knew the two of them supported someone important.

Dushyant jumped down and landed awkwardly. Jayanth approached him. Straightening quickly, he yelled at Jayanth. "Ride to the front. Save the princess." After watching Jayanth spin around, Dushyant ran to the rear. His guard followed him.

Seeing the two of them, the tall escort shoved their prisoner. The prisoner lost his balance and lurched forward, instinctively thrusting his right arm toward Dushyant's chest to stop himself from falling. Their eyes met, and Dushyant recognized the thin frame and the gray hair. Prince Bhimasena. Lalitha's father. He had been a fool. *A mighty fool.* Unknown to Dushyant, the real prince had traveled in one of his wagons. Prince Bhimasena had remained a captive all along. Which of his men had orchestrated this charade?

The tall man cried out and thrust his dagger forward. The blade glided toward Prince Bhimasena. For a brief instance, Lalitha's face drifted through Dushyant's mind. He could not let any harm come to her father. Dushyant collided with the prince and sent him slumping to the floor. Dushyant felt the dagger crunch against his upper arm. The prince screeched from below as Dushyant's blood dripped onto his chest. Dushyant staggered backward and shuddered as he hit the carriage. He felt trapped.

The tall escort moved slowly toward him, his eyes burning. As he came closer, Dushyant's frozen muscles began to work. When the man lunged toward him, Dushyant jumped and spun out of his reach in one smooth move. The escort fell to his knees.

Dushyant took a step back and swung his sword. The weapon wailed, and its sharp edge plunged into the ribs of the tall escort. With a rasping breath, the man collapsed to the floor. The bearded man leaped out of the way of his falling comrade and gazed at Dushyant with a mad gleam. His guard rammed into him, causing both of them to fall.

Dushyant hit the bearded man between his eyebrows with the pommel of his sword, causing him to howl and faint. Then, he pulled his guard up. The nest wig came loose and stayed on the ground. The young man kicked the false hair in disgust.

"What is your name?" Dushyant asked. Knowing his name would mean Dushyant would worry for his safety, but he wanted to bear that burden.

"Sendhan."

"Sendhan, keep him alive. I want to question him later," ordered Dushyant. He heard weapons clanging and men shouting. He had no time to rest. He bent down to cut off the ropes binding Prince Bhimasena. The prince gazed at him in confusion. "I am King Dushyant, and I will convey you safely to your daughter." As he scooped the prince in his arms, Dushyant staggered under his weight.

"Help the king," yelled the guard while pressing his foot on the bearded man who stirred, and the other drivers, who had watched the battle frozen in place like statues, came to life.

"Our king," muttered one in disbelief, gazing at the disheveled, dirty, and blood-covered king. Shaking his head still, the cart driver helped carry the prince to his wagon. Dushyant took the reins and hurried the bulls. The air in front rippled with tension. Horses neighed, and the lone elephant trumpeted. The smell of blood assaulted his nostrils. He knew blood seeped from his arm, but he dare not rest. His eyes sought the princess on top of the elephant, but it was empty. Where was the princess? His heart thundered against his chest. He saw a flash of green ahead. He prodded the bulls to run, wishing he had wings to fly to her.

An arrow slammed into the side of his cart, piercing the wood. Before Dushyant could react, a second arrow flew at him. Dushyant deflected it with his sword. A madness raged in front of him. Some called for a fight while others cautioned restraint.

Coming to a precarious stand on the moving vehicle, Dushyant yelled, "Stop the fighting. I come in peace."

Jayanth heard him and echoed his cry. For a moment, everyone stared at him in a suspended state. Dushyant's eyes searched for her in the chaos. He found Lalitha standing in the middle of a circle of men, her hair fanning out of the bun and her face contorted. Seeing her alive and unhurt, a strange emotion flooded his body. *Joy.* He nearly laughed in delight, but that way led to peril. He suppressed his feelings for her. When she saw him, her eyes opened wide, and her hand covered her mouth. Then an arrow came flying by, and commotion rose again.

That arrow did not come from the Garthapuri tower. It seemed to come from the woods nearby. "General Ayobahu, kill or capture the archers," commanded Dushyant, looking away from her. Her anger or fear, he will face later. A group of horses rode toward the trees.

Dushyant slowed down his cart as two guard members joined him on their horses. Then he saw the broken bodies lying on the ground. Kanva, still in chains, lay flat on his stomach with an arrow sticking out of his back. His stomach twisted at the sight of the dead man. Dushyant never had the chance to talk to his father's murderer. A few feet away, his crown rested on the gravel, glinting in the light. With his heart in his throat, Dushyant sought his mute guard, who had dressed as the king. He found Amudhan a few feet from the crown, nursing a wound on his leg. A large bruise on his cheek turned blue. Still,

Dushyant was glad to see Amudhan alive. His eyes swept past Amudhan and landed on something terrible. Stretched beside Amudhan with a dagger protruding from his stomach was the fake Prince Bhimasena. Dushyant's stomach dropped to the ground. He'd allowed his faceless enemy to trick him.

A few yards from Lalitha, he halted the cart and jumped down. The young man with the simple gold crown stood beside her, his sword drawn. That must be Prince Giridhar. A sudden rage to sink his dagger into Giridhar's heart coursed through Dushyant. Shocked, Dushyant clenched his jaw. Lalitha's eyes shot daggers at Dushyant. "You deceived me," she said, her voice breaking with the weight of her emotion. Dushyant wanted to pull her against his chest and deny her allegations.

"Lalitha, is that you?" called a feeble voice from his cart, startling them.

2 1

LALITHA

"Father?"

Dushyant, disguised as an older man, strode to the back of the wagon and helped someone out. Why did Dushyant conceal his appearance when Lalitha expected him?

As a gray-haired man emerged, "Father," said Lalitha and ran to him. Dushyant supported him with a hand on his shoulder, but he moved aside as Lalitha flung herself into her father's arms.

Her father staggered back with a smile, grabbing onto Lalitha. "Give me a day or two to recover," he said as Lalitha took a step back to inspect him. While her father looked pale and thin, she saw no outward sign of injury or broken bones. At least Dushyant had not resorted to torture. She remembered Puru's words about her father being a valuable prisoner. Puru, who was Dushyant in a masquerade, could have released her father earlier. Rage bubbled in her stomach at his deceit and her naivete.

Dushyant's hands hovered nearby. The blood congealed on his arm bothered her though Dushyant appeared unaffected by it. He'd nearly killed her father and did not deserve her pity.

Lalitha glared at him and then put her arm around her father's waist. "Lean on me," she whispered.

Her father briefly pressed his lips to her head. "I missed you," he said, and they started walking. She matched her father's slow pace.

"Prince Bhimase—" started Dushyant, but Lalitha interrupted him.

"You have done enough damage. Leave us alone," stated Lalitha, with heat coating her words.

Dushyant stared at her with his face blank. "I am determined to escort Prince Bhimasena to safety," he said and signaled to his men. Half a dozen of his men formed a semi-circle around them.

She ignored the king and guided her father to a horse. With Giridhar's aid, her father mounted the mare.

"Giridhar, I did not expect to see you," said her father, looking at the prince.

Giridhar dipped his head. "Aunt Padmavati invited me, my lord. I am grateful to see you alive. Lalitha did not want you to miss her wedding."

Heat rushed to her face at Giridhar's implications, and she felt Dushyant's eyes on her. She cursed herself for letting the king affect her so much. Her father glanced at her, and she shook her head slightly, not wanting to discuss this matter with Dushyant's gaze piercing her.

Lalitha climbed onto the back of the kneeling elephant, and it slowly rose to its feet, causing her seat to sway from side to side.

Soon, their procession moved toward the castle. Dushyant followed them on a black stallion, his eyes drilling a hole into her back. He'd imprisoned her father and nearly killed him today. Did he expect her to be grateful?

Near the fort doors, Dushyant said, "My lord, there are a few unsettled matters between us." His eyes glanced at Lalitha. "I seek your audience to discuss them."

Her father turned to Dushyant. "King Dushyant, I don't know why, but you saved my life just a few moments ago. I am grateful for that. And I have several questions about the past few days and would like to get some answers. Come back to our palace tomorrow. Garthapuri will be ready to show you a guest's hospitality."

As the fort doors started closing behind them, Lalitha looked back through the gap and saw Dushyant gazing at her. Frustration rose in her at his infuriating behavior. Did he save her father's life or pretend to by instigating the harm first? He did deceive her with the Puru charade. She wished he would disappear from her life. A small voice in her mind contradicted her. No, she did not want him out of her life.

Father and daughter entered the king's chamber.

"Bhima," her uncle exclaimed and sat up. Lalitha rushed to arrange the pillows behind his back.

"Brother," her father said and touched her uncle's feet in respect.

Her uncle's eyes misted. "I had nearly abandoned any hope that you would return, Bhima."

Her father stood beside his brother. "I never imagined Dushyant would set me free. And what happened does not make sense." Three deep lines creased his forehead.

"Tell me everything that has happened since you left the palace," her uncle urged.

"Though we fought gallantly, Dushyant and his men overpowered us. His men threw me in a dark dungeon cell with mice for company. When he first came to visit, he questioned me about Kanva. I told him Kanva was justified in killing his father and refused to answer further questions."

Her uncle leaned forward and touched his brother's wrist. "Did they torture you?" he asked, worry tinting his face.

Her father shook his head. "It was strange. Instead of being punished, they moved me to a better cell and brought me decent meals. They even let me wash once in a while. Then something even stranger happened about a fortnight ago. Dushyant ordered them to move me to a tiny room with simple but adequate furniture. I had access to books and even the sun once in a while." A fortnight ago? That was when Dushyant must have returned to Vidarpur after their encounter. Did Dushyant make these changes because he regarded her with fondness? A gentle warmth spread through her limbs.

Her father paused and gazed out the window. Lalitha could hear the chirp of birds faintly. "How did you escape, Father?" she prompted, breaking the silence.

Her father sighed. "That is a mystery I hope King Dushyant can solve. In the company of two guards, I was walking in circles around a small garden. The majestic cliffs rose all around me. Then suddenly, arrows flew in and lodged in my guards' throats. While I frantically tried to look for the source of the weapons and save the two men, I heard footsteps. As I glimpsed, a masked face appeared, and something hard hit the side of my head." Lalitha gasped at hearing this. Her father reached out to her and squeezed her palm. "I lost awareness. When I woke up in a dark room, my feet and wrists were bound, and I sensed a rocky surface underneath me. All the gentle treatment from before vanished. Under a sky lit by stars, men with their faces covered tossed me into the back of a covered wagon. They fed me a tasteless gruel, and I could not tell how many days had passed in the dark. And then I tumbled outside our palace today."

"Outside the palace, you said King Dushyant saved your life. How did he protect you?" asked Lalitha, her heart squeezed tight.

Her father rubbed his forehead. "I was bound inside the carriage and did not know what was happening. Suddenly, the man who had kept watch over me dragged me out. Sunlight blinded me after being in the dark for a very long period, so I could not see very well initially. I thought he and another man were prepared to attack me. When my eyes adjusted, I noticed Dushyant shove me aside and fight with the two of them. Dushyant wore a disguise, but I recognized him. He then freed me from my bonds and carried me to another cart. He mumbled something about delivering me to you, Lalli. I cannot make sense of his actions." He looked down at his soiled clothes. "I need a bath," he said, wrinkling his nose.

As Lalitha walked back to her chambers, she tried to make sense of her father's story, but she only came up with questions. Why did Dushyant kill her father's guard and move him at night? Dushyant had sent a message that indicated he would free her father, so all this mysterious transportation appeared bizarre. And who attacked her father today? They must be Dushyant's men, so why did he fight his men? And who shot at them in front of the castle to instigate a scuffle? Lalitha plopped down onto a bench inlaid with ivory and folded her legs underneath her. If Dushyant cared for her, why did he act so coldly? Or was Lalitha mirroring her feelings onto him?

Agamathi strode into the room. "Did King Dushyant keep his promise? Is Prince Bhimasena back in the castle?" she asked rapidly without pausing for breath.

Lalitha gazed at her friend. "My father is alive and well. And King Dushyant did free him. But he wore a disguise," paused Lalitha, her mind traversing what she heard from her father and what she witnessed.

"Disguise? Why? He'd already sent us a messenger about his arrival."

Lalitha shook her head in frustration. "I don't understand many things that happened today."

Lalitha narrated what occurred to her friend, hoping that would clear the muddy picture in her head. It did not. "My father has invited him tomorrow, so I hope he can clear up some of my confusion."

Agamathi smiled slowly. "I am eager to see the king who stole your heart."

Lalitha looked at her friend in mock anger. "He looks like a bat with overgrown ears." She remembered how well she fit into his arms, her head resting on his chest and his chin on her head. No, that was Puru. An illusion that did not exist.

During the mid-day meal, her parents sat across from each other while Lalitha occupied the seat next to her father. Her father glanced at her mother furtively from beneath his thick lashes while her mother avoided looking in his direction. With the worry about her father lifted, Lalitha relished the sweet and mildly spicy coconut rice more than the other occupants at the table. Her mother barely touched the food, while her father ate absently.

Once the servants cleared the plates, her mother rose to stand next to a window. Her father, still seated at the table, gazed at her silhouette, a yearning etched on his face. *He loved her still.*

With her back to the room, her mother asked, "My lord, do you approve of this marriage between Lalitha and Giridhar?"

"Last time I met the boy, he was still playing with a wooden sword. I have had no time yet to form a view. Regardless of my lack of knowledge about him, the decision lies with *our* daughter." At his emphasis on our, her mother turned to look at him. Their eyes met momentarily, and her mother spun around as if she feared what she saw in his eyes. Her father's eyes never left her mother's face. "I promised Lalli she would be able to choose her groom, and I intend to keep that promise."

"The queen does not care for your promises," her mother muttered.

Her father chuckled with no mirth. "Leave the queen to me.

She will allow us to hold a swayamvara as long as Giridhar attends it."

"If the other contenders are lowly noblemen, the prince will shine like a diamond among rocks. Lalli would be a fool not to garland him," said her mother.

"I don't intend to wed a prince," said Lalitha. When both her parents stared at her, she felt heat rise to her cheeks. "I want to rule this kingdom. A prince will relegate me to the sidelines hosting feasts and dances," she continued, determined to make her views known.

"Not all princes are tyrants," whispered her father as he gazed at his wife. Lalitha felt her heart squeeze tight.

Her usually serene mother appeared perturbed, and her lips quivered. "Not all princes," repeated her mother in a broken voice and fled the room. Her father grimaced like she'd whipped him.

2 2

DUSHYANT

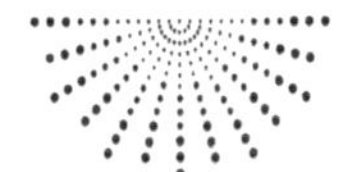

Dushyant prided himself on controlling his emotions. He thought demonstrating anxiety or excitement was a sign of weakness. Today, he twitched with impatience as the royal healer treated his wound. He tapped his foot and drummed his fingers. Jayanth watched him like an eagle from a dark corner of his tent.

He remembered Lalitha's revulsion as she gazed at him, and he grimaced. "I can bring something for your pain, my Majesty," said the physician, mistaking his expression.

"That is not needed," mumbled Dushyant. The girl continued to haunt him despite his effort to shut her out. Was this how his father felt after his mother's death? A seed of sympathy for his dead father germinated in his heart. He barely knew Lalitha, while his father had lost the mother of his three children. Maybe, Dushyant had judged him too harshly.

"My Majesty, there is no damage to the bones, so this should heal quickly. I will come back to check on you tomorrow," said the physician pulling him out of his musing.

Dushyant thanked him, and the healer bowed before departing.

Dushyant rose to his feet and paced the room. Like a man swimming against the current, Dushyant turned his thoughts to other matters. Prince Bhimasena did not escape his prison. Someone had kidnapped him and planned to kill him today. When he imagined Lalitha's horror of finding her father harmed, his stomach rose into his throat. By sheer luck, he'd saved the prince's life. Who was the traitor in his midst? He cursed his foolishness in staying away from Vidarpur till his father's death. Apart from Jayanth, he had no close ties. And Jayanth had spent the last two years in his company.

"Jayanth, there is a deadly viper among my men, ready to strike me. I have been a fool not to recognize it," said Dushyant, pausing in the middle of his tent.

Jayanth, whose alert eyes had been watching him closely, nodded. "Someone intended to slay the prince and blame it on you."

Dushyant tugged his ear. "If their plot had succeeded, it could have started a war with Garthapuri." And doomed his chances with Lalitha. She was never far from his mind.

"Only a few men can execute something of this nature, my King," whispered Jayanth, as if the walls had ears.

Dushyant neared him. "I can count the men with this capability on my fingers: Minister Panini, Chief Guard Samudra, General Ayobahu, and Advisor Upananda."

"General Ayobahu has been here all along," said Jayanth, scratching his chin. "But he could have henchmen carrying out his orders in Vidarpur."

"He commands all my standing army," Dushyant agreed. "And he was here for the finishing touch with Prince Bhimasena."

"Minister Panini and Chief Guard Samudra both had ample opportunities to kidnap Prince Bhimasena," said Jayanth.

Dushyant clenched the hilt of his sword. "Advisor Upananda

traveled with me to Vidarpur, but he could have orchestrated the whole affair."

"Only two of these men are warriors."

"Samudra and Ayobahu," said Dushyant. Suddenly, Dushyant remembered the man who had accompanied Prince Bhimasena in the wagon. "I want to question the man we captured earlier," said Dushyant and hurried outside. Jayanth followed him like a shadow.

They entered the dark enclosure quietly. A man stood stiff against a wooden pillar. It was him—the long-bearded man. The reason for this unnatural posture soon became apparent. His hands were twisted behind him and tied together. And his soldiers had attached the prisoner's neck to the post with a coir rope. Whip marks crisscrossed his bare chest.

A horsewhip stretched tautly between Ayobahu's fingers. "Tell me who ordered you to kidnap the prince," rasped Ayobahu as he approached the bearded man, his pale scar glinting against his dark skin. Raising his arm above his head, Ayobahu snapped the whip savagely across the man, snatching the hair on his beard.

"Mercy!" screamed the man, his teeth clenched in pain. "The tall man who died today was the one who knew. Teju was my cousin's brother-in-law. He got a bag of copper coins from someone important. I don't know who. It was a dangerous secret, he said. We killed the guards and hid the prince in a cave. Then, we loaded him onto the cart, and I stayed with him on our journey to Garthapuri."

"What was your plan when you reached Garthapuri?" asked Dushyant in a quiet voice. Heads turned to look at him, and men parted, so he had a clear view of the bearded man.

"I don't know. Teju told me to keep the prisoner alive, and I fed him gruel in the cart." Tears streamed down his chin. "King Dushyant, I got greedy for coins and followed Teju. Punish me for that. But I don't know any plans." It appeared the man uttered the truth. Dushyant glanced at Jayanth, and he inclined his head in agreement.

"General Ayobahu," called Dushyant and walked to a corner. Ayobahu handed the whip to another and followed him.

"Did you find the archers in the woods?" asked Dushyant.

Ayobahu wiped the sweat on his forehead with a cotton rag. "We found a dead man who appeared to be a sellsword. His throat was slit. There were signs of another man in the vicinity, but he'd escaped before our men reached that spot."

"Do we have men in pursuit?" Dushyant asked and watched him closely. Could he be the traitor? What would Ayobahu gain from betraying him? The answer came to him. Control of his kingdom through Sundari's son.

Ayobahu sighed. "I did, but they have returned empty-handed." Convenient to hide the identity of the man pulling the strings of these puppets.

"Don't give up so easily," Dushyant said, keeping his voice neutral. "Send them back to scour the area. Have them talk to the villagers. Maybe someone saw something."

Ayobahu opened his mouth to say something, but after glancing at Dushyant, he shut his mouth and merely dipped his head. Dushyant noticed the tightening of his jaw. Either the general thought this was a futile activity, or he was trying to figure out how to fool his king. Neither served Dushyant well.

Dushyant had other matters to discuss. "Is Kanva dead?" Dushyant remembered the lifeless form he'd seen earlier that day.

Ayobahu nodded. "What do we do with the corpse?" he asked.

"Cremate him and store the ashes in a clay pot." Dushyant would hand Sundari her father's ashes. He was no closer to solving the mystery of his father's death. Frustration mounted in his chest, and he quashed it with difficulty. "Our prisoner appears to be telling the truth. Send him to Vidarpur under guard. I will mete out his punishment when I return."

Ayobahu regarded him like he was seeing him with new eyes but did not disagree with him.

"Any news of my sisters?" asked Dushyant.

Ayobahu shook his head. "I will send a messenger to find out the latest," he replied. "Who will accompany you tomorrow to Garthapuri, my Majesty?"

Dushyant had not considered the matter. "I will tell you tomorrow." Dushyant returned to his tent with mounting irritation.

Dushyant had not avenged his father's death. He had no idea who was plotting his downfall. And Lalitha refused to vacate his mind.

Amudhan walked in to relieve Jayanth, and Dushyant realized he'd not checked the wounded men. "Amudhan, should you be here?"

Amudhan smiled widely. He touched his chest with his palms to indicate he was well.

"He only suffered minor bruises," said Jayanth.

"Jayanth," said Dushyant and approached him. "Find someone trustworthy to shadow General Ayobahu and report back to me," he whispered.

Jayanth searched his face. "I will, my king," he said.

"Have someone talk to the long-bearded prisoner. Become friends with him. He may drop clues about the man who handed them coins." Jayanth bowed his head and departed.

"Amudhan, let us go visit the injured men." Dushyant went to a large tent housing the wounded soldiers. Some rested on wooden cots while others sat on benches. Dushyant stopped to talk to each of them, and his men readily shared their stories with him. Dushyant thanked them as he moved to the next. Most of them were men his age.

An arrow had pierced one young man's right eye, and he sat

at a bench with a patch covering his injury. "When I returned home, I was going to marry. Now, she might reject me," he said, scratching the bench with his nails. His problems did not end there. He could no longer serve in the army and had to find another trade.

"I will write a scroll to her describing your bravery." The man with the eye patch looked at Dushyant with tears pooling in his one good eye. Dushyant pressed his shoulder and moved on.

"How is your arm, my Majesty?" a young man with a wrapping around his knee inquired.

Dushyant glanced at it and smiled. "It could have been worse."

As he emerged from the healer's tent, some of his soldiers invited him to join them for the evening meal. Someone fetched a tree trunk for his seat. "This is not a throne—"

"I can almost imagine it as my throne," said Dushyant while he sat on it. A thin man handed him a plate made of large dried lotus leaves, and Dushyant ate the rice, listening and chatting with his men.

When Dushyant came back to his tent, a calmness settled over him. Whatever other uncertainties he faced, his duty as the king was clear. That duty came first and all else a distant second. He leaned on a chair and took out his cloth pouch. Exhaling slowly, he opened it. A dull silver anklet rested at the bottom, and he pulled out the jewel that had adorned Lalitha's ankle. Setting aside the bag, he rubbed the metal, alternatively despairing about his chances with Lalitha and worrying about his growing feelings for her.

Jayanth strode in and dismissed Amudhan. His alert eyes scanned the tent.

Dushyant remembered the loss Jayanth had suffered. "How did you forget your wife?" Dushyant asked, still holding Lalitha's silver anklet.

"I have not forgotten her, my king. She remains in my thoughts constantly."

Dushyant looked up and stared at his head guard. "How do you even get up in the morning?" Did he still think about taking his life?

"It is hard sometimes. Then I think of you and my duty to protect you, and then I am ready to face the day," said Jayanth and shifted to face him. "Most days, I remember her and our life together fondly. She brought me much joy."

"Joy?" asked Dushyant, mystified. Wouldn't grief color those happy memories?

Jayanth's eyes brightened, and the corners of his mouth shifted up. "Initially, I could only think of her loss. But when I met you, and you gave me new purpose, I slowly recalled all the little ways she brought me cheer." He smiled widely, showing his teeth.

"My father never enjoyed life again after my mother's death," said Dushyant. Why did he never recover?

"That was a pity. Especially when he had three children to remind him of the delight she brought into his life."

Dushyant's heart sank. He'd abandoned his father. Would he have healed if he'd remained in Vidarpur? Dushyant grabbed the pouch and dropped the anklet inside.

"My king, if you permit me, I will say something on my mind."

Dushyant blinked his eyes to hide his pain and then gazed up. "Yes?"

"Do you intend to marry?"

Confused by the question, Dushyant inclined his head.

"How do you plan to cloak your heart, my king? Are you planning to never comfort your wife when she is in pain? Never share her joy? Never hold your firstborn child in your hands?"

Dushyant staggered back like he was stuck. He had not thought about these things. He assumed he would marry and raise his children while his heart remained untouched. Would it?

"Avoiding love does not prevent pain. It does prevent you from enjoying life. Please reveal your feelings to Princess Lalitha. I have watched her, and she shares them."

He was not strong enough. If he lost Lalitha, he could never bear it. Better to forget her. He did not say any of that to Jayanth. "I have a duty to this kingdom, and I cannot risk it by repeating my father's mistakes."

"My majesty, you are choosing a life of regret. You deserve happiness. Ask her father for her hand." Dushyant pictured waking up in the morning and gazing at Lalitha's sleeping form next to him, her lips murmuring his name. An intense longing seeped into him. Then he imagined her dying in his arms, blood trickling out of her stomach and covering his fingers. No, he could not face her death.

23

LALITHA

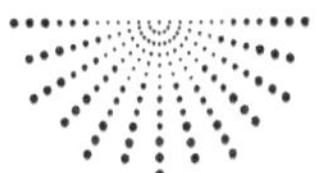

Her father arrived in her room, and his eyes were drawn to a large tapestry hanging on her wall. The red silk cloth embroidered with silver and gold threads depicted the Garthapuri castles. The artwork belonged to her mother, who had gifted it to Lalitha. Only Lalitha did not realize back then that it was a parting present. Many times since she'd wanted to set it on fire. But something had held her back.

"I had given this to your mother after our wedding," he said softly. Lalitha could hear the raw pain in his voice.

"Crafted by our artisans. It is beautiful," she said and hooked her arm through the crook of his elbow to lead him to her bench covered with lotus floral forms rendered in ivory.

Her father gazed at the white flowers contrasting with the dark wood surface. "Another piece of our superior craftsman-ship," he said as he sat down. Then he reached and clasped her arm. "I talked to the queen. She agreed to your swayamvara. Her nephew, Giridhar, will be invited, along with Garthapuri petty chiefs and noblemen."

"Father, I don't need a master, which is what Giridhar will be," Lalitha snapped in irritation. Though her mouth uttered

Giridhar's name, her mind dwelled on Dushyant's face. Pain ripped her body when Lalitha realized she and Dushyant might never fit together. She felt trapped in darkness with no light to guide her out. She nearly screamed out in frustration.

"Did your mother teach you that?" he asked, his eyes weary, pulling her out of her misery.

"No. Even if she did, I wouldn't listen to her," said Lalitha.

"You should listen to her and respect her. She is your mother." Her father stroked her wrist gently.

"She gave birth to me. And forsook me. You have been more a mother to me than her," said Lalitha, tears misting her eyes.

Her father put his arm around her and pulled her against him. "Don't blame her for my mistakes. I was not a good man to your mother."

"I don't—" Lalitha started, but he waved her off.

"You are old enough to hear the story now, Lalli," he said, staring at her. What did he see when he looked at her? Did he see her mother's long tresses or his brown eyes? Slowly, he reached up and tucked her hair behind her ears.

"Your mother was the daughter of a petty chief, and I was visiting her father." He paused and looked at his fingers. "I was walking to the stables when I saw her. She was wearing a green sari and looked like spring itself. She scolded some boys about a kitten they were harassing and picked up the tiny cat in her palms and nestled it against her throat. She wandered away without seeing me while I watched her receding figure mesmerized. She'd braided some hair in the middle, and the rest flowed to her waist." Lalitha styled her hair the same way after she washed it. She watched her father swallow.

"I saw her next at the temple, offering bananas to the devotees. She gave two to a young girl who limped. When the devotees left, I stepped in front of her and held my hand out. She placed the last banana on my palm and then glanced at me. Seeing the prince, she blushed and lowered her eyes." Her father's mouth shifted up. "I asked her father for her hand." Then his smile faded away, and he squeezed her hand. "Her father did not know how to refuse the prince, so he said yes."

He rubbed his nose. "Your mother sent a message to meet me in her garden. I went, assured of my reception. With tears in her eyes, she begged me to withdraw my demand to marry her. She wept, and instead of sympathy, rage filled me. I demanded the reason. She said she loved someone else. I felt betrayed and stomped back to my room." Lalitha sat up straight, afraid of what came next.

Her father slumped on the bench. "It did not take me long to find the boy. I challenged him to a duel and killed him." Lalitha gasped in horror. She could not imagine her gentle father committing this act of rage. Her father held out his right hand. "In this hand, I clutched a dagger and stabbed his heart. Blinded by anger, I stabbed him, over and over again, while he pleaded for mercy." Her father grasped his forehead in his palms. His face contorted in pain. Stunned by her father's violence, Lalitha forgot to breathe. "Then I married your mother. I realized my mistake when I exchanged the wedding garlands with her. She performed the rituals like a corpse, with no spark in her. I brought her to Garthapuri and tried to make amends. When you were born, I thought she'd forgiven me. She cherished you and sang to you. But when your brothers died soon after birth, she—" A lone tear trickled down his cheek. "I was a monster, and she paid the price."

Lalitha stood up to move away from her father, horrified. "You murdered the man Mother loved?" Hot tears stung her eyes, and she turned her back to him.

"I have repented for my actions, Lalli. Every day since. I will bear whatever punishment you want to mete out, but don't shun me."

Lalitha took a deep breath and spun around. He'd remained faithful to her mother and had been a dear father to her. Her father rose to kiss her head. "Your mother never abandoned you. She never stopped caring about you." She understood why her father insisted on holding a swayamvara for her. He wanted her to have the choice he'd denied her mother.

Lalitha wandered to her mother's chamber. Light from a brass oil lamp spilled a yellow glow around the room. Her mother sat cross-legged on a mat, reading a scroll. She glanced up at her daughter. Without uttering a word, Lalitha sat beside her and leaned her head on her mother's shoulder.

"What is wrong?"

"Nothing," said Lalitha, suppressing the many things she wanted to say. Her mother put the scroll down and rubbed Lalitha's back gently. They sat in warm, cozy silence.

Her parent's story affected her. "I am scared of marrying the wrong person," said Lalitha, her eyes damp. If her gentle father was capable of such heinous acts, what could happen to her at the hands of the wrong man? How would she recognize someone right for her? Lalitha did not want her mother's past. Terror gripped her throat.

Her mother pulled her into a hug and smoothed her hair away from her face. "It is okay to be scared. When you were young, I was terrified of all the things that could happen to you," she whispered. "But you proved to me how brave and resilient you are. Giridhar is a virtuous man. If you choose to marry him, he will treat you with respect and be an able partner in ruling this land. The choice is yours. Trust your heart. The right man will make you feel warm and safe."

That night, as stillness draped over the world, she remembered Dushyant's arms around her. She'd felt safe wrapped in them. Her mother asked Lalitha to rely on her heart, and hers whispered Dushyant's name. As she slipped into a deep sleep, she dreamt of his warm mouth leaving a trail on her skin.

* * *

"THEY ARE HERE," said Agamathi from the balcony. Lalitha resisted viewing the arriving royal party. "I see him," added Agamathi and went silent.

Her impatience won, and Lalitha edged toward her friend and peeked out from behind her. A dozen horses rode in a neat formation, and one of the lead men held an eagle flag that fluttered gently. Lalitha scanned the crowd, and it did not take long to spot the man wearing the crown. King Dushyant stood out like the full moon among the night sky filled with tiny stars. She'd never seen him in his royal outfit, so shock reverberated as she gaped at him arriving on his black stallion. Blue sapphires glinted from his gold crown as he gazed up, his eyes searching for something and then landing on her.

He tugged his ear, and a smile erupted on her face. For all the royal attire, he was nervous. Dushyant noticed her look and brought the hand that had clutched his ear in front and pretended to inspect it while the corners of his mouth pulled up, transforming his face. A tingle spread through her at sharing this private moment with him amidst others.

Agamathi turned and viewed her, a teasing grin on her face. "I did not know you had progressed to reading each other's minds."

Lalitha ignored her taunt and inspected the rest of Dushyant's retinue. The man behind him looked suspiciously like the commander she'd met, though his mustache was thinner. His roving eyes caught hers, and he dipped his head. Lalitha felt a tug in her stomach like she'd seen him more recently.

"That man looks familiar," said Agamathi. If Agamathi recognized him, he must have come to Garthapuri with Dushyant. Then it struck her. He'd come disguised as Jayanthi. Lalitha could immediately see the similarities.

On the other side of Dushyant rode a man with a scar. Lalitha knew him instantly. Dushyant had called him his cousin but likely was no relation of his. The joy of earlier fled.

Dushyant had woven a web of lies, and she'd fallen for it. How could she trust him?

She walked in and collapsed on her bench. Hot tears pooled in her eyes. Agamathi rushed to her side. "My lady, what is it?" she asked, kneeling beside her.

"I don't know him at all," Lalitha said, wiping her eyes roughly. Till someone unveiled his identity, Dushyant hid behind Puru. All his actions were designed to apprehend Kanva. And she'd foolishly let him sneak into her heart.

"My lady, if he'd deceived you, no good will come to him. But I cannot imagine him unaffected. Give him a chance to explain himself. If his words are unsatisfactory, I will help you throw him out."

Lalitha smiled at the image of her petite friend dragging the mighty king. "We can ask Nambi to aid us," said Lalitha. Still, she could not shake the image of Dushyant's deception from her mind.

24

DUSHYANT

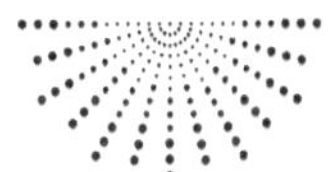

Prince Bhimasena, Lalitha's father, wearing a simple gold band on his forehead, stood at the top of the steps leading into the palace. Dushyant dismounted and handed the reins to one of his men.

"King Dushyant, I am glad to be out of chains so that I can welcome you to the Garthapuri palace," said the prince, walking down the stairs. Dushyant heard the taunt, but he chose to ignore it. Instead, Dushyant dipped his head to the prince while his eyes searched the crowd. A woman waved an arati plate around his face to ward off evil. As he climbed up, young girls showered him with flowers—no Lalitha.

"This invite a month ago would have avoided our clash," said Dushyant, with no animosity.

"Kanva is dead, putting an end to the hunt," replied the prince.

"If only," said Dushyant. He still had a traitor to root out.

Prince Bhimasena gazed at him sharply but did not probe. He escorted Dushyant to a large hall that held a long table. Light streamed in through the windows on one side of the wall. The windows were inadequate for the room and kept it semi-dark.

163

"Queen Padmavati," said Prince Bhimasena as an older woman with an elaborate crown approached them. Dushyant bowed his head.

"King Dushyant, welcome to Garthapuri," she said pleasantly.

"General Ayobahu," introduced Dushyant. "And my head guard, Jayanth."

"This is our minister Kapila," said Prince Bhimasena, leading Dushyant to a seat. The Vidarpur men sat facing the window while the Garthapuri delegation sat in the darkness.

Dushyant waited for Queen Padmavati and Prince Bhimasena to take their seat before dropping down to his. Jayanth stood behind him while Ayobahu occupied the chair to his left. Advisor Upananda had taken ill this morning, and Dushyant decided to leave him behind.

"King Dushyant, I assume you know the tale Kanva narrated when he sought refuge here?" asked the queen, her eyes alert.

Dushyant reminded himself that she was a veteran ruler and not one to be underestimated. "Yes, my lady. I was honor bound to hunt him to avenge my father's death."

"Kanva has perished, and I am home, so we can call a truce," said Prince Bhimasena in a mild tone. "Though, I am curious as to why your men kept me hidden in the dark wagon for days and attacked me yesterday."

Before Dushyant could answer, he heard the tinkling of bells from an anklet. Lalitha! His heart thudded like he'd run uphill, and the hair on his neck rose. He resisted the urge to turn around and gaze at her. Instead, he straightened in his chair and watched the reaction on the faces before him.

Prince Bhimasena and Queen Padmavati looked past him. Bhimasena's face brightened while the queen frowned.

"Lalitha, come join us," waved the prince.

She walked past him, and Dushyant was aware of her every

step as she made her way to the front. Without glancing at him, she perched beside her father.

Dushyant forgot the question and peered at Lalitha. She wore a yellow sari that looked like the soft morning sun. Pearls decorated her neck and ears. Her thick hair was braided with jasmine flowers. He felt jealous of the blossom that hung over her ear and caressed her skin. His heart sang when his eyes fell on her lips.

"King Dushyant," someone called, and Dushyant heard them through a fog. Jayanth touched his arm, and Dushyant nearly jumped.

"If you were going to release me, why all the mystery and ill-treatment?" Prince Bhimasena repeated his question.

Dushyant recollected his place and observed the people in the room. Bhimasena rested his elbows on the table while the queen leaned back on her chair. Dushyant avoided gazing at Lalitha lest his mind wandered again.

Looking Prince Bhimasena in the eye, Dushyant said, "When I arrived in Vidarpur, my men told me you had escaped my prison."

"Escaped?" echoed the prince.

Dushyant nodded. "I thought you would return to Gartha-puri, so we headed here. That is when I realized you had been kidnapped, and I fought to save you."

Queen Padmavati smirked. "You have lost control of your kingdom, young king."

Irritation flared inside Dushyant, but he suppressed it. "You are right, my lady. As a new king, I have not yet gained complete control of my land. Traitors are plotting behind my back. I wish I had a chance to talk to Kanva. He might have shed some light on it."

Dushyant felt rather than saw Lalitha's gaze. He glanced up, and their eyes met. "When is Princess Lalitha's swayamvara?" he asked. Color rose in her cheeks at his question, and matching heat rose in his throat.

"In seven days," said the prince, regarding his daughter fondly.

Then, Dushyant uttered words that he did not plan to state. "Prince Bhimasena, allow me the honor of attending Princess Lalitha's swayamvara." Horror rained on him. Why did he utter these words? He'd intended to forget her. He sensed Lalitha shift in her seat, but he kept his eyes on her father. Something propelled him to say these words, and he seemed to have no control over them.

Prince Bhimasena studied him like he was a new insect who had flown into his room. "Swayamvara? As a guest?"

"As a suitor," answered Dushyant. Lalitha gasped, and Dushyant glanced at her. Her eyes breathed fire and kindled a spark in his stomach. In vain, he'd tried to repress his feelings for her. But to no avail. He loved and admired her against his judgment. He could not take his words back. He did not want to retract them. While his heart struggled, his face remained a mask.

She seemed to struggle with emotions of her own. "No," she spat, tossing her head.

Dushyant heaved his head up, shock reverberating in his chest. "N-No?" he stuttered. While he'd worried about his feelings, he'd not contemplated her reaction.

"Why do you want to attend the swayamvara?" She did not wait for his answer. "Garthapuri has remained an independent kingdom for generations, and I am not going to jeopardize that."

He stared at her with his mouth open. "Your kingdom? You think I am doing this for Garthapuri?" He wished he did this to annex her land. Not because she caused flutters in his stomach.

Her chest rose and fell in anger. With difficulty, Dushyant

drew his eyes to her face. He was surprised he'd not turned into ashes from the blaze raging in her eyes.

Abruptly, she heaved up, her chin jutting out. "No," she stated forcefully and stormed out. Dushyant sat stunned. A murmur rose around him as he realized she'd rejected him. He should be pleased that she'd prevented him from walking down the path paved with mistakes. Instead, he felt gloom descend on him.

25

LALITHA

*L*alitha collapsed on the bench nestled among neem trees taking in gulps of air. Light filtered through the leaves and created a pattern of shadows on the ground. She stared at the dirt without noticing anything. She did the right thing by rejecting Dushyant. Why did her heart feel torn then?

A caterpillar crawled onto her thigh, and she brushed it off, wishing she could push the king off as readily. Dushyant had caused trouble from the moment they met. He had lied to her and hid his identity. He did not deserve her trust. Then, she remembered his lips on her mouth, and her body ached.

She heard footsteps and lifted her head. Dushyant stood at the edge of the small clearing watching her intently. Her eyes landed on the man next to him.

"Jayanthi?" she asked, wanting confirmation of his trickery.

"Jayanth, my lady," the man bowed. "Head guard for King Dushyant."

"You were willing to dress as a woman for your king," she stated, observing him.

"I am willing to die for him, my lady," said Jayanth.

She saw a flicker of emotions on Dushyant's face. "Your king is a fortunate man."

"He saved my life once, my lady. I am eager to repay my debt," said Jayanth, glancing at Dushyant. Dushyant swallowed but remained quiet. However, his large ears turned red, betraying his emotions.

Would Jayanth state the same words in Dushyant's absence? Regarding the broad man, she thought Jayanth would be more effusive in his praise if his king were not present. "How did you find me? You should not be here," she stated and turned away.

"I brought them," said Agamathi, appearing behind Jayanth.

"You—" Lalitha started, anger coating her words.

"Please listen to the king, my lady," she whispered and moved away. Jayanth vanished, too, leaving Lalitha alone with Dushyant.

"There is nothing for us to talk about," she said, her back to him. "You are the king of Vidarpur. If I marry you, Garthapuri will become yours."

She heard his feet shuffle. "I don't care about Garthapuri."

Fury filled her chest. "You don't care about my land," she hissed.

"Not in the way you are accusing me," he said coldly. Then, he said, "This is a mistake. I should leave."

She turned to face him, her insides twisting. "Go away then. I was right. You wanted to use me to capture my land. What will you do now? Attack our fort?"

Something flickered in his eyes. Real emotion. "If I wanted to annex your land, I would have seized you when you were injured and helpless."

She shifted to him, wanting to know why he'd treated her with kindness. "Why didn't you?"

His eyes moved to her lips and lingered there. "You haunt me. Day and night," he said as if the words were torn out of him.

Was he blaming her for his misfortunes? "How dare you?"

she started and faltered as she gazed at him and saw his tight mask slip. He appeared tormented and troubled. Something stirred in her. He frequented her thoughts too. "That is not a good reason for you to attend my swayamvara," she said gently. If he'd declared he had feelings for her, her answer would be different.

He chuckled without any joy. "What will be a better excuse? My undying love?"

Anger spread through her at his scorn. "From you, no reason is good enough. You have already deceived me several times, and I would be a fool to fall for your ploy again."

He regarded her intently. "I owe you an apology for concealing my name from you," he said.

"And for imprisoning my father," she added.

Dushyant remained silent. Frustrated, Lalitha cried, "It was all lies." Tears gathered in her eyes.

"Not all of it," he said softly. "Not how I feel about you." He stepped close to her and gently wiped under her eye with his thumb. He towered over her, and she craned her neck to look up and saw a storm brewing in the previously calm ocean of his face. Her stomach tightened. She wanted to wrap his arms around her and let him comfort her. For a brief moment, he appeared alive and not a wooden doll. But that was an illusion. No, his feelings were likely a myth too. Everything about Dushyant was made up like a statue formed out of clay.

But she needed to know. "How do you feel about me?"

"Confused," he said. Lalitha waited for him to elaborate. "One moment, I want to spend an eternity with you. Next, I never want to see you again."

At least he was honest and did not resort to lies. "You are wooing me with your words."

"I am no poet," he mumbled. The space between them filled with heat. Neither moved.

"How about telling me the truth for a change?"

"I like your spirit," he said, his mouth shifting up. The tiny movement brightened his face. He should smile more often. She did not realize she uttered those words out loud till an actual grin erupted on his face.

Somehow, the gap between them narrowed. Lalitha was not sure who had moved and did not care.

"If you are not doing this for my kingdom, why do you want to be one of my suitors?" she asked, her heart hammering against her chest. She felt his warm breath on her cheeks.

"I-I want to marry you," he stammered, his eyes a pool of molten gold. A lump formed in her throat. Lalitha did not imagine it all. Dushyant did care for her even if he had difficulty expressing it. His thumb brushed her chin, sending shivers down her back. She wanted to bury her face in his chest.

"Why," she asked, leaning into him. She longed to hear more.

Dushyant did not answer. His thumb traveled to her lower lip, and she drew a sharp breath. "I did not realize what was missing in my life till you came galloping into it. I want you to be mine," he whispered as he bent his head. Her lips parted in anticipation. She wanted to belong to him, too, and tried not to think of what kept them apart.

"My lady," said Prince Giridhar sharply, and they jumped apart. Giridhar halted a few feet from them, his gaze darting between Lalitha and Dushyant, his lips pressed into a thin line. Agamathi walked behind Giridhar, twisting the end of her sari around her index finger, her mouth opening and closing. Lalitha felt like a child caught wearing her mother's jewels. Then anger swirled in her stomach. She did nothing wrong except for falling in love with a man who could not be hers. That pain was hers to bear.

Lalitha sneaked a look at Dushyant. His mask was up, but he stayed within her arm's distance. Their union would not be in Garthapuri's interest. She knew it, but her heart protested against the unfairness.

She heard fast-approaching steps, and Jayanth loomed in front.

"My Majesty," said Jayanth. "The princesses are missing," he whispered in Dushyant's ear, but she was close enough to hear the words.

Dushyant's head pulled up. "My sisters?"

Jayanth nodded.

With a glance at her, Dushyant spun on his heels. Then he turned back. "Farewell, my lady." Sadness swelled between them, and he vanished.

26

DUSHYANT

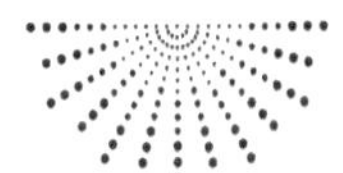

"What did you mean my sisters are missing?" Dushyant knew what missing meant, and it worried his stomach.

"My king, a messenger arrived from Chief Guard Samudra this morning. He'd sent some men to escort the princesses back to Vidarpur, but his men found no trace of them on the king's road. Two men continued to your aunt to see if the princesses had returned to her. Another pair arrived in Vidarpur to share the news with the Chief Guard while the rest were searching for them," recited Jayanth without slowing down his pace.

His stomach dropped to his feet. "Where is the messenger? I want to talk to him."

Jayanth led him to a small room with no windows. In it stood General Ayobahu and another man who only reached the general's shoulders.

The man bowed when he saw the king. Jayanth shut the wooden door behind them, and it creaked loudly.

"Are you the messenger from Chief Guard Samudra?"

"Yes, my Majesty."

"When did you leave Vidarpur?"

"Three days ago. I rode all day and even into the night to reach you quickly. I had a note from the Chief Guard that allowed me to trade my horse each day." Dust coated him from head to toe, and he had bags under his eyes.

"Relate the message," ordered Dushyant.

"My Majesty, Chief Guard had sent a dozen men to escort Princess Kanika and Princess Ambika to the palace. Our men found evidence of a scuffle on the king's road but no sign of the princesses—"

Dushyant leaned forward and furrowed his brows. "What kind of evidence?"

The messenger shrugged his shoulders. "I don't know, my king."

Dushyant imagined broken chariot wheels and bodies oozing blood. He rubbed the bridge of his nose to drive away these pictures. "Continue."

"Two men departed to Jaisalpur to see if the princesses returned to your aunt. And two men traveled back to Vidarpur to share the news with the Chief Guard. The other men stayed to search for them. The Chief Guard dispatched me immediately to bring this information to you."

Dushyant's hand shook slightly as he retrieved a silver coin from his pouch. "I am grateful for your speedy delivery of this message," he said, swallowing the lump in his throat.

The man bowed again with his palms touching and accepted the coin.

Dushyant walked to a corner and faced the wall. Tears stung his eyes. If anything happened to his sisters—even the thought caused him unbearable pain. A boy, bald as a melon, drifted into his mind. He'd buried Mahabahu deep in his mind. With the fissures caused by his sisters' disappearance, Mahabahu floated up to agonize him. Making a fist, he pushed hard against the stone surface, paralyzed with fear.

"King Dushyant," called Lalitha, and the door creaked loudly as someone opened it. Wiping his eyes roughly, he turned to the door.

Lalitha stepped in and scanned the room. She stood like an enduring flower amid pale withering leaves. Her gaze fell on him, and she strode to him. Her arms rose toward him and then fell to her sides. "What happened to your sisters?" she asked, a deep line creasing her forehead.

"They seem to have disappeared on the way to Vidarpur," said Dushyant. Only someone who knew him well would hear the tremor in his voice.

Her frown deepened as she leaned forward. "Why are you still here? Rescue your sisters and punish the culprits," whispered Lalitha, breathing fire into his veins. Her expressive eyes infused him with spirit.

Dushyant wanted to pledge his allegiance to her in love and loyalty. Instead, he stood tall and dipped his head. "Please express my gratitude to Queen Padmavati and Prince Bhimasena. And explain the reason for my hurried departure." There was more he wanted to say, but the words fled as he gazed at her upturned face. Dushyant felt torn about leaving Lalitha. He foolishly wished she could accompany him.

With a sign to his men, Dushyant marched to the stables. His farewell took on a final tone as he realized he might never see her again. Even if he did meet her, she would be married to someone else. He tried to put her out of his mind.

As their horses rode toward the Vidarpur Garrison, the Garthapuri fort doors shut behind them. He rode on without a backward glance while his tingly skin felt her against his heart.

"I will hand-pick 50 men, my Majesty. We will find the princesses," said Ayobahu as they dismounted. Dushyant regarded the general. Was this his plot? Will his 50 men betray him?

"No time to hand pick men. Ask an entire unit to get ready," ordered Dushyant.

"My Majesty, with a traitor in our midst, I wanted to be sure about the loyalty of the men I picked," whispered Ayobahu, repeating Dushyant's thoughts.

"We will deal with disloyalty swiftly," said Dushyant coldly and marched into his tent. Soon, he emerged in his battle armor.

Advisor Upananda stumbled in front of him and doubled down into a fitting cough. Wiping his mouth, he rose. "I heard the news, my Majesty," he rasped.

"Send a messenger to the villages on our way to get horses ready for us to swap. You can stay here and get well," said Dushyant and mounted his horse.

They pitched no tents and cooked no food. They traveled swiftly like the wind, stopping to eat what food they obtained in the villages. At night they exchanged their tired horses and rode on, resting only during the darkest parts of the night. Though he shut his eyes and settled on the ground, sleep never claimed him. After his mother's death, his aunt arrived in Vidarpur. Noticing the state of his father, she took him and his sisters under her wing. When he'd traveled to Jaisalpur with his sisters and their aunt, seven-year-old Kanika kept a steady stream of chatter while he pretended to sleep. As their chariot rattled along the narrow roads, she exclaimed about every rock and tree. Kanika drew him out of his shell, and soon Dushyant started pointing out the foxes hiding in the tall grasses and monkeys swinging in the trees. Without his sisters, Dushyant would have spiraled into despair. They kept him sane. Staring at the sparkling stars, he prayed silently.

As a fitful sleep claimed him, his mind dredged up a past he'd submerged—his cousin Mahabahu. When they arrived in Jaisalpur, they met their four cousins. Out of them, a boy his age drew his attention. While the younger cousins jumped and squealed, Mahabahu stayed quiet. Dushyant had thought him a year or two younger than him. He was mistaken. Mahabahu was older.

His aunt had told Dushyant that he would share Mahabahu's room. That night, while the light from the full moon poured in, they lay side by side in matching beds. Mahabahu stared through the windows, his bald head gleaming like the surface of the moon. Dushyant had cleared his throat a few times, wanting to ask Mahabahu what had happened to his hair. But no words came out. Tired from the journey, he shut his eyes. "Tell me a story," said Mahabahu. Dushyant opened his eyes to see Mahabahu turned toward him, his face in the dark.

"What story?"

"Yours."

"Mine? It is a dull tale."

"I have never left this palace. So let me decide if it is dull. Is your palace the same as mine?"

Dushyant had shrugged. "Mostly. But our castle is carved out of a hill."

"Hill? With boulders?"

"With caves."

"Caves? Did you hide in them?"

Dushyant yawned. "Sometimes." Sleep had claimed him.

Mahabahu and Dushyant had become unlikely friends. During the day, Dushyant would ride horses, play with his sisters, and train with swords. At night, he would narrate all that happened to Mahabahu, who absorbed them like parched earth drinking water. He would ask him strange questions— what color was the sky from the top of the banyan tree? And Dushyant would climb the tree again to find out.

Dushyant knew something was wrong with his cousin. Mahabahu rarely left his room, but in the dark, while they talked, he seemed normal. Or Dushyant pretended he was normal.

One night, Mahabahu called out to him after he'd closed his eyes. "Dushyant, do you believe in prayers?"

"Hmm," Dushyant muttered.

"In the old stories, if one chants hard enough, a god will arrive to grant them a boon."

"What will you ask for?" Dushyant asked in a sleepy voice. No boon would bring his dead mother back.

"I want to fly," said Mahabahu, the boy who could not walk.

One morning, two years after Jaisalpur had become home, the heat from the sun had woken him up.

"Mahabahu, why did you let me sleep?" asked Dushyant, stretching his hands above his head. His cousin's voice would usually wake him up as the sun rose. That day, Mahabahu did not stir from the other bed.

Dushyant's mind was still sluggish from the night as he approached his cousin. "Mahabahu." No response. Dushyant had shaken him then. The cold lifeless body moved limply. No sound came out of Dushyant as he fell back.

"My Majesty," a voice called, and Dushyant woke up drenched in sweat.

"Time for us to move," said Jayanth.

Dushyant nodded and tugged his ear. He washed his face in cold water. While it drove remnants of sleep away, it did nothing to drive away his nightmare. Dushyant had hidden in the woods after finding his cousin's corpse. A search party had found him lying between two thick roots with his knees pulled to his chest. Dushyant thought his aunt would send him back to his father. Terrified, Dushyant whispered over and over again that he did not hurt Mahabahu. He was given a new chamber, smaller than the one he'd shared with Mahabahu. No one came to punish him. No one came to comfort him either that night. The next morning, his sisters, Kanika and Ambika, found him sitting on the floor. They flew into his arms and sobbed on his shoulders. Their grief opened up his, yet he'd never cried over his dead cousin. But, no boy had claimed his friendship ever since.

Jayanth brought a brown stallion to him. Dushyant imagined his cousin, Mahabahu, flying in the relentless blue sky, visiting places he never saw in real life. With a sigh, Dushyant locked him away in a dark corner of his mind and rubbed the coat of the horse. Soon, they rode under the glittering stars.

In the wide open space, his fears returned to haunt him. Dushyant imagined finding the corpses of his sisters, and his stomach twisted into a tight knot. The past and the future merged to form a tempest. He struggled to breathe. Then, Dushyant remembered he was a king. He would not let any harm befall Kanika and Ambika. He repeated the words like a prayer.

Mid-day on the third day, they arrived at the sight of the skirmish. With the sun blazing overhead, they halted several yards away from the evidence of the scuffle. A broken chariot. Many footprints. No corpses, though. General Ayobahu jumped off his horse and walked around the area, his eyes rooted to the soil.

Dushyant slid off his mount and stood watching Ayobahu mutter curses under his breath. The commander heading the search approached Dushyant.

"Are the men who went to Jaisalpur back?" asked Dushyant.

"Yes, my Majesty. The princesses have not returned there."

His throat constricted painfully, and he cleared it. "How many men did my sisters leave with?"

"About half a dozen."

Half-a-dozen. Then at least ten must have attacked them to overpower them. The image of Mahabahu wafted into his mind. Dushyant could not bear to think of his sisters as dead.

Suddenly, Dushyant could not breathe, so he wandered away from his men, gasping for air.

He heard Ayobahu gather a few men and give them orders. Dushyant wanted to tear apart every house in the neighboring villages till he found Kanika and Ambika.

Dushyant heard footsteps and sniffed his emotions in. "My Majesty, we will find them alive," said Ayobahu in a gentle tone. Dushyant glanced at him. "Chief Guard Samudra dispatched our spies here. I expect to hear from them soon. It is hard to keep something like this under the lid for long."

Dushyant stared at Ayobahu to see if he betrayed any signs of derision. Dushyant only saw concern. "We will wait one day. Tomorrow, I want heralds in all the surrounding villages announcing a reward from me for news about my sisters."

Ayobahu's prediction came true. One of the spies arrived that evening as they set up camp. Jayanth, Ayobahu, and he gathered to hear him. "I pretended to be a drunk yesterday and a lame beggar today. One of the devotees asked the priest if the decrepit temple by the stream was open. The devotee thought he saw smoke there last night. The priest seemed surprised and shook his head."

"King Lambhodara wanted to renovate it, but it had fallen further into disrepair," said Ayobahu, rubbing his scar. "It would serve as a good hiding place."

"What do we do?" asked Dushyant, his mind spinning like a wagon wheel.

"We wait till nightfall. In the middle of the night, we surround the temple, and at dawn—"

"I don't want to wait," said Dushyant with his hands on his hips. If Ayobahu was in league with the culprits, he did not want to give them a chance to move.

Ayobahu opened his mouth to say something, stared at Dushyant, and then shut it.

Jayanth cleared his throat.

Dushyant glanced at him.

"We can send a priest to light the lamp at the temple."

Dushyant brightened. "With a servant or two to clean the area."

Ayobahu joined in. "Our men can hide in the trees and by the stream outside. I will find the men."

Dushyant interrupted him. "One of them will be my guard, Sendhan." He wanted a trusted man in that temple. And Sendhan fought beside him outside the Garthapuri palace and helped him save Lalitha's father.

Two covered carts, with four men in each, drove to the temple, the second cart a few yards behind the first. Jayanth and Dushyant rode in the second carriage. Squeezed tightly in the dark, Dushyant could hear the other occupants' inhalation and exhalation over the sound of the rickety cart. He wondered if they could hear his pounding heart as he observed the outside through a gap in the wooden planks. He saw cows grazing in the meadows. As the carts passed, they looked up with a mouthful of grass. As they had planned, the cart in front stopped at a place where they could watch the temple entrance. The cart driver, General Ayobahu in disguise, jumped down to inspect his wheel. He kicked one of them, likely breaking it in the act, and cursed loudly. Their wagon slowed down as it approached them.

"What is wrong, brother?" asked their driver, pretending to help a fellow traveler.

"My wheel is broken, and I need to take this food to a wedding feast," said General Ayobahu, holding his head in his hand.

Their driver, a medium-sized archer whose bow was concealed under blankets, hopped down. With their heads nearly touching, they inspected the broken wheel. A light wind rustled the trees.

Dushyant spotted their two boats drifting past the temple.

Their covers hid weapons underneath while the four sailors could wield the oar in a battle.

Dushyant saw the grass move. He knew his men with mud on their faces crawled on the ground to approach the temple courtyard. His guard, Sendhan, wearing a turban and holding a broom, accompanied a priest in a white cotton dhoti. One of the younger soldiers wore a sari and carried a basket of flowers. The broom hid a dagger, and the flowers concealed an ax. The priest chanted hymns in praise of God Shiva.

Dushyant noticed it just as his three men saw it. "The temple door is locked."

Dushyant saw Sendhan gesture wildly with his arms but could not hear the words. Then Sendhan picked up something from the ground and hit the lock with it. "They are breaking in," Dushyant narrated.

"Sensible. I was worried Sendhan would climb the wall and meet a pointy knife on the other side," muttered Jayanth.

Dushyant saw the six mud crawlers reach the wall under the shade of a large tree. One of them swung his legs over a branch and climbed into the trees, disappearing from his view. The others stood up slowly with their backs to the brick courtyard wall and stepped toward the door.

Soon, the rusty lock gave way, and Sendhan removed the chains. The priest and Sendhan pushed each door open with their shoulders while the *flower woman* stood to the side, his posture alert.

Crows cawed and flew overhead from their nests. The temple courtyard and the inner sanctum came into view as the doors slid open.

Sendhan moved forward first, his broom sweeping the debris away. The priest followed with the *flower woman* by his side, his chanting growing louder. The mud crawlers advanced to the doors.

Sendhan climbed the first step to the sanctum and started

brushing the dirt away. The tree climber swung down on a branch. Holding the large trunk with his ankles, he meowed. One of the mud crawlers fell to the ground and crawled to him. The tree climber waited till the crawler approached him. Dushyant assumed the climber communicated something to the crawler. Then the climber disappeared into the leaves. The crawler returned to the wall and leaned into the man beside him. Then two of them peeled away and went to the back.

"The tree climber saw something and asked our men to move to the back," said Dushyant. One of the boats reached the shores by the temple, and the two rowers hopped out and dragged the craft onto the sand. Then, one of them removed a net from the boat and cast it into the water while the other started rubbing something onto the wooden planks of the vessel.

Dushyant could bear it no longer. He turned inside to Jayanth. "Let us—"

Suddenly, he heard a cry outside and saw Ayobahu yell, "They are escaping through the back. Grab your weapons." The two drivers held their weapons ready and ran to the temple.

Four archers hopped out of the wagons with a bow in their hands. They slung a quiver of arrows onto their shoulders and marched forward.

Dushyant looked at Jayanth and his two other guards. "Let us join them," he said, his fist gripping the hilt of his sword. Once out of the tiny enclosed space, all four drew their swords and strode forward. Leaves crunched under their feet, and squirrels scattered up the trees on hearing them approach.

"To the back," said Dushyant and ran to the side of the temple walls while the archers positioned themselves by the open door and nocked their arrows.

Branches growing close to the wall scratched their arms and necks as they hastened to the stream.

The mud crawlers fought with a handful of men, and the

boatsmen joined the battle. Axes clanged against shields, and men darted around trees, creating a cacophony of noises.

With a cry, two men rushed at Dushyant with their swords drawn. Dushyant jumped aside and deflected with his blade. These were skilled men trained in warfare. The first thug attacked him again and then leaped aside while the man behind thrust his weapon at Dushyant. Dushyant spun and evaded their sharp blades and then slashed one of them across his shoulder. A fountain of blood spurted on his face.

The hurt man backed away quickly while the other attacked Dushyant from behind. Coward! As the weapon skimmed his lower back, Dushyant used his momentum to roll on the ground and kick his opponent's ankles. The man lost his balance and stumbled backward. With rage fueling him, Dushyant cried as he rose onto his knees and stuck the lower belly of the second thug. He hit his mark, and his target howled in pain.

Dushyant wiped his eyes with the back of his hand and rose. No sign of his sisters. He saw a small back door that stood open. He spotted his guard, Sendhan, through it, fighting inside the courtyard with two men, and rushed to his aid.

One of the thugs turned to him and attacked with a ferocious jump. Instead of defending himself, Dushyant thrust his sword. The thug did not expect it but jumped aside in time to escape his blade. The thug countered and cut the air with his sword. Dushyant parried the blow, but the sharp edge still slashed his hip.

Gritting his teeth, Dushyant rammed his head into the shoulder of the thug and plunged his dagger into his throat. Blood gushed out, and Dushyant knocked the thug down.

Dushyant glanced around and saw Sendhan press his fingers into his stomach to stem the flow of blood. Dushyant tore his dhoti and tied it around Sendhan's mid-section.

He then scanned the temple courtyard. Bodies of men,

severed limbs, and weapons defiled the place of worship. "Where are my sisters?"

"They are not here," said Sendhan through clenched teeth.

"Not here?" Dushyant repeated the words, befuddled. Then in a cry of fury, he yelled, "Where are they?"

27
LALITHA

When Lalitha heard the news about Dushyant's sisters, she stood like a statue. Giridhar asked her a question, but her mind was far away. Hearing no response from her, Giridhar muttered something and stormed out.

Then Agamathi touched her elbow. "My lady, what happened?" she asked.

Suddenly, Lalitha came to life. Among all his lies, Dushyant had mentioned one truth about himself—his sisters. She took it to mean he cared for them deeply. "I have to do something. I will come back and explain," said Lalitha and followed Dushyant. When she found him, he looked drained of color, and his shoulders drooped. Seeing his anguish, she took it upon herself to spur him to action to save his sisters.

Now, Lalitha watched Dushyant ride off through a small window wishing she could accompany him and help him find his sisters. While she watched his back, she muttered a prayer to Goddess Durga to keep him and his sisters safe.

Another thought nagged her. The swayamvara was in 7 days. Dushyant would be too far away to attend the event. Though she tried to convince herself that this was better for Garthapuri, her heart refused to listen to reason.

She stood by the window till the fort doors shut behind the king. As the guards put the heavy iron bolt in place, Lalitha felt like hope had fled with the king. Sighing, she sought her father and found him in her uncle's chamber. Hearing voices, she paused at the threshold.

"Dushyant will be an ill match for Lalitha," her aunt, Queen Padmavati, proclaimed. "He will annex the kingdom to Vidarpur, and what your forefathers built for generations will be lost."

Her father remained silent while staring at a rug. Her uncle glanced at his brother. "Kingdoms grow and shrink. Vidarpur is larger than us, and Dushyant will offer Garthapuri better protection." Her father gazed up. "His heirs to Vidarpur will carry Garthapuri blood."

"What do we know about Dushyant? Giridhar is my nephew and is trustworthy," argued her aunt.

Lalitha entered the room, and all eyes turned toward her. "King Dushyant received some news about his sisters and has departed," she said. Her stupid eyes misted, and she blinked rapidly to hide any trace of her anguish.

Her father rose and approached her. "He has left?"

She nodded, avoiding his gaze.

"Is he coming back for your swayamvara?" asked her aunt.

Lalitha took a deep breath in. "It is unlikely he will attend." Her father put his arm around her shoulders and squeezed it. That touch nearly unraveled her. Lalitha wanted to bury her head in her father's shoulder and sob. With difficulty, she muttered, "I will leave you to your discussion."

"Join me for the mid-day meal," her father said as he regarded her.

Lalitha returned to her chamber and curled up on a chair

with her legs tucked under her. She did not know how long had passed as she stared at the walls, her mind in turmoil.

"My lady," said Agamathi as she entered.

Lalitha peered at her through the tears pooling in her eyes. Agamathi rushed to her side and reached for her hands. Grasping Lalitha's right hand firmly, Agamathi said, "I saw the king leave."

"He has gone to his sisters." A lone tear spilled down her cheek. "He will not be able to attend my swayamvara."

"Ask your father to put off the swayamvara, my lady. Or call it off altogether."

Lalitha shook her head and wiped her tears with her sari. "This is for the best."

"How can this be for the best? You care for him. And he cares for you."

"How do you know?" asked Lalitha with a hunger in her voice.

"I could tell from the way his eyes caressed your face. Not when you were looking. He hid his feelings then. But when your focus was elsewhere, he glanced at you with tenderness and despair."

Lalitha laughed and rubbed her nose. "He is adept at hiding his emotions. But messages have already gone out for the swayamvara. We cannot change the day."

She strolled to her father's chambers with a heavy heart. "Princess Lalitha," called Prince Giridhar.

She halted, embarrassed and guilty about her earlier behavior. She heard his footsteps draw nearer as she stood still in the hallway.

"I am leaving, my lady."

"Leaving?" she asked and gazed at him. She wished he tempted her. But her heart rejected him like a day-blooming lotus flower shunning a full moon on an autumn night.

"I have overstayed my welcome here—"

"King Dushyant has departed," blurted Lalitha with a slight tremor.

"Departed?"

Lalitha nodded, her voice too choked with emotions for her to utter any words.

"Is he returning to attend your swayamvara?" Giridhar asked, shifting to view her.

Lalitha shook her head.

"Allow me to offer a piece of advice. Abandon the swayamvara and ask your father to arrange your marriage with the king." He turned to gaze at the sky.

Lalitha laughed with no joy. "You think it is that easy?"

He glanced at her. "No, it is not easy. Nothing about our lives is simple. But you will regret not trying." He spoke with heavy regret.

"What happens to the girl in your play? The one who fell in love with a king?"

"Shakuntala? While her heart was torn from the long lovelorn absence of her king, she remained faithful to him. The rest, you have to watch yourself," Giridhar said, a note of longing entering his eyes.

"Shakuntala," repeated Lalitha. "What was the king called?"

Giridhar shrank from her at the question, and weariness was etched in the lines around his mouth. After a long pause, he uttered the name like it hurt him to say it. "Dushyant."

It was only a silly play with no connection to reality, but her heart raced as Lalitha heard the name. "Stay to watch the end of my marriage drama, my lord," said Lalitha. "You may yet play a part in it."

"Whatever happens, I will hold your heart blameless because love leaves us blind," said Giridhar. "I will stay to watch you become a warrior's bride." With that, he strode off.

Warrior's bride. That could mean anyone because none but warriors were invited to her swayamvara. She continued to her father's chamber. Her mother sat across from him at the rose-wood table inlaid with tiny silver stars in an intricate pattern that matched their positions in the sky. Lalitha took the seat next to her mother. They uttered no words as the servants served the food. Watching her parents, Lalitha wanted to divide herself into two, one half for each.

Spicy pumpkin stew served over rice on a silver plate tasted like mud in Lalitha's mouth. After attempting to eat, Lalitha gave up and leaned back. Lalitha saw her father glance at her mother frequently like he was blind to everything else around him. Now that she knew their story, she could see the guilt mingled with love in his gaze.

"When did you meet King Dushyant?" her mother asked.

"This morning," answered Lalitha, confused.

"Before yesterday, Lalli. Your father told me what happened this morning. Dushyant saving your father's life appears tied to his desire to attend your swayamvara. There seems to be a shared past between the two of you." Lalitha gazed at her mother and saw no rebuke there.

Lalitha sighed. "I did not know he was King Dushyant. He called himself Puru and escorted me to the Garthapuri castle."

"You traveled with him alone?" her father asked, his eyebrows raised.

"Nothing untoward happened," said Lalitha, heat rising in her neck.

"How many days did you travel with him?"

"Three," whispered Lalitha. She saw her parents exchange a worried look.

"If it gets out that you spent time alone with the king, your prospective suitors will decline to attend the swayamvara. The honorable thing for King Dushyant to do is to marry you," said her mother, reaching out to stroke her hand. Dushyant wanted to wed her. That thought brought her no comfort.

"Lalli, I wanted you to choose your groom. That is why I

organized the swayamvara. Do you care for Dushyant?" her father asked, his brows knitted.

Lalitha stared at her lap, unable to speak, as emotions churned in her stomach. Dushyant's face flashed in her mind. When Lalitha considered the possibility of never uniting with Dushyant, her heart tore into pieces. Did that mean she cared for him?

"Is he worthy of you?" asked her mother, squeezing her hand.

With trembling lips, Lalitha inclined her head. Though he hid his name, he never tainted his honor or hers.

"If he attended the swayamvara and you did not have to worry about Garthapuri's future, would you place the garland around his neck?" asked her mother, with keen insight into her emotions.

Lalitha glanced at her with misty eyes. "But I cannot set Garthapuri aside," cried Lalitha.

Her mother put her arm around her shoulders and glared at her father. "You are not the sacrificial lamb for Garthapuri. Even if you did renounce your happiness, would that make you a better ruler? It will only make you bitter."

Her father rose and walked around the table. Standing behind her, he bent to kiss her forehead. "Your mother is right. The swayamvara was for you to find a partner to share your life with. The ceremony was not for choosing a regent for Garthapuri."

Lalitha hauled up and moved to face her parents. Her mounting frustration caused her breath to come in short gasps. "You talk as if I can choose a partner without considering the harm to Garthapuri."

"My child, if the man loves you, he will not cause harm to your kingdom," said her father. Her mother shifted to face him. "And I am still alive. Let me worry about Garthapuri."

Lalitha put her hands on her hips. "You want me to trust Dushyant blindly? How did that work for the two of you?"

Her father flinched as if she'd whipped him. Lalitha stammered, "I-I did not—"

"No, my child. Don't retract your words." He turned to face her mother. "Charu, when we walked around the fire seven times, we had vowed to cherish and protect each other. I betrayed my marriage vows to you. Not by being unfaithful. But by being blind to your needs. My foolishness kept you away from your daughter, an act that caused great harm to both of you." Tears streamed down Lalitha's cheeks as she watched her parents. "Will you forgive me?" Her father choked on the last words.

Her mother placed her elbows on the table and buried her face in her palms. Her shoulders shook gently, and Lalitha ran to her side and knelt beside her. Her mother leaned into her shoulders and put her arms around her daughter's neck. Lalitha stroked her mother's back gently as she wept.

Slowly, her mother straightened while wiping her eyes and turned to her father. His eyes glittered with tears. "Bhima, I made my share of mistakes. I never trusted you to share my feelings with you." Her mother sniffed loudly.

"I cannot blame you for not trusting me. Not after how I reacted when you first shared your secret with me," said her father. He must mean his duel with the boy her mother had loved.

"Since that tragic start, you have made amends through your actions. We cannot put our lives back together. But I can let go of my grudge which I have held and allow us both to heal." A drop of tear glinted on her chin. "I forgive you," her mother whispered.

Lalitha moved between her parents and put her arms around them both. They held her tightly. Her father smoothed Lalitha's hair while her mother squeezed her hand.

"I set you free, Bhima," her mother said, looking up at him. "Marry again. That will set Lalitha free to follow her heart."

Her father laughed dryly. "Let us worry about our daughter's marriage first."

They both regarded Lalitha as she inspected her wishes. Her smitten heart revealed itself readily. Like a river seeking the ocean, she sought Dushyant's company. Blood rushed to her cheeks, betraying her thoughts, but modesty kept her from stating her feelings.

"I will repeat my question, Lalli," said her mother, understanding her reluctance. "When you hold the garland of blossoms twined with leaves, will you move past King Dushyant to the next suitor?"

Lalitha shook her head. "I will place the wreath around his neck," she whispered.

"That settles it," said her father.

"Are you canceling the swayamvara?" her mother asked.

"Messages have already gone to the eligible noblemen, and they will start arriving soon. I will send a messenger to Dushyant inviting him to the swayamvara."

"His sisters are missing. He might not return in time," said Lalitha, worry pooling in her stomach.

"Then, we will wait for him. We can keep the assembled suitors engaged with feasts and festivities for a few days."

"How about Giridhar?" asked Lalitha. Guilt pricked her heart.

"We will place him ahead of King Dushyant in the line, and you can walk past him. He will be disappointed by your rejection, but he would not risk Dushyant's wrath," stated her father.

As if emerging from an underwater cave, Lalitha heard the chirping of birds outside. Her heart soared like an eagle flying over hills. Hope sprouted in her, sending shoots into her limbs. Enclosed in the arms of her parents, Lalitha allowed herself to relax.

The next few days, the city prepared for the wedding of their favorite daughter. Servants hung strings of mango leaves at the various entries into the castle to ward off evil. Maids drew intricate rangoli with rice flour on the courtyard floors. Flowers, birds, and lamps came to life in their drawings. Helpers polished the brass and silver lamps till they gleamed.

Her mother opened her jewelry box for Lalitha to view. "All of these are yours," she said, pointing to golden necklaces, earrings, waist belts, tiaras, hair clips, and bangles set in milky white pearls, red rubies, corals in the color of sunset, and diamonds that rivaled the night stars. Lalitha held a necklace shaped like a wreath of jasmine flowers set with pearls against her neck and inspected herself in the mirror. The jewel sparkled against her dark skin.

Her aunt, Chitra, entered the room. "Finally, you are glowing like a bride," she commented as she approached them. Lalitha smiled shyly. "You are going to break many hearts."

"Those men will recover by marrying other brides," her mother dismissed any concern for their well-being.

Her suitors started arriving in the city in horse-drawn chariots. Agamathi peered at them from her balcony while Lalitha reclined on a chair. Her friend kept her informed about their appearances. "The nobleman from the west has a mustache that rivals your hair."

Lalitha grinned. "He must keep it oiled."

Agamathi smirked. "His first love is going to compete for his affection. You don't want to come second in a man's life, my lady."

Agamathi spotted another. "The young man from the east is tall. But his father is the striking man. Look at the boy cower in front of him."

Lalitha laughed. "I want him to cower in front of me. How will I ever achieve that?"

Agamathi snorted.

"I see a lone horse racing toward us. The man hopped off even before the animal stopped. He is running up the steps."

"That must be a messenger," said Lalitha and heaved up. "I will visit my uncle to find out more." She hastened through the palace halls past the servants cleaning the torches hung on the walls.

She met her father near her uncle's chambers, along with another man of medium height. He looked vaguely familiar. "He is the royal envoy I sent to Dushyant," said her father as they continued toward the king's chamber.

Lalitha glanced at the man to see if he'd brought good news. The man betrayed no emotions.

"Brother, our messenger has returned," said her father as they crossed the threshold. Then, her father helped his brother to sit up. Lalitha rushed to the other side and arranged the pillows to make her uncle comfortable.

"What news do you have?" asked her uncle.

Lalitha paused with a blanket in her hand.

"King Dushyant has perished in a fire, my Majesty."

Lalitha stood like a statue.

"Perished?" repeated her father, but he sounded like he stood in a well.

"Yes, my lord. While he tried to rescue his sisters, his enemies set fire to the hut in which they held the two princesses. All three perished in the fire, and only charred bones remain."

Lalitha collapsed, and a pit of darkness swallowed her.

2 8

DUSHYANT

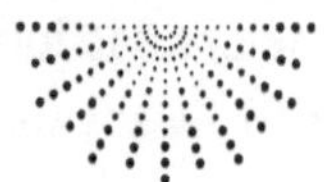

Fuming, Dushyant searched the temple, fervently seeking his sisters.

The man dressed as the priest, bloodied and battered, staggered down the stairs from the main sanctum. "The princesses are not here. But I found this."

He held out a gold bangle, and Dushyant grabbed it. Set with pearls, it resembled jewelry worn by his sisters. Fear choked his throat, leaving him speechless. Dushyant clutched his sword, fighting the urge to chop everyone down into pieces.

General Ayobahu approached them with a limp, sweeping the surroundings with his eyes. Noticing a man moan, he pounced on him. Holding the wounded man's throat in an iron grip, Ayobahu whispered, "Where are the princesses?"

"They moved them. I don't know where," the man gagged, his eyes bulging.

Moved? Was it a ploy by Ayobahu to hide his sisters? Dushyant almost stormed to his general's side to slash his head off. He tugged his ear hard to restrain himself, nearly pulling his earring off.

Jayanth hurried to another man lying on the ground and

pressed his feet on the wrist of the man. "When did they move them?"

The man cried out in pain. "Yesterday. They are not far from here."

Jayanth increased the pressure on his hand. "A-a barn of some kind," the man on the ground stuttered.

"Cows," gasped the other man in Ayobahu's clasp. "I heard the men complain about cows." Ayobahu sprang up.

Dushyant glanced at him. "General, round up the men here and see what more you can find. Jayanth and Sendhan, let us go find my sisters."

The two men joined him, and they strode out. "Where will we find this barn?" asked Dushyant, tucking the bangle into a cloth pouch.

"It would be in a secluded place, my Majesty. One of our men is from this area. I will ask him to guide us."

"Trustworthy?"

Jayanth nodded and led them to the local man.

He scratched his beard when Jayanth posed the question. "A remote cow barn? There is one about a mile away, near a farmer's fields. There is also a run-down stable further in the forest, but that place is deserted."

"Does this farmer milk his cows?" asked Dushyant, with his brows furrowed.

"Yes, he supplies milk for many families around here."

"That can't be it. Guide us to the abandoned structure," ordered Dushyant.

Dushyant and his guards, Jayanth, Sendhan, Amudhan, and their local guide, rode to the forest. At the edge of the forest, they dismounted near the towering trees. A light wind rustled the leaves and scattered them down. Tying their horses, Dushyant and his men proceeded on foot. A strange smell assaulted his nostrils as he entered the woods.

"Fire," cried Dushyant and dashed off. His feet pounded the

ground while his heart throbbed. Through the treetops, Dushyant saw smoke rising into the air. He burst into a clearing and saw flames licking a wooden structure.

As he was about to rush toward the building, Jayanth grasped his arm to hold him back. "My King, allow us to inspect the area first."

"Sendhan, check the surroundings for men hiding," ordered Jayanth. Sendhan raced off. "Amudhan, to the hut."

Dushyant bristled against the restraint but contained himself. He noticed Amudhan holding an ax and a long shield. Using the ax, Amudhan chopped off the burning wood, causing soot to disperse, and made his way in. When he disappeared into the fire, Dushyant's impatience won. Pushing Jayanth away, he hurried toward the blaze.

"Kanika, Ambika," screamed Dushyant as he entered the blackened property. His heart was its own blade twisting inside him. Smoke and fire obscured his view. With a crackling sound, a post collapsed on him, burning his skin. As he fell, the cloth around his shoulders caught fire. Dushyant watched in horror, his hands pinned under the bar. The heat singed his skin and caused his eyes to water. Suddenly, someone ripped and tossed the blazing fabric away. Powerful arms pulled him up, and the post hit the ground, and spat sparks.

Jayanth dragged Dushyant out, and Dushyant slumped on his knees, coughing.

Amudhan walked out with scorched skin and burnt eyebrows. Gasping for air, he shook his head to indicate he found no sign of them.

Dushyant hit the ground with his fist as tears blinded him. Suddenly, he remembered something. "Was there a rope around the post that crumbled?"

Amudhan darted in again. Before Dushyant's worry for Amudhan's safety turned real, Amudhan ran out coughing. He held a burning coil and threw it on the ground. Jayanth stamped the sparks out.

They escaped. Hope sprang like a fire fueled by wind. "Join Sendhan," Dushyant ordered the local man. "Jayanth and Amudhan, let us go search for my sisters," he said and leaped up.

The three men spread out in the woods while Dushyant called out his sisters' names. "Kanika, Ambika."

When they were a few yards away, a loud boom erupted. "The building," said Jayanth. Dushyant saw black smoke rising from the destroyed structure.

They continued for several feet when Dushyant saw a piece of silk stuck to a thorny bush. He removed it gently and inspected it. The gold threads weaved into the soft red fabric looked like something his sisters would wear. "Kanika, Ambika," he yelled and dashed into the bushes, not noticing the thorns tearing into his skin.

"Brother?"

"Kanika," he ran toward the sound. He searched behind the thick shrubs—no sign of them.

Ambika liked to climb trees. He glanced up with his heart pounding and noticed two figures hidden among the leaves on a thick tree branch. Their eyes widened in their soot-blackened faces as they saw Dushyant. His sisters! Dropping his sword, Dushyant held out his hands to catch them. They jumped into his arms one after another, and he clasped them to his chest. The two girls held him tightly and broke into a sob, wetting his skin. A wave of emotions hit his chest as he stroked their hair and backs. They were alive.

With her cries winding down, Kanika straightened. Letting go of them, Dushyant shut his eyes. He wanted to curl up on the ground in a fetal position. That would be unseemly for a king. He felt tossed in his feelings like a leaf tossed in the wind. They were alive. He trembled all over.

"Brother?" Kanika touched his shoulder gently.

A gasp escaped him. They were alive.

"My king," said Jayanth from somewhere close. "The princesses are safe."

The words tore out of him. "Not because of any power I had to keep them from destruction." He shook violently, and the ground scattered with fallen leaves swayed with him. He had to live in constant fear of losing them. A bolt of lightning could spear his heart anytime and crush it. His sisters and Lalitha could vanish without a farewell. A king in name, what could he do against such fate? Grief choked him.

"Dushyant?" Ambika's voice shook like she was near tears.

That tone pierced his hazy mind. He pushed all fear into a tiny corner of his mind. Gradually, he lifted his eyes and regarded them. Their matted hair, burnt cloth, and scorched skin anguished him. Still, a small corner of his heart sang at the sight of them.

"You are alive," whispered Dushyant and reached out to smooth Ambika's hair.

"Not for lack of trying on their part. They tied us to a post and set fire to the hut," ranted Ambika.

"How did you escape?" asked Dushyant.

Kanika held her hands out. Dushyant saw the burn marks on her wrist. "We positioned ourselves so that the rope had slack. Once the fire crept closer, we slid around till the blaze was toward our back. We let the flames slice the rope and crawled out."

He pulled them into another hug and kissed their heads. "You climbed a tree," he said. To love them meant to worry about them. Live in constant fear. Did that perpetual dread drive his father to his madness?

"We were not going to let those hideous men capture us again."

"Do you know who was behind your kidnapping?" asked Dushyant, pushing out his other worries.

"No," said Kanika. "But it is someone who pulled our father's strings. At least that was what one of the men stated."

"Our father?" asked Dushyant, puzzled.

"They never spoke in our presence about anything meaningful. But, I provoked them. In anger, one claimed the end was near for us. As our father had perished, so will we, he stated." Kanika's eyes blazed as she spoke. "We will not let them destroy our kingdom, will we?" asked Kanika while her fingers dug into his arm.

"No," said Dushyant. "We will restore it to its former splendor." First, he would find his foe and bring him just reward.

"Clear the cobwebs and traitors," said Ambika.

"Fill it with music and dancing drums," added Kanika.

"We will awaken the painter's brush and bring our caves to life," said Dushyant, remembering his mother's words. She wanted to paint elephants in lotus brooks, maidens descending stairways, and grass-sprouted flowers. Now, the caves had grown black with long neglect. And even the moon no longer wanted to shine its light on their floors and hid behind clouds. It was his duty to restore the city to its glory.

Dushyant heard footsteps. In one fluid motion, he stooped to pick up his sword from the ground and pushed his sisters behind him. Jayanth and Amudhan stood ready like tautly drawn bows.

Sendhan and the local man emerged from behind tree trunks. Their eyes found the princesses and brightened.

"Did you find the men who set the hut on fire?" asked Jayanth.

"We found tracks on the ground and followed their path. We heard noises but never came close enough to count them."

"There were four of them," said Ambika.

Sendhan inclined his head. "They found our horses and escaped on them. We decided to return here instead of pursuing them on foot."

Dushyant pondered what to do next. He was no closer to finding the monster behind the attacks. All eyes turned to him, waiting for his command. Like a snake hiding in the grass, his foe concealed himself. Dushyant needed a way to drive him into the open. His gaze fell on Amudhan. Blisters started to form on his fire-singed skin.

"Jayanth, I have an idea. Let Amudhan return to Ayobahu as the lone survivor. He can claim the king has perished in the fire."

"Perished?"

"Proclaim the king is dead," said Dushyant.

29

LALITHA

*L*alitha roamed through cremation grounds, dying embers lighting her way on a moonless night. The smell of burning flesh assaulted her nose as she searched for Dushyant's ashes. She was no wife of his to mourn him. Yet, every part of her called out his name. Then she came across a smoking pyre, and a glitter caught her eyes. A golden crown shone in the flame, mocking her. She picked up the hot metal and clutched it to her chest, unaware of the pain caused by the scalding jewel, and wept for the man she loved.

"My lady," someone shook her shoulders, and Lalitha opened her eyes in confusion. "You were wailing in your dream," said Agamathi with concern.

Lalitha felt the wetness on her cheeks. Her desolate mind knew she would never make any new memories with him. She looked at her friend, regret echoing in her eyes at her failure to comprehend her heart. "I loved him," she whispered.

* * *

THE RED BLOSSOMS on the Asoka tree seemed to droop in sadness. The sun hid behind the gray clouds. It seemed like the universe mourned the death of Dushyant. On the eve of her swayamvara, Lalitha wanted to beat her chest and cry out in anguish. Instead, she gathered ivory-colored flowers from the Champa tree with Agamathi and placed them in her woven jute basket. Lalitha held one delicate flower between her fingers and remembered Dushyant tucking a blossom into her hair. That memory cocooned her for a brief moment, bringing her respite from her grief. Then, Lalitha saw a wilting flower dangling on a short branch. She plucked the brown-tipped blossom and set it in the basket along with the others. A wilted garland signified her doomed life. She could not live in her past however much she wished. She had to face the future without Dushyant. Her heart broke into a thousand pieces.

Laughter drifted in with a gentle breeze, but Lalitha had forgotten how to smile. She should have been ecstatic that her father was free and her mother was with her. But she was nauseated because Dushyant haunted her every thought and emotion. Sensing her mood, Agamathi plucked the buds quietly. A dove called out to its mate, and Lalitha glanced in the direction of the sound. An answering call came from a few yards away, and a sigh escaped her. Love claimed her heart briefly. Now, only an empty hole stood in its place. A void she would fill with duty and tradition.

She looked at the half-filled basket. "This is enough flowers. I will string them with leaves," said Lalitha. Agamathi peered at her friend without a word.

They returned to Lalitha's chambers avoiding all the places offering amusement and merriment for the visitors. Lalitha placed the basket on a table and dropped onto her bench. Her life would alter tomorrow. She would choose a groom from among her suitors and marry him. She would become a stranger's wife pledging true commitment to him. Lalitha swallowed the lump that rose in her throat.

Agamathi hovered nearby like a mother bird watching her hatchling take flight and fall. "My lady, time heals all wounds. In a few years, you will drown in giggles from girls who look like you, wake up to kicks from soft feet that have never walked, and cuddle with warm babies. Like the sun appearing after a storm, joy will surround you."

As Agamathi talked, Lalitha imagined little boys with big ears like their father. Her stomach twisted in pain as she banished that vision from her mind. That dream was dead. Lalitha should let it go. But her heart had a will of its own, and it latched on to an image of Dushyant.

Lalitha heard the rustle of silk saris, and Queen Padmavati strolled in with two maids. Lalitha rose and stood with her chin on her chest.

"Lalitha, I am hosting a feast and then a dance in your honor. You will be seated on the balcony while your suitors mingle in the hall, longing to catch a glimpse of you." Her aunt halted next to Lalitha and lifted her niece's chin. "You have a rare opportunity to shape your destiny. Not many brides have the freedom to choose their husbands. Don't squander it."

Lalitha gazed at her aunt with misty eyes, unable to hide the anguish sweeping through her.

"Give us a moment alone," commanded the queen. The maids and Agamathi left the room.

Her aunt sat down and patted the spot next to her. Lalitha lowered herself to the seat. "I was once a young bride filled with dreams. I thought my dreams came true when I was crowned the queen of this land. Then, your uncle fell off his horse. Fate cursed him to a bedridden existence. My desires took a tumble that day."

Her aunt moved the thin gold bangles on her hand. Lalitha reached out and squeezed her knee gently. "Like a blossom that never fruits, I withered on my stalk. Young and healthy, fate doomed me to a barren existence."

"Aunt Padma," Lalitha whispered, touched by her aunt's pain. Lalitha noticed the fine lines around her mouth.

The queen gazed at her. "I know you are mourning the loss of your first love. Save the tears, Lalli. If destiny gifts you with children, you will lose a few before they walk. You will lose boys who run and climb on battlefields. Girls will be wed and sent off. A queen's life is a path filled with obstacles that break your heart at every turn."

Lalitha imagined the bleak world that her aunt had painted. Sorrow drowned her. "What is the purpose of my life then?"

"Not to seek joy but to bring light into the lives of others," stated the queen. "You can help your father rule. You can make life easier for your peasants. You can guide your children to achieve what was denied you. You can support your husband in fulfilling his desires."

"A life of service," said Lalitha, wiping her eyes.

"While living in the castle, yes. There is no need to seek a monastery. Get ready, my child. Wear your silks and gems as your armor." Her aunt leaned to kiss the side of Lalitha's head.

That evening, Lalitha sat in an ornate silver chair on the balcony. Brass lamps that hung from the wall cast a mellow light around her. Her yellow silk sari glowed like molten gold, and the diamond jewelry around her neck sparkled like stars in the night sky. Down below, her suitors craned their necks to view her. The smoke from the lamps hung as a veil around her.

On the stage, God Shiva's celestial bow rested on a bench. A dancer dressed as a prince flexed his muscles and spun toward the table to the rhythm of drums. He set one hand on the long bow and tried to lift it. Failing, he placed both hands and grunted and puffed. As the music reached a crescendo, he collapsed on the floor, unable to move the bow.

Rama emerged on stage to melodious Veena notes and

approached the bow. With his palms touching, he shut his eyes and uttered a prayer. Then, slowly, as the music built up, he reached the bow and lifted it overhead. The audience erupted into cheers. As Rama strung the bow, it broke into two halves. Seetha, clad in a red sari, swayed toward Rama with a jasmine garland. Lalitha moved to the edge of her chair to witness the next scene. As auspicious flute notes wafted into the air, Sita placed the garland around Rama. Despair engulfed Lalitha as she realized her swayamvara would not have a similar happy ending. A dozen dancers swirled onto the stage to celebrate the union of Rama and Sita.

Unable to bear the jubilation, Lalitha fled the room and found solitude on a terrace. The moon hid behind the clouds to avoid witnessing her sorrow.

Lalitha heard footsteps and spun to see her mother slide beside her. Her simple clothes looked out of place next to her vibrant attire.

"You witnessed the happiest moment of Sita's life," said her mother.

Lalitha glanced at her. Her mother stared at the tops of the trees.

"She only knew anguish in her life afterward," said her mother, bitterness coating her words.

"Sita enjoyed moments of joy in the forest," stated Lalitha, thinking of her journey with Dushyant.

Her mother remained quiet for a few moments. They could hear the folks leaving the dance hall. "How are you going to choose your groom?" asked her mother.

"Choose?" asked Lalitha, still caught up in Sita's tale.

"How will you decide who is worthy of you?"

"I will listen as each suitor is introduced and then—" faltered Lalitha. How would she decide if the man in front of her was the right match?

Her mother reached to adjust the thick necklace around

Lalitha's neck. "When Sita was a child, her ball rolled behind the celestial bow. The girl effortlessly lifted the bow in one hand to retrieve her toy. Her father witnessed this. He decided a man worthy of her should be able to string the bow."

"Rama lifted the bow proving himself suitable." Lalitha frowned. "A contest? Isn't it too late to inform the suitors of the rules?"

"It is acceptable to reveal the contest rules to the gathered suitors tomorrow. Your father can take care of that," answered her mother.

"Do we have an ancient bow for the suitors to string?" asked Lalitha.

"Lalli, this is not a matter for jest."

"How will I decide what trial to hold?" Lalitha did not want to hold any games. She wished to wed Dushyant—an impossible desire unless he woke up from his death.

"What quality are you looking for in your groom?"

Quality? If she could not marry the man of her dreams, she could at least ensure the well-being of her kingdom. Lalitha wanted a husband who would not hinder her rule of Gartha-puri. An idea took root in her mind.

As Lalitha walked back to her chambers through the dark halls lit by oil-wicker lamps, she heard a whisper. "Princess Lalitha, beware. There will be an attempt to kidnap you tomorrow."

Startled, Lalitha scanned the surroundings. Whoever spoke was well hidden. Why would anyone want to kidnap her on the day of her swayamvara?

30

DUSHYANT

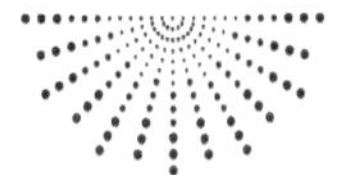

"Who is Lalitha?" asked Kanika, her hands on her hips.

Startled, Dushyant stammered, "No-Nobody. Why do you ask?"

Kanika smirked. "Because you were whispering nobody's name in your sleep."

Curse Lalitha for haunting his dreams. After traveling non-stop for the last few days, he succumbed to a short rest only to be tormented by Lalitha. "She is the Garthapuri princess," said Dushyant reluctantly.

"And why is her name on your tongue?" asked Kanika, raising her eyebrows.

Heat rushed to Dushyant's face. "Since when do you question your older brother?"

"It must be serious if you are avoiding my question. I can always ask Jayanth," said Kanika with a playful smile.

Dushyant knew his sister would not rest till his reply satisfied her. He glanced at Jayanth standing a few yards away and talking to Sendhan. "I met Lalitha when she was traveling back to her kingdom. I grew fond of her," said Dushyant and tugged

209

his ear. "But nothing can come of it. Her swayamvara is in three days, and I am here in Vidarpur." It pained him to utter those words. In three days, she will marry someone and be out of his reach, even if she remained in his nightmares.

"Brother! I can see that this girl means a lot to you. Go to her swayamvara—"

"Enough, Kanika," said Dushyant, in a tone that discouraged further conversations on this subject. He needed to forget Lalitha. That was the prudent way.

Dushyant heard the snapping of twigs and spun toward the sound.

"My Majesty, your plot has succeeded. You are dead to the world," proclaimed Jayanth.

Dushyant brightened. "The jackals and wolves will come out now that the danger from the tiger has passed. Let us unmask them. Do you have our disguises?"

Jayanth nodded.

Leaving Sendhan and the local man to guard his sisters, Dushyant and Jayanth set out on foot in the dark. Near General Ayobahu's hastily erected makeshift camp, they hid behind a tree. Dushyant looked up and spotted a black and brown centipede with stripes like a tiger. This insect crawled down the tree trunk with its dozen or so legs. The movement resembled the waves crashing on a shore. Dushyant shifted slightly to allow the bug to reach its destination, wondering if he could ever command his troops to move in such unison.

Jayanth hooted like an owl, and one of the soldiers approached them cautiously. Dushyant stayed hidden while Jayanth stepped out of the shadows.

"Commander Jayanth, I heard—"

"Don't believe everything you hear, Soldier. Where is Amudhan held?"

"In that tent," the soldier said while pointing his index finger toward a midsize cloth structure illuminated by flaming torches. "Is the king—"

"Soldier, sometimes ignorance is bliss. Can you get me inside Ayobahu's trunk?"

"Commander, I have sworn loyalty to Vidarpur and her king. If the king is hurt or worse, why are you here?" Dushyant noticed that the soldier ignored Jayanth's request.

"I am here seeking the truth," said Dushyant taking a step forward.

Alarmed, the soldier moved back, staring at Dushyant like he saw a ghost.

"I am the king you swore an oath to. Can you arrange for us to be in Ayobahu's trunks?" asked Dushyant.

"My M—"

"Being dead suits my needs, so don't reveal this to anyone," ordered Dushyant.

The soldier swallowed and nodded.

Shortly after, Dushyant folded his long frame onto the bottom of a large wooden trunk, with Ayobahu's silk dhotis and shawls covering him. Jayanth crammed his broad frame inside another crate. Then stillness descended around them as they waited in the dark for Ayobahu's return. With his back flat against the side and knees bent, Dushyant peeked through the tiny slit in the box, inhaling the stale air. His short sword pressed against his hip, reminding him of the danger surrounding him. If Ayobahu was the traitor, Dushyant made it easy for his general to dispose of him.

Time slowed to a crawl, and Dushyant's body ached from being twisted into the tiny space. The burns he suffered in the fire, though minor, increased his anguish. Something crept up his right leg, and he had no room to crush the insect. The musty smell inside the box gave Dushyant a headache, and his chin drooped in tiredness. A bright light outside made him squint, and Dushyant blinked his eyes rapidly.

Dushyant heard the shuffling of feet, followed by a rustling sound. Two pairs of legs crossed his vision, one covered in silk and another in cotton. The cotton-clad legs stood still while the silk-clad ones moved in and out of Dushyant's sight. A nervous quietness stretched around them.

"General Ayobahu," said a voice, breaking the long silence. "The men who went looking for the king have returned."

"Send them in," said Ayobahu and froze at the edge of Dushyant's view.

Dushyant held his breath, though the stomping of feet he discerned would have muffled any noise he made.

"What did you see?" Dushyant sensed an urgency in Ayobahu's question.

"The structure was burned down, but we found this."

Dushyant could not see what they showed to the general. After a pause, Ayobahu said, "Hmm. It could be the king's." Dushyant remembered his shawl that had caught fire. Did a piece of that fabric escape the flames? Another pause. "What else did you see?"

"The ground was covered with foot tracks. One set led further into the forest. Another set led to the edge of the forest and converged with hooves prints. That is how the traitors must have escaped." Traitors? Did they mean men loyal to him or the ones who kidnapped his sisters?

"Any sign of charred bones in the structure?" asked Ayobahu.

"None we could find." A mistake on Dushyant's part. He should have left some animal bones in the hut.

Footsteps receded. Dushyant heard the sound of wood scraping on the earth. And one leg stretched into his view, with heel down and five toes up. Dushyant assumed Ayobahu had sunk into a chair.

"Jayanth was loyal and trustworthy. Where did he disappear without a trace?" asked Ayobahu. Dushyant noticed a slight tremor in the general's voice. Did the general worry that his treachery was going to come to light?

"What do we do now?" asked another male voice that Dushyant did not recognize.

"We have to return to Vidarpur soon. Get me the last message from Minister Panini. I placed it in that trunk." Trunk? There were no scrolls in his. Dushyant saw a pair of feet head toward Jayanth's chest. He grasped the hilt of his sword. What would Ayobahu do if Jayanth jumped from the box? Someone slid the bolt and lifted the lid of the trunk. The hairs on the back of Dushyant's neck rose. With his heart hammering in his ribs, Dushyant prepared to spring out.

"I found it," answered the soldier who had aided their entry into this room. Dushyant nearly sighed out loud on hearing his voice. The soldier did not give away Jayanth's location. Closing the box, he crossed the room to General Ayobahu.

"I don't know who to trust," said Ayobahu in a distant voice. Silence ensued. "Soldier, bring Amudhan here. We have recovered no remains to prove his claim. I want to question him more."

Dushyant tugged his ear. He'd seen nothing to confirm or deny Ayobahu's role in the kidnapping of his sisters. With a sense of despair, he waited for Amudhan's appearance. His body protested for staying in the distorted posture.

"Blah," Amudhan bleated and stumbled to the ground. Dushyant realized with a shock that his guard's hands and feet were bound. Someone pulled him up roughly.

"The men I sent found no dead bodies. What did you and Jayanth do to the king?" asked Ayobahu in a menacing tone. He throttled Amudhan's throat.

Amudhan made strangled sounds, and Dushyant fought the urge to reveal himself. "I want to hear only the truth," Ayobahu whispered. "Bring him a plate of grain, so he can write on it."

Random noises erupted, and then a silver plate appeared. Amudhan held up his arm.

"Untie his right hand," ordered Ayobahu. A soldier freed Amudhan's right hand but placed the left hand behind his back and tied the cord around his waist.

Amudhan started tracing on the rice.

"Princess——missing," read the soldier.

"Yes, I know that," said Ayobahu.

"Hidden in hut," read the soldier. "King died in fire."

Ayobahu snatched Amudhan's hair roughly. "Where is the king's body? Where are the princesses? Where is Jayanth?"

"Ba," cried Amudhan in pain.

"Answer me," said Ayobahu and released him.

"I fainted," read the soldier.

Ayobahu slapped Amudhan hard across his cheek, causing his face to swing. "You are the king's guard. You swore an oath to protect him with your life. You failed that oath," yelled Ayobahu.

Amudhan whimpered and wrote on the rice.

"I came to tell you the news. Give me a sword. I will kill myself," read the soldier in a halting voice.

"Do you think me a fool? I will behead you with my sword," cried Ayobahu, drawing his sword.

Dushyant started lifting the lid of his chest. He did not want Amudhan to perish on his behalf, though Jayanth would argue he was doing his duty. Dushyant got ready to command Ayobahu to drop his sword.

"General, if the king is dead, it is best to take Amudhan to Vidarpur palace with us. We can punish him after he shares the news," said the soldier.

Ayobahu grunted and let the sword drop back in. Dushyant let out his breath and allowed the lid to close silently.

"Soldier, take Amudhan back. Search for the traitors who

fled on horses. The princesses could still be alive," ordered Ayobahu.

Footsteps faded. The general slumped to the floor and crossed his feet. He leaned forward and buried his face in his palms. "My king, I failed you," he whispered. "I don't know who betrayed you," he said in an anguished voice.

Dushyant desperately tried to figure out what Ayobahu's words meant while his mind churned through everything he heard. Was Ayobahu still loyal to his king? Dushyant's face grew hot under the layers of clothes while his heart pounded wildly with a strange mixture of fear and hope.

After a long while, Ayobahu wiped his nose and stood. Then he vanished from Dushyant's view. Dushyant ignored his throbbing feet and pondered Ayobahu's actions. Confusion reigned in his mind. Sensing they were alone, he pushed open the lid of his trunk and peeked—no sign of any life. Fully opening the box, Dushyant sat up.

"Jayanth," he whispered.

Jayanth's head appeared through the gap in the chest beside his. Soon, the two men crawled out of Ayobahu's room. As they crossed the field, leaves crunched under their feet.

"Who is there?" called a guard. He lifted his torch over his head and swiveled side to side. Dushyant and Jayanth crouched behind a copper pot. Dushyant could sense Jayanth was ready to pounce on the guard if he spotted them.

"Meow." A cat strolled in front of them.

"It was only you," said the guard and lowered the light.

Dushyant and Jayanth reached the safety of the woods and paused to catch their breath. "I need to tighten security around our camps," said Dushyant, standing on his toes to stretch his legs. Then, he glanced at Jayanth. "Would you have killed the guard?"

"If he threatened your life," said Jayanth, gazing clear-eyed at the silhouettes of the trees. "My Majesty, would you have saved Amudhan's life back there?"

"I am not a monster to let my people die without me putting up a fight to save them," Dushyant said calmly.

"My Majesty, your life is worth hundreds of ours."

"Why?" Dushyant stared at the ground and took a few deep breaths. "I have not done anything worthy yet." In the absolute stillness, he could smell the crisp air.

"Because, unlike us, you can never say no, even if you want to run from your duty," whispered Jayanth.

"I am not afraid of the sacrifices I have to make," said Dushyant while he remembered Lalitha's upturned face.

"That makes you worthy, my king."

A lump caught in Dushyant's throat as he soaked in Jayanth's kindness. Neither spoke for a while as they walked swiftly.

"Do you still doubt General Ayobahu?" asked Jayanth.

"Tell me what you think."

"I think he is loyal to you."

"I am not ready to issue a judgment on him yet, but he is not my top suspect."

"Where next, my Majesty?"

"Vidarpur Castle," answered Dushyant.

When he returned to his sisters, they assailed him with questions. Dushyant answered them patiently. "Ayobahu is not my main suspect. I am going to Vidarpur with Jayanth. Sendhan will stay with you—"

"No, dear brother. You are not leaving us here," said Kanika.

"The men who kidnapped you are still out there. I don't want to jeopardize your safety."

"What could be safer than traveling with you?" asked Ambika.

"Don't argue with me," started Dushyant.

"My Majesty, it will be prudent for us to stick together," said Jayanth.

Dushyant glared at Jayanth.

"They can dress as boys to avoid suspicion."

In the dark, the six of them set out as a wedding party returning home. The local man wore a red bridal sari, and Sendhan dressed in a yellow dhoti of the groom. Dushyant adorned his scratchy gray beard, and Jayanth became Jayanthi in his blue sari. The princesses wore a loose top garment and a dhoti to pass as brothers of the groom.

"Brother, if we walk all the way to Vidarpur, you are going to miss Lalitha's swayamvara," whispered Kanika in his ear.

Dushyant's stomach dropped to his feet on hearing Lalitha's name. What if news of his death reached her? Would she mourn him? What foolish thoughts, Dushyant chided himself. Kanika was right. Traveling on foot would take them too long.

Before Dushyant spoke his mind, Jayanth said, "I will find us a cart."

Soon, they rode on two carts. Sendhan drove one with the local man and Ambika. Dushyant managed the other with Jayanth and Kanika.

As the sun rose above Nandri hills, Dushyant said, "Jayanth, find a safe place for my sisters on the outskirts of the fort. You and I have urgent business inside."

"There is a trustworthy woman we can leave them with," Jayanth said. Noticing his strange tone, Dushyant turned to look at him. His head guard blushed under his gaze.

"Jayanth, your demeanor tells me she is special," said Kanika.

"I guess it is apparent," Jayanth answered with a sheepish grin.

"Are you going to marry her?" asked Kanika, giving him a searching glance.

Jayanth's blush deepened. "Yes, my lady. With the king's permission, I hope to wed her."

"You never told me," Dushyant scolded.

"My Majesty, I apologize. There was never a good time to bring her up," said Jayanth, squirming in his seat.

Four years ago, Dushyant had saved Jayanth before he flung himself off a cliff. Jayanth had lost his wife and wanted to end his life. "I am glad you found another to share your life with," said Dushyant. His father had never healed from his mother's death. Would Dushyant be like his father, looking for Lalitha in everyone and everything, unable to let go, never letting anyone else get close to his heart? Or would he mend like Jayanth?

"I owe you my gratitude, my Majesty. You brought purpose into my life and allowed me to recover."

They stopped outside a modest house. Clusters of bananas from trees growing on one side of the house greeted them. Jayanth went in first. After a few moments, he waved at them from the threshold.

Dushyant entered the single-room house and gazed at the woman who beamed at them. She wore a plain cotton sari, and simple silver studs adorned her ears.

Jayanth shut the door. "This is Kantha, my king." His head guard, who would not hesitate to step in front of a spear aimed at his king's heart, looked at Kantha with obvious fondness. Jayanth's happiness leaked into Dushyant's heart and turned into emotions of sorrow. Would there ever be another woman in his life like Lalitha? No matter which corner of the world she lived in, he could never forget her.

Kantha bowed from her waist with her palms touching.

"We will celebrate your wedding in the palace," smiled Kanika. Dushyant nodded his agreement, his tongue tied.

Leaving his sisters with Sendhan and the local man, Jayanth and Dushyant made their way to the foothills.

Hearing the thunderous gallop of horses, they hid behind a large boulder. Jayanth peeked around it. "The flag bears our eagle symbol."

Dushyant edged closer to the other side of the rock and

looked. About 50 horses trotted past him with the riders in full battle armor. One man, in particular, caught his attention. "Chief Guard Samudra?"

"Headed to a battle," remarked Jayanth.

Dushyant watched in horror as the men cried, "Death to Ayobahu." These men must think General Ayobahu caused his demise. With his fake death, Dushyant had unleashed terror. Could he stop his generals from killing each other?

3 1

LALITHA

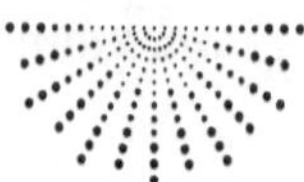

"Kidnapping?" asked Agamathi, tying a string of white jasmine around Lalitha's bun.

Lalitha tightened her pearl earrings while the night reluctantly bid farewell to earth. "That is what I heard yesterday."

"Why would someone want to kidnap you today?"

Lalitha shrugged her shoulders while sliding gold bangles onto her wrist. "To stop my swayamvara?" Lalitha adjusted her pink sari in the color of a lotus bud and gazed at her reflection in the mirror. An empty shell with no dreams stared back at her.

Agamathi sighed. "You are going to break many hearts today."

None more than hers. Lalitha's hopes and desires stayed inside her, eating away her body like a caterpillar preying on new spring leaves. "Not if I am carried off," said Lalitha lightly. She did not take the abduction threat seriously. Why would someone risk seizing her from the palace?

"Any news from Vidarpur, my lady?"

A pit opened in Lalitha's stomach on hearing that name. "There are reports of unrest since the king's death." She wished

220

Dushyant's demise was a nightmare that would vanish once she woke up.

A knock sounded on her door, and Agamathi opened it.

"Lalitha!" exclaimed her aunt as she entered the room. "You glow like a pearl fetched from the depth of the ocean. A pearl has no need to seek, for it is sought."

"Thank you, Aunt Padmavathi," said Lalitha while thinking it was a strange message before her groom choosing ceremony. She would be the seeker today.

"I have come to take you to God Krishna's temple so you can pray for wisdom and strength," said Queen Padmavati.

Lalitha wanted to talk to her mother and father that morning to discuss her idea for a contest. "I don't want to be late, Aunt Padmavati," said Lalitha.

"Don't be silly. You need the divine lord's blessings on this auspicious occasion. Come, Child. I have the chariot ready."

"That temple is outside the fort, Aunt Padmavati," persisted Lalitha. "Can we visit the Goddess Durga temple that is close by?"

"Lalli, you are not going to war. In matters of heart, you need God Krishna's grace. This god is known to grant the wishes of young maidens." Unlikely he would resurrect Dushyant.

Soon, Lalitha and her aunt rode toward the temple outside the palace compound. Lalitha glanced at the men accompanying her. "Where is Nambi?" Lalitha asked, noticing her trusted guard was not among them.

"He is helping your father," replied her aunt.

The city dwellers paused in their morning routines to wish her well, and Lalitha dismissed Nambi from her mind. She thanked them graciously, hoping to choose the right partner for their well-being as well as hers.

They arrived at the temple as the sun hid behind the trees. "You stay here. I want the priest to invoke the spirits of the celestial elements before you enter," said Queen Padmavati and descended from the chariot.

Lalitha smiled at the early morning devotees. A beautiful rangoli drawn on the sandy entryway using rice flour drew her eyes. The intricate design depicted six lotus flowers with petals on the outside and stems joining in the center. A flock of pigeons descended atop the pattern and blocked her view. As she tilted her head to see them better, her carriage rocked, and in climbed Prince Giridhar.

Before she could question him, he yelled, "Go," and the charioteer tugged the reins, and the horses took off. Four other riders flanked them on either side.

Lalitha rose from her seat. "Prince Giridhar, stop the chariot. What do you think you are doing?" A breeze rolled in, whipping her clothes around.

He gazed at her. "I am abducting you so I can marry you," he shouted above the wind.

"Giridhar, has a demon spirit invaded your mind? Today is my swayamvara. I intend to choose my own husband. Let me go."

Lalitha grew worried as she watched Giridhar laugh like he had lost touch with reality. She did not even bring her trusted knife with her. Will her aunt raise the alarm once she notices her missing?

Suddenly, Giridhar leaned in and whispered, "I warned you yesterday." Then loudly, "Forget the swayamvara. I intend to make you mine."

Lalitha grew cold. "Is my aunt aware of this plot?" she asked quietly.

Giridhar looked at the horizon but inclined his head. No one was going to rescue her.

"Prince Giridhar, my father will avenge you for this," proclaimed Lalitha in a normal voice.

"My father-in-law will not hurt me," said Giridhar.

The carriage swayed side to side, and Lalitha collapsed onto the slender bench. If Giridhar married her, her father and uncle would not hurt him. Curse her aunt for trapping her. Hot tears stung her eyes. She glanced at the still-standing prince and met his eyes. She saw no triumph in them. Why did he warn her yesterday? And why did he agree to this heinous act today?

"My father forced my mother into marriage. It did not end well for them," said Lalitha.

Giridhar grimaced for an instant. "I hope you and I can forge a better future." He sat beside her, leaving a foot-length space between them. "I will take better care of you."

"Even if your king wishes otherwise?" asked Lalitha sharply.

He shrank from her as if stung by a scorpion. Lalitha knew she spoke the truth. Giridhar would obey the commands of his brother, the king. And she would be a puppet in their hands to rule Garthapuri.

As she approached the crossroads, she saw two roads. One headed south to Vidarpur, and the other headed west to Nidhapur. As her chariot turned toward Nidhapur, she saw a dust cloud on the road from the south. In the blink of an eye, four horses emerged.

"Help me," she screamed, not knowing if the riders were friends or foes. "Help!"

32

DUSHYANT

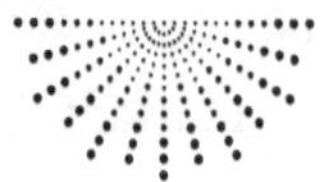

Dushyant grunted as he moved a rock while Jayanth stood guard. An opening appeared behind the stone. Dushyant peered into the gap, and a bat fluttered out, almost hitting his face. Making sure nothing else hovered nearby, Dushyant crawled into the space on his knees. The jagged edges scratched his skin as he crept through the narrow passage. The sound of flowing water reached his ears, and he emerged into a slightly bigger cavern with room for four people. Dark rocks greeted him on all sides while a faint glow came from below. Dushyant moved further in to give room for Jayanth.

His guard peeked into the hollow on the floor. "About a ten-foot jump into the water. I will go first." He leaped into a pool of water and disappeared from sight.

Dushyant waited for Jayanth's head to float above the surface. As Jayanth swam to the edge, Dushyant jumped into the water. With the weight of his weapon pulling him down, he touched the bottom of the pool. Kicking his feet, he swam to the top. Looking around, he spotted Jayanth climbing out and followed him.

Once on solid ground, Dushyant squeezed the water out of

224

his dhoti. "Let us claim my kingdom back," he said and moved in the direction of the castle.

Quietly, they advanced through the twisted tunnels carved from the caves. The dank odor faded the further they went. Dushyant's foot slid on the uneven path, and he grabbed onto a sharp rock for support. There was hardly any wind down here, and he could hear his pounding heart. Taking a breath, he used his hand to feel his way forward.

"Someone is coming," whispered Jayanth.

Dushyant saw flickering light reflect on the walls of the cave to their right. These tunnels were used by the royal family to enter the palace unnoticed or to flee it. The king's guards patrolled them. Was it one of his guards? Regardless, he should stay hidden from sight. He scanned the area frantically for a hiding place before they were spotted.

"In here," murmured Jayanth, and he took cover inside a tiny cavity hidden by a partial rocky formation. Dushyant squeezed beside him.

"I heard guards outside my room whispering about the king's death. Is it true? Is he really dead?" asked a female voice.

"I heard the same rumor and cannot confirm or deny it," answered a gruff male voice.

Dushyant could make out a woman and two men in the glow of the flaming torch. They walked toward them.

"Where are you taking me now?" asked the female.

"Her voice sounds familiar," Dushyant whispered.

"If Dushyant is dead, what will happen to me?" asked the female.

Sundari! Dushyant recognized the voice of the woman who had accused his father of besmirching her honor. He glanced at her stomach for the telltale pregnancy bump.

"Why, you will be the queen regent, ruling this land till your child comes of age," replied the man. Dushyant pressed his lips together.

Sundari paused. "What if that puts my life in danger?" She slid a ring on her finger up and down. The green gem sparkled in the light.

A memory flashed in Dushyant's head. He stepped forward and drew his sword. "That should not be your only concern." Dushyant sensed Jayanth shift beside him into an attacking posture.

"King D-Dushyant," Sundari stammered.

The two guards with her recovered from their initial shock and reached for their weapons. Jayanth pounced on the man with a broken front tooth and threw him to the rocky ground. A hand-to-hand combat ensued.

Dushyant stuck the pointy edge of his sword into the throat of the broader man and drew blood. "Surrender to me, and I will spare your lives," said Dushyant. His opponent lunged forward, seeking an opening to strike a fatal blow, but each time he failed due to Dushyant's swift reflexes. Dushyant parried every thrust from his opponent's blade, dodging left and right while keeping his guard up high. On a normal day, Dushyant and Jayanth would have defeated the two men in no time. But, Jayanth and Dushyant were tired after being on the road for several days with no sleep. Their movements grew sluggish, and they reacted to their opponents' attacks slowly. The clank of metal against metal filled the air as they clashed swords, the traitors gaining an advantage over them. Jayanth fell to the floor while his opponent pinned Dushyant to the wall of the cave.

"I am your king," hissed Dushyant while pushing hard against the blade edging toward his neck.

The sound of running feet distracted the broad man, and Dushyant used that opportunity to slide away. Jayanth struggled with the man with the broken tooth, and Dushyant despaired about his inability to help.

"Commander Jayanth?" Two city guards appeared.

"Help him," yelled Dushyant. The two new men split and came to aid them, and the tide shifted in their favor.

One of the new men surged forward and delivered a flurry of blows to Jayanth's opponent. Jayanth used this chance to scramble up and join the attack. Jayanth and the new man advanced on their opponent, who was now backed into a corner. The man tried to fight back, but it was no use against the two. Soon he lay on the ground. Jayanth stepped on his wrist, causing him to yelp and let go of the handle of his dagger.

Dushyant's opponent raised his hands above his head in surrender. The torch he held nearly touched the ceiling. "My king, forgive me. I never intended to harm you."

Eyes wide, Sundari stepped back.

"Get their weapons one by one and make a pile there," Dushyant ordered. Soon, a collection of weapons lay on the ground. Dushyant took the torch from his combatant, and Jayanth used their shawls to bind their arms behind their backs.

"We were watching Sundari on Commander Jayanth's orders," said one of the men who arrived to save them.

"March," said Jayanth and pushed the two traitors in front. Dushyant walked beside a nervous Sundari, who kept glancing at him.

"Who gave you that emerald ring?" asked Dushyant in a quiet voice. He'd seen it before on Advisor Upananda's little finger.

Her face scrunched into an unsightly contortion, and she moved her hand behind her back. "No one," she screeched.

"You can lie to me and face my wrath. Or tell the truth to earn my mercy," said Dushyant coldly.

A sob escaped Sundari. "Spare my baby, my Majesty."

"Who is the father?" asked Dushyant, though he had a suspicion.

She looked side to side as if expecting assailants to leap at her from behind the rocks and then wailed loudly.

"Let us head to the main palace," said Dushyant, and Jayanth inclined his head. After marching through a maze of winding tunnels, they stood under the king's room. Jayanth placed one of their prisoners under the trap door and climbed on his shoulders to open it. He pulled himself up and slid onto the floor. Dushyant heard strange noises as Jayanth moved around above him.

"Help Jayanth," ordered Dushyant to one of the city guards, and he followed Jayanth. Dushyant could hear Jayanth issue a command. "Fetch the minister."

Jayanth peered down and dropped a silk dhoti. "To tie them together," he said.

The other city guard placed the two prisoners back to back, and Dushyant helped him tie the cloth around them.

Time stood still as Dushyant waited in the underground cave, his mind racing through the past two months. Like a moth caught in a spider web, he'd allowed others to influence him without understanding their motives. A mouse ran around the corner while Sundari continued to cry.

Footsteps thundered above. Two more soldiers dropped down and bowed to him. They brought bundles of rope.

"Find out where these two were taking her and then throw them into our dungeon," ordered Dushyant to the city guard. Then he faced the two new men. "Guard her and wait here for my next command," said Dushyant.

Jayanth let down a ladder. "Sundari, I will take that ring from you," said Dushyant. She sniffled and handed it to him. Dushyant climbed the rungs to reach his father's chambers.

"My Majesty, it gladdens this old man's heart to see you alive," said the minister as Dushyant pulled himself up.

"Why did Samudra march with an army?" asked Dushyant, wasting no time.

"One of our spies arrived this morning with a message that

you had died in a skirmish. I advised Chief Guard Samudra to wait, but he wanted to confront General Ayobahu."

"I am alive. We need to stop Samudra and Ayobahu from killing each other." Dushyant walked to the sitting room and found dried palm leaves. "I will pen my orders to them," commanded Dushyant.

Dushyant wrote two identical messages and sealed them. "*I am alive. Come to the castle immediately.*" The minister dispatched two messengers with these letters.

"Now for the difficult part. The two men we captured were taking Sundari somewhere. Take her as bait and find out."

The minister stared at him with his mouth open. "Sundari?"

"She is in the tunnel below. There is no time to waste," urged Dushyant, spurring him to action.

After setting these things in motion, Dushyant collapsed on a chair. "Jayanth, send someone trustworthy to fetch my sisters."

Alone in his father's chambers, he glanced at the life-like sculptures carved on the rock walls. An elephant with a lone rider marched to a battle. The delicate carving of the rider's crown indicated royal heritage. On another side, a prince in full armor fought with a spear. Dushyant approached the carving of the young prince and traced his face. Dushyant saw a mixture of hope and fear reflected in his posture.

When the minister returned, he found his king seated at the table. Dushyant asked, "Where is Advisor Upananda?"

"Upananda is still at the Garthapuri border."

"Send men to escort him back to the castle. And fetch our goldsmith."

The goldsmith arrived shortly after, and Dushyant handed him the ring. He inspected it carefully. "I made this for the queen."

"My mother?" She was the last queen of this land.

The goldsmith nodded. "But the queen never lived to wear it. I also made matching earrings and a necklace."

"Did you give the set to the king?"

"No, my Majesty. King Lambhodara was grieving, and I did not want to intrude. I mentioned the jewels to Advisor Upananda, and he sent a servant to pick them up."

The goldsmith handed the jewel back to Dushyant. Dushyant thanked the man. As he turned to depart, Dushyant asked, "Did my father commission more jewels?"

"Yes, my Majesty. A coral set including arm bands and waist-bands, a diamond tiara, and a few more. I gave the jewels to the king's servant."

After he left, Dushyant paced the floor. Like a rain settling the dust in the air, some parts of his father's life became clear to him.

"Should I fetch your father's servant?" asked Jayanth. Dushyant nodded at his guard, who stood unobtrusively in a corner.

"Prince Dushyant." His father's servant bowed from his waist. Then realizing his mistake, he said, "Apologies, my king. I left your father's belongings as is. I can clear them out so you can move in."

Emotions choked Dushyant at the thought of moving into the king's chambers. "That can wait. How was my father's health this past year?"

"Nothing unusual in his health, my Majesty."

Dushyant observed the man rubbing his palm on the side of his thigh. "What was normal for him?"

The servant squirmed.

"I am your king. You can speak freely."

"Since your mother's death, the king sustained on poppy's milk. He may abstain for the few weeks you visited, but—"

Dushyant spun to gaze outside the window and clasped his hands behind his back. How did he miss all this?

"What did you do with the jewels you picked from the goldsmith?"

"Most, I kept them in a box in the king's bedroom. Some I handed to Advisor Upananda at the king's request. Should I bring them?"

"No, not now. Who visited the king in his room?"

"Advisor Upananda came daily to seek the king's view on matters of governance."

Dushyant half turned and glanced at the man over his shoulder. "Did he speak with the king's authority?"

"Yes, the king himself told me to follow Advisor Upananda. He kept the kingdom running."

Dushyant's mind raced to connect the dots like a maid's fingers connecting the dots on a rangoli. "Did a woman named Sundari visit the king?"

The old servant seemed to struggle with some great feeling. "The king was faithful to your mother's memories. But Advisor Upananda said the king wanted to see the lady alone. So I left her with him. She did not stay for long."

Dushyant looked at the thin wisps of cloud floating in the sky. Upananda had planned this meticulously.

"My Majesty," the servant said. "The king left you some of your mother's jewels for your wedding. Should I bring it?"

Dushyant nodded absently, not registering the man's words. The servant placed a box on the table and lingered nearby.

Dushyant dismissed the man. The servant paused near the door. "In honor of your mother's memory, your father invited dancers from all over the kingdom to come and dance. All others enjoyed the feasts while he mourned her."

A lump rose in Dushyant's throat as the door shut behind the servant.

He walked to the table and traced the ivory carving on the ornate case with his index finger. Why did his father leave him this for his wedding? It was locked, but his father's servant had left the key behind. Idly, his mind elsewhere, Dushyant opened the box. Inside glittered what appeared to be his mother's jewels. He picked up a sapphire choker, and the colors of the ocean sparkled in his hand. As he placed the necklace back inside, his eyes caught a scroll hidden under the jewels. Moving the glittering stones aside, he removed the scroll. His father had sealed it.

With trembling fingers, he opened the letter.

"Dushyant,

On a rare lucid day, I am writing this letter. Son, you just departed Vidarpur after a brief visit, and I will revert to my dependency as before. But today, I wanted to beg your forgiveness. At fifteen, you have grown into a young man far more capable than I ever was. Your wit and valor moved me. But, in an unguarded moment or two, I saw your repulsion when you gazed at me. I don't blame you. I have wronged you.

Your mother was stronger than me. She always knew what to do. She was my truest friend. I never learned to love myself. When I looked in the mirror, I only saw what was ugly in me. Only her eyes reflected what was good in me. Without her, I did not know how to live. Your mother's smiles and faith in me kept me whole. Without them, I was wretched and hollow. So, I sought her ghost to keep me company. I have lived in the past.

These last few days, you have reminded me of the future. Unlike mine, this future of yours is filled with shining light. The duty that was a burden around my neck, you wear lightly. You have made me hopeful for our kingdom. I know I have been a poor imitation of a father, but I am proud of the man you have grown into.

One day, a girl will capture your soul. Don't place the responsibility for your happiness on her. That is too much load for another person to bear, living or dead. She is there to share your joy, but you find your own purpose.

Where I failed, I pray you succeed."

Tears pricked Dushyant's eyes as he remembered his brief visits to see his father. He'd judged the man harshly. Thinking him without virtue, Dushyant had never attempted to aid him.

His mother had filled the world with her generosity and kindness. He, like his father, had learned to absorb her light but never emit it. His father glimpsed something in Dushyant that gave him hope for the future. Maybe, he was not doomed to repeat his father's mistakes.

As the sun climbed overhead, the minister entered his chamber in a hurry. "Advisor Upananda was hiding outside the city, waiting for Sundari. When he saw our soldiers, he tried to escape. Our men snatched him after a brief encounter."

Dushyant rose from behind his table. "Where is he?"

"He is locked up in a cell in our dungeon. I housed Sundari next to him."

Simmering like a boiling stew, Dushyant strode to the dungeon. On seeing him, Upananda wailed, "There has been a mistake."

Ignoring his pleas, Dushyant stood in front of Sundari's locked door. She sat on the bare floor with tear-streaked eyes. "Only the truth will save your unborn child," he said.

Her head jerked up.

"Who is the father of your child?" asked Dushyant, regarding her intently.

Upananda howled like an animal caught in a hunter's net. Sundari trembled all over.

"We are searching your houses for any jewels, gifts, and letters. If you lie, you will face my wrath," said Dushyant, his tone leaving her no doubt that he intended to carry out his threat.

"He is," whispered Sundari while pointing her chin in the direction of Upananda's cell.

"Say his name," ordered Dushyant. The howling from Upananda grew to a feverish pitch.

"Upananda," mumbled Sundari wiping her eyes with the end of her sari. A cloud lifted from Dushyant's head. Whatever his other faults, his father was an honorable man.

"She is lying," yelled Upananda.

"Why did you tell me you were carrying my father's child?" asked Dushyant.

"I believed Upananda's tales and thought it was good for my child. Like a fool, I lusted for the gold and silks. I want none of it. I only want my child to live." She broke into a sob.

"Your father, Kanva, died believing your lies," said Dushyant.

Her crying intensified.

"Release her and keep her under guard in her old room," ordered Dushyant. Then Dushyant strode past Upananda. "Chain him and bring him to court."

Donning his crown, Dushyant sat on the Vidarpur throne, holding his scepter in one hand. Upananda stood in front of him, whimpering like a frightened child. "Your actions led to the death of King Lambhodara. In the name of justice, I will give you a chance to defend yourself."

"I d-did," stammered Upananda, flapping his hands frantically. "I did my duty. Your father was a weak ruler, and I did Vidarpur a tremendous service by removing him." Upananda wept loudly, his whole body shaking.

Revolt filled Dushyant at the sight of the man still harboring his lies. "You exploited a man's grief," he stated sternly.

"You are better than him," appealed Upananda. "You will lead us to glory."

"Is that why you plotted to take my throne with your child? " Dushyant asked.

"That child is not—"

"Enough of your lies, " he said. "You kidnapped my sisters to harm them. "

"I never intended to harm them, " Upananda said.

"You admit to abducting them, then? " Dushyant said, his voice growing stern.

Upananda stuttered incoherently in response.

"When I wanted peace, you took Prince Bhimasena from my

prison to start a war with Garthapuri," Dushyant continued, remembering his fear of what could have happened if Lalitha's father had died. She would have never forgiven him. "Do you still claim to be doing your duty?"

Upananda muttered under his breath.

"What evidence have we recovered, Minister?"

"It appears Sundari did not trust him completely. Against Upananda's instructions to burn his letters, she kept two of them hidden in a trunk in her house. One letter proclaims their dreams for their son will come true. The other warns her about the need to continue their deception. The letters are addressed to a lover. We also found royal jewels in her possession."

"That idiot woman," erupted Upananda, rage reddening his face.

Dushyant turned to Minister Panini. "What is the just punishment for his crimes?"

"Public hanging."

"No need to delay justice. Read his crimes and hang him today. After her child is born, Sundari will work at the palace temple. She will receive no payments for her service. Only food and a place to stay."

"You will regret this, Dushyant," barked Upananda. "You will fail like your father because you are weak."

Dushyant stared at him coldly. "No more than you."

Later that day, Dushyant met with Minister Panini, General Ayobahu, and Chief Guard Samudra in the small council room. He glanced at each of them. They lowered their chins, unable to meet his eyes. "You did not serve my father well," he stated.

"My Majesty—" they started in a chorus.

Dushyant held up his right hand to halt them. "I am giving you a second chance. A ruler needs advisors willing to speak the truth to his face, especially about his erroneous ways. Be my eyes and ears. Counsel me about my faults."

General Ayobahu prostrated on the floor, and others

followed. "My king, accept my apologies. Your charity and wisdom speak of your righteousness. I am honored to serve you faithfully and loyally."

Dushyant returned to his chamber with a heavy heart. "I failed my father," he said as he removed his crown and held it in his palms.

"My king, you were a mere child when your mother died. You cannot be responsible for the actions of a grown man. While love causes great pain, it is also the best balm to ease your pain. Your mother's death caused deep sorrow in your father. Instead of finding love to ease his pain, he became addicted to poppy milk."

"If I had stayed in Vidarpur and comforted him, he might still be ruling this land."

"Maybe. We cannot change the past, my king. The wise among us learn from our mistakes."

"A king belongs to no one," said Dushyant, thinking of Lalitha. He wanted to be tethered to her for this life and the next.

Jayanth guessed his state of mind. "My Majesty, a king belongs to everyone. And a wise queen is a precious gift. Please do not throw it away."

"If she ceases to exist, I will forget my duties. Like my father." Dushyant's chest tightened and cramped. He was afraid of loving her, of losing her. Why did his ability to restrain his emotions feel like a defeat?

Jayanth looked at him. "When I married my wife, I thought I had found bliss. But now I know love is also worrying about our dear ones and grieving for them. That love was what made me a complete man. I also know that people we love are never lost to us, even if they die." Dushyant tugged his ear, remembering his mother's touch.

"Brother," called Kanika, and his sisters ran into his room.

"We heard all the news. What a dreadful man. He betrayed our father's trust."

"He is facing punishment for his wicked deeds," said Dushyant walking to his window.

"Brother, are you going to the swayamvara?" His sisters faced him expectantly, their eyes shining.

Dushyant pondered that question. Did he want to live a life of regrets, fearful of letting anyone into his heart? In his mind, Lalitha shone like a lotus amid dull leaves, waiting for his answer. Passion filled his heart as he spun to face the room.

33

LALITHA

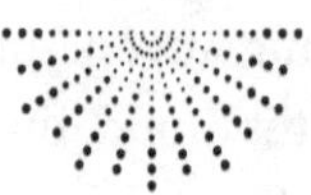

As her chariot turned west, Lalitha craned her neck to look behind. The four horses rode past the crossing toward Garthapuri.

"Help," she cried feebly, tears of anger stinging her eyes.

"Lalitha," began Prince Giridhar, looking concerned.

She felt like a child, tired, frustrated, and not in control. "Don't talk to me. I thought you an honorable man, but you are abducting me against my wishes. Admit it. Our life together will be no better than my parents. It'll be worse. What do we share besides our royal breeding?"

"Lalitha, most princes and princesses are married to complete strangers to strengthen their alliances. At least we are not strangers."

"And that is what hurts me most," she sneered.

Giridhar reached to grab her hand, but Lalitha slapped it away. "Don't touch me."

"No need to treat me like I am enjoying myself. You are not the only one forced into this marriage," he snapped.

"Is that supposed to make me happy? That we are both miserable?" she shouted.

"With Dushyant dead, what could possibly make you happy?" He locked his hands over his chest.

She felt like she'd drowned in a well, unable to breathe or surface. What she wanted was lost to her. Now, she only knew what she did not want.

The earth trembled, and she heard the sound of galloping horses. She leaned out and saw four horses fast approaching them. They looked like the same four she'd seen earlier. She did not know what caused them to change their minds and come in her direction. She yelled, "Help."

"Halt," commanded a voice that sounded familiar to her ears. The soldiers accompanying them spun around to face the newcomers.

"Giridhar, stop this madness," pleaded Lalitha.

He drew his sword and shifted away from her. "Faster," he yelled to the charioteer.

Lalitha heard the clash of metal against metal, the neighing of horses, and the clatter of the chariot wheels, still racing away.

A single horse trotted toward her. Did her kidnappers defeat the others? Her chest rose to her throat, cutting off her breath. The horse drew alongside her carriage, and she glanced at the rider.

"Dushyant!" she exclaimed, her heart nearly exploding. He was alive.

"Lalitha?" he questioned at the same time. His eyes fell on Giridhar. "Where are you taking her?" Dushyant glared at him.

Giridhar looked at his feet. "We heard the news of your death," he said. His knuckles grasping the hilt turned pale.

"He is abducting me to marry me against my wishes," blurted Lalitha, tears blinding her eyes. Another rider appeared on Giridhar's side. Jayanth!

"Giridhar, I don't want to hurt you. But I won't hesitate to kill you if you harm her," said Dushyant and transformed into a king before her eyes. Authority derived from his ancient heredity stood as his shield and his ability to control his emotions as his armor. What a fool she'd been ever to think he was an ordinary man.

"No," flapped Giridhar, flustered by Dushyant's imperious presence.

Dushyant glared at Giridhar with icy cold eyes and tilted from his horse toward her.

Understanding his intention, Lalitha rose from her seat. Dushyant extended his arm, and she leaned toward him. He grasped her waist and lifted her off in one fluid motion. Straightening, Dushyant placed her in front of him.

"You are alive," said Lalitha and touched his cheek. Her heart pounded against her chest. "You are alive," she repeated senselessly and flung her arms around Dushyant's neck and wept on his shoulder. Her action nearly caused her to slide off the horse.

Dushyant pulled her back and held her waist tightly. "Apologies for causing you distress," he murmured into her hair, gently stroking her back.

"I would never hurt her," mumbled Giridhar bringing her out of her reverie.

Lalitha sat straight and wiped her eyes.

Jayanth hit Giridhar's head with the handle of his ax. "There, you have a battle wound for your efforts," said Jayanth.

Giridhar looked at Lalitha. "I wish you well, Princess. Don't despise me," he said. "Go," he shouted, and the chariot took off without her.

Lalitha noticed the sharp cuts and bruises on Jayanth's arms. She turned to inspect Dushyant and locked her gaze with his. "I thought you were dead," she said again, her voice choking with emotions. She'd lost all hope and had surrendered to a life without love.

Dushyant stroked her cheek with his thumb. "I started that rumor to smoke out some vermin in my house."

Lalitha blinked her tears. "Did you succeed?"

"Upananda, who served as my father's advisor, plotted to usurp the throne with his own child. Kanva believed his lies and killed my father in a rage." Dushyant's face contorted in pain for a brief moment. Recovering, he turned his stallion toward Garthapuri.

"What an evil man."

"Upananda was punished for his crimes," said Dushyant with a stoic expression.

They passed unhorsed wounded soldiers on the ground. Dushyant's two men held the reins of two empty horses each. She regarded them. She saw knife cuts on one man's chest. The other had wrapped a cloth around his bleeding arm. Lalitha glanced at the riderless animals. As an unmarried girl, custom would dictate she rode separately, but she'd no inclination to leave the warmth of Dushyant's arms. She nuzzled against him, and he shifted slightly to place her back against his chest. "Are your sisters' safe?"

His face brightened. "Yes. I came to attend the swayamvara at their urging."

"I will express my gratitude to them when I see them," Lalitha whispered, drinking in his familiar scent. "I thought no one heard my pleas for help. What made you return?"

"I was in a hurry to reach Garthapuri before you chose your groom, so I ignored the cry at first. Then, I thought of you and my sisters. I knew I could not face any of you if I abandoned a lady in need of my aid." He gazed at her tenderly.

"Why were you in a hurry to come to my swayamvara?" Lalitha asked, with a teasing smile on her face.

Dushyant wore a solemn expression. "My dear Lalitha, I thought my father was a weak futile man. But in the past few days, the scales have fallen off my eyes. My parents shared a unique bond, and her loss left him drowning in a sea of grief. I was too young to help him, and a man he trusted led him astray. My father found comfort in poppies and became detached from reality. But he never betrayed my mother. I only saw his pain of the last decade, but then I remembered their shared radiant life. I was afraid of loving you with my whole heart. Not anymore. Neither of us knows what the shapes of our lives will be tomorrow. All I know today is what I feel for you is real. What began between us on your journey home only grew in strength. The future is as fragile as a fresh-budding blossom filled with promises of spring. A frost might wilt it, but I am hopeful for a blooming summer. If you still reject me, I will return you safely to Garthapuri and take your leave."

Lalitha moved the bangles on her hand, touched by his trust to open his innermost thoughts to her. "My feelings for you have evolved. In my heart, I knew all the time. But I held on to foolish views and avoided acknowledging the truth. When I heard of your death, I realized too late that I loved you," she whispered, heat rushing into her face.

Dushyant looked at her strangely. "You knew your heart, yet you were going ahead with the swayamvara."

Guilt swept through her. "Dushyant, I was devastated but did not have the luxury of mourning you publicly." Dushyant pushed her hair out of her forehead, giving her strength to continue. "I had a duty to my kingdom and was prepared to marry a stranger. I might not have loved him but was ready to offer him my loyalty and fidelity. Does that make me wicked?" Lalitha sighed.

Dushyant took her hand in delicate possession, brought her knuckles to his lips, and kissed them lightly. "Only brave. I envy your ability to act fearlessly. I was afraid of losing you, so I was prepared to live a life of regrets with my heart untouched. I lacked your courage to lead a full life, even if it meant despair and pain, along with bliss and joy. I was going to wallow in self-pity." He gazed at her so tenderly that she wanted to melt into him.

"You give me too much credit. Only when I thought I had

lost you forever did I learn that your death did not stop my love for you. I could have learned to live without you, but now, I have no wish to."

"You grieved for me, but you did not break. You hid your scars and faced your life like a soldier. There is so much for me to learn from you. I lied earlier. I don't intend to walk away quietly. Till you are married, I plan to fight for you."

"Will you force me to do something against my wishes?" she asked, lifting her brows.

Dushyant looked affronted. "Never that. It is still your swayamvara, and I will be one of your suitors pressing my case."

Her heart soared on hearing his words. "There is one condition for me to choose you," she said and gazed at him.

He smiled at her, and happiness leaked out of his every pore. Lalitha was surprised to see this unusual exhibition of his feelings. "Only one?" he asked as if he was ready to give her anything she asked for.

"Garthapuri would remain an independent kingdom. One of my sons will rule it after my uncle."

"Your son?" he teased her, his grin extending from one large ear to another.

Lalitha knew she turned crimson. "Our son, if you accept my condition." Her mind wandered to a boy who looked like the mirror image of his father.

"It is not Garthapuri that I seek," said Dushyant. He gazed at her with fondness and warmth and made her heart bubble with joy. "I have a request of you as well."

She arched her brows at him.

"When we marry, will you honor me by being my queen?"

"Queen of Vidarpur?" she interrupted him.

"Yes. My mother was our last queen, and she was much beloved by our people. I know that you will capture the hearts of Vidarpur citizens." He hesitated briefly and then plunged ahead. "My father never groomed me to rule, and I have struggled to govern. One of my advisors plotted behind my back, and I had to fake my death to capture him. I don't know who to trust." He gazed into her eyes. "You have been trained all your life to reign your kingdom. Help me be a better ruler."

Lalitha swallowed. She understood the depth of Dushyant's love for her to reveal his vulnerabilities. All these years, Garthapuri occupied her thoughts and deeds. She had only given thought to how her husband might aid her in ruling her kingdom. She'd never contemplated what role she would play in his life. She had been abominably selfish like her father, who had failed to consider her mother's needs. That thought ashamed her. She tried to breathe through the thorns prickling her throat. She would make amends for her selfishness. She would grow to be worthy of Dushyant's affection. His request tugged something in her. He believed her capable. "Do you trust me to assist you?" She'd done nothing to earn it.

He offered her the faintest of smiles. "I would trust you with my life."

His words lingered in her heart. Was this how marriage worked? Based on mutual trust that was neither fleeting nor weak? One that would endure as long as they both did their part. But she could not abandon her kingdom. "Dushyant, I cannot forsake Garthapuri."

"I will never ask you to," he replied swiftly. "My sword will be yours to command to defend Garthapuri. And your acumen can serve both kingdoms."

Her father was alive and healthy, so Garthapuri was in reliable hands for now, giving her time to learn about Vidarpur. Another worry sprouted in her head. Where would they live? She turned her body toward his. "I don't want to live apart from you. How do we split our time between the two kingdoms?" asked Lalitha.

If the question surprised or startled him, he gave no indication. Instead, he looked at her solemnly. "Neither do I wish to spend time away from you. I am the king of Vidarpur. Would you consider it your home?" He added hurriedly, "We can spend as much time as needed in Garthapuri."

Traditionally, a wife's place was beside her husband. While Lalitha never sought a traditional marriage, she wanted to create a life with Dushyant. She should not let her parent's marital failures chain her. She could forge a better union. She had faith that Dushyant would keep his word. "Dushyant," she choked with emotion. "I will strive to be a worthy queen of Vidarpur."

Before they could say more, they encountered a small army led by her father. She moved away from Dushyant and sat with a straight back.

"Lalitha," exclaimed her father. "Did this man kidnap you?" he thundered.

"No, Father. He rescued me from Prince Giridhar."

"Giridhar?" A puzzled frown appeared on her father's face.

Dushyant pulled the reins and halted his horse. He jumped down and helped Lalitha dismount.

"Prince Giridhar was planning to wed me against my wishes." She approached her father, and he pulled her into a hug. As they separated, she whispered, "I suspect Queen Padmavati knew of his plans."

Her father pressed his lips together. "I will deal with that matter later. Your suitors are waiting for you. Let us return to the castle."

Lalitha looked at Dushyant to make sure he followed her. Suddenly, she noticed dark patches of blood that blotted his dhoti. "You are hurt," she exclaimed and moved to rip the ends of her sari to make him a wrap.

"Don't mar your sari," Dushyant said, covering her hand with his palm.

Her father cleared his throat, and Lalitha nearly jumped out of her skin.

Dushyant pulled his arm away. "I am fine," Dushyant whispered and mounted his stallion.

One of Dushyant's guards brought her a mare. Reluctantly, she climbed into her saddle, missing Dushyant's warmth. They rode swiftly and reached the castle as onlookers gathered to watch them. As they reached the palace stair entry, her father gazed at her kindly. "I will give you a few moments to clean up."

Lalitha climbed the stairs with her heart soaring. At the top, she encountered a furious queen.

"What is he doing here?" hissed Queen Padmavati, staring at Dushyant.

"Why did you force Giridhar to abduct me?" countered Lalitha, rage bubbling in her stomach.

"I only had your welfare in mind," stated the queen without answering her question. Then she spun toward King Dushyant. "Where is my nephew? Did you hurt him?"

"Only his pride," answered Dushyant, all earlier signs of joy wiped away from his countenance.

"Queen Padmavati, did you play a role in this attempt to force my daughter to marry Giridhar?" asked her father, not attempting to hide his anger.

"Only because you insisted on this sham swayamvara. She is seventeen. What does she know about choosing a husband? My nephew, Giridhar, was a fit companion for her." Her aunt looked at Dushyant with derision. "Your father, King Lambhodara, was a madman who neglected his children and kingdom."

Dushyant regarded her with icy calmness. "My father grieved for my mother."

"He should have married again instead of moping around," her aunt snapped.

Dushyant regarded her father. "Men are capable of constancy in their love. Even when all hope is lost," he said. Her father gazed at him and swallowed. Lalitha knew of her father's love for her mother and the one-sided nature of it.

Queen Padmavati regarded them with contempt. "Kings cannot act like ordinary men. Nor can future queens."

"I have not forgotten my duties," said Lalitha, her hands trembling.

"If Nidhapur attacks us—"

Dushyant interrupted her. "Vidarpur will come to your aid." He looked at Lalitha. "Our union will strengthen the ties between our two kingdoms. Your water can help my farmers. My gold can replenish your coffers." Lalitha saw a new future ahead of her—a partner who would share her burden. The two of them, arm in arm, would work to better both their kingdoms. A bright future filled with love and hope.

"Leave, my child," urged her father, bringing her back. "I want to start the swayamvara at the auspicious time."

With a skip in her step and a smile on her face, Lalitha walked through the castle. As she reached the hallway to her chamber, her mother called out to her, " Lalitha." Her mother was with her sister, Aunt Chitra, and they both hurried toward Lalitha. Her mother pulled her into her arms. "I was worried about you, my child. I did not want my fate to befall you."

Lalitha's heart swelled at this show of affection from her mother. "Dushyant returned from the dead to rescue me," she murmured.

Releasing her, her mother gazed at Lalitha with tears sparkling in her eyes. "Let me help you," she said and hooked her elbow into Lalitha's arm. Aunt Chitra took her other arm, and they slow-marched to her room.

"I guess you don't need a competition to pick your groom today," her mother said with a grin as she fixed her daughter's hair.

Aunt Chitra wiped her face with a wet cloth as Lalitha smiled at her mother. "Dushyant is alive," Lalitha said in a wonder-struck voice.

"Let us not keep him waiting," said her mother, and they

escorted her to the large hall. Faint notes from the string instrument, Veena, floated in the air as Lalitha stood at the threshold holding the Champa flower garland. Head bowed, she peeked at the gathered through the corner of her eyes.

"Do you want to meet some of the other suitors before—" started her mother.

Lalitha noticed yellow silk-clad legs approaching her. "You look like Goddess Saraswati, Lalli," said her father. "Let us meet the young men vying for your hand."

With that, he conducted Lalitha into the hall. "Anga, son of Anupa, will become chief of his lands after his father. He distinguished himself in recent battles and has risen in the Garthapuri military. He will support you ably in governance."

Lalitha glanced at his youthful face and bare chest blemished by battle scars. "I hope Anga will serve as my general one day," she said with a bow.

The blossoms of her garland danced as they moved to the next candidate.

"Avanti is wise and wealthy, twin gifts that rarely reside in the same person. He would be a fit companion for you," stated her father.

Lalitha rejected him gently. "He is worthy of my gratitude, and I hope he will serve as my minister."

Queen Padmavati pushed Avanti aside and held out a sword. "This sword represents Giridhar. He is a prince of Nidhapur, a kingdom with deep ties to Garthapuri. He hails from a royal family with a glorious past. His kingdom is favored by fortune—"

With tremendous control, Lalitha swept aside the urge to shake her aunt's shoulders. "I am sure the prince favored by fortune will find a princess worthy of him."

Seeing this, her father decided not to torment Lalitha anymore and led her straight to where Dushyant stood. Dushyant's eyes sparkled like the ocean under the sun. "King

Dushyant of Vidarpur. High lineage, bravery, and virtue are all at his command."

Lalitha looked at Dushyant and was swept away by the adoration emanating from him. He was fully dressed in gold and splendor. Centuries of power spilled from his visage without any stony arrogance. Yet, he retained something oddly boyish in his looks, his face tilted down to her with excitement and a touch of impatience. Sweet, strange hopefulness filled her at this sign of restless eagerness from him. The promise of something miraculous fluttered in her chest. She wanted to savor this moment when her future unfolded with him in it. Tongue-tied, Lalitha started to stand on her toes to reach Dushyant. He bowed his head at the same time to help her place the wreath around his neck, and the people around her broke out in shouts of joy. Their eyes met, and suddenly all else vanished, and her world stood still with only two people in it: him and her. His gaze caressed her tenderly, and she wanted his hands to envelop her.

"Lalli, I will help you change into your wedding sari," said her mother, breaking the spell.

"Wedding?" asked Dushyant, sounding dazed.

"Today is an auspicious day. If we miss it, we will have to wait a fortnight," answered her father, watching the king.

Dushyant glanced at her. "If my parents were alive, I would have suggested waiting for them to bless our union. Instead, I would follow their advice not to put off a good deed," he said.

"Your father does not want to give Queen Padmavati another opportunity to thwart your marriage," her mother murmured as they walked back to her chambers.

As her friend Agamathi, Aunt Chitra, and her mother helped her drape the red silk wedding sari embroidered with gold thread, Queen Padmavati entered her room.

"You chose the king of Vidarpur against my advice," she said with a deep frown between her eyes.

"You kidnapped my daughter to marry her against her wishes," her mother snapped.

Queen Padmavati put her hands on her hips. "The daughter you abandoned to join a monastery?"

Her mother's body trembled as she folded the sari pleats. Lalitha covered her hands and knew what she had to say. "Aunt Padmavati, Mother, you both mean a lot to me. And I know you both love me. Can you please set aside your differences for one day?" Lalitha took turns looking at each woman.

Her mother wiped her eyes. "My lady, I never thanked you for taking care of my daughter."

"Our daughter," the queen amended. Then she sighed. "Lalli, I hope your trust in Dushyant is well placed, and your union brings you joy."

Soon, Lalitha stood in front of Dushyant and exchanged wedding garlands. As yellow rice and flower petals showered on them, Dushyant whispered, "My queen," in her ear, his lips breaking into another smile. She was used to his caged smile, struggling to be released from behind pursued lips and twitching eyebrows. What spirit caused this change in him? It could not be her. Heat spread to her face as she gazed at him. A priest tied her sari to his dhoti, and Dushyant clasped her hand to walk around the sacred fire. His calloused palm squeezed her hand gently, spreading warmth through her body. With each of the seven steps, they exchanged vows of love, loyalty, fidelity, respect, and eternal companionship.

Without letting go of her hand, Dushyant guided her to her uncle and aunt to seek their blessings. As the newly wedded couple touched their foreheads to the ground, the king and queen of Garthapuri showered them with yellow rice. "King Dushyant, Lalli is the princess of our hearts. While her angry outbursts don't last long, her loyalty does. Take good care of my child," said her uncle, patting her head gently.

Dushyant looked at Lalitha with a twinkle in his eyes. "I am aware of her worth and my fortune."

"Did you not hear what my uncle said about my anger?" she whispered with a teasing smile.

"Anger? You? You are the warm breeze on a summer day."

They approached her parents, who stood a few feet apart. "If you stood closer, we can seek both your blessings," said Lalitha. Her father slid toward her mother, still leaving a foot between them. As she frowned, Dushyant squeezed her hand, reminding her of this fragile, precious love they shared. She let her breath out, and as a couple, they touched the ground in front of her parents. As she rose, her father embraced her. "Lalli is a fighter. Don't break her spirit," her father said as he released her and blinked his misty eyes.

"I am depending on her to buoy me," said Dushyant.

Her mother hugged her tightly. "Unlike me, you always showed wisdom beyond your age. Let that light your path."

"The people are eager to see their princess and her chosen consort. Your chariot is waiting," said her father.

Dushyant helped her into the carriage and sat beside her. "I am trying not to dwell on how radiant you look lest I behave less than civilly," he whispered in her ear while the horses trotted.

34
DUSHYANT

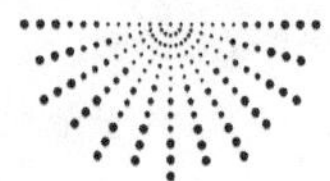

ushyant had no sense of home in Vidarpur or with his aunt in Jaisalpur. He had thought that part of him was dead. But today, being wedded to Lalitha felt like a home-coming to him. He'd believed himself cursed, but now he knew he was lucky. He was no longer the king who hid his heart. His emotions broke through the dam he'd built and flooded his veins with happiness. His mind caught the odd details about her that he'd never noticed before in another person. Her coral necklace set in yellow gold glittered with multiple colors of a sunset and shone against her throat. The pattern of her earring matched the gold threading on her sari. Her kajal-lined eyes looked deceptively innocent, but he knew not to underestimate her.

A sudden desire to be alone with Lalitha pierced Dushyant--to find his way through all the layers of her. Seated beside her on their chariot ride through her city, Dushyant tried hard to maintain some semblance of composure. He took her hand in his and traced her wrist with his thumb. Like a flower bud opening its petal to the first rays of the sun, she gazed at him.

"A winged horse," she whispered in his ear. He raised his

brows while his mind reeled from the touch of her lips against his skin. "So the two of us can fly into the mountains away from the crowds." His spine tingled to hear her echo his thoughts.

She turned toward the hundreds of people thronged to see them. That they loved their princess was apparent to him. They regarded him with curiosity.

"I suspect I am falling short in their eyes," murmured Dushyant as Lalitha gracefully accepted the people's well wishes.

"You are thinking of my father and uncle," she said, half turning to look at him. A mischievous grin floated on her lips. "For them, no one could be a good match for me. The people on the street are more accepting. Look at them gaze at you in wonder. They probably think you won me in your conquest. A king who came to conquer their land instead conquered their princess' heart."

Dushyant gazed at her profile. Her thick lashes cast shadows on her cheeks while wisps of hair curled near her ears. "A king who came to fell his enemy instead fell for their princess."

Her face broke into a wide grin that caused him to smile as well. "The princess was fortunate to stumble upon the king on her journey. Otherwise, she would have settled for a chief when she could have aspired higher."

"The fortune rests with the king," he interrupted her. A mellow warmth radiated from her and heated his core. "I was lost, meandering through life. You captured my heart and set me free."

She laughed, sounding like the pattering of raindrops on leaves. "We found each other then. I need you like a tree needs its roots. You keep me grounded."

"If I am the root, you are the branches reaching for the clouds pushing me higher."

"My head is in the clouds sometimes," she said.

"Only sometimes?" he jested.

She arched toward him gracefully like a slender branch swaying in a breeze. Her knee nudged his, and that banal touch sent him reeling. "You won't begrudge a girl her dreams," she asked, her lips tilting up.

"Not if you share them with me," said Dushyant. A faint blush spread on her cheeks as they arrived back at the castle. Somewhere in the sky, two birds sang back and forth to each other.

A familiar man dismounted from his horse. "I have met him before," Dushyant said to Lalitha.

"That is Nambi, one of my trusted guards. He helped me rescue you," answered Lalitha.

"I will have to thank him."

"There is a better way to express our gratitude. He is in love with my friend Agamathi. Before we leave for Vidarpur, let us arrange their wedding."

Joy rang in his ears at her using our and we. "That can be our first deed as husband and wife," he said, a smile splitting his face.

The festivities continued into the night, and he had eyes only for Lalitha. Her red silk sari hinted at her curves as she reached across to point something out to him. In the brass wicker lamp, her gold earrings shimmered against her skin as she nodded at something. As she sat beside him for a feast served on a banana leaf, her necklace cast a rainbow of light on her throat.

* * *

FAINT INDISTINGUISHABLE VOICES from the gathered royal dignitaries floated up as Dushyant made his way through the dark hallways. Soldiers and servants bowed to him, recognizing his crown, if not his face. He paused near her chamber to view the stars sparkling in the cloudless sky. He walked the last few paces, and a large wooden door with brass knobs loomed in front of him. A guard opened it, and he stepped inside. While his eyes adjusted to the dim light, the door shut behind him. Lalitha rose from a bench like a beautiful nymph coming to life.

It was not clear who led whom, but they were seated side by side. Brushed by the light spilling from a lamp, Lalitha glowed in the darkness. A lone jasmine flower sat in the folds of her sari like a bright star fallen from the sky.

"Dushyant, have you—lain with. . ." she asked, hesitant.

"I have not." His answer was plain. He had plenty of opportunities that his wealth and title threw his way. But, seeing his father broken had restrained him. Until he met Lalitha, Dushyant had suppressed that side of him. And now, he yearned to touch every part of her. He kissed her lightly on the forehead as she looked at him, her eyes wide.

"What if you don't like it?"

Dushyant laughed. Just her breath on his skin sent tremors through his body. "Why wouldn't I like it? I love you."

Lalitha turned her body toward him and touched his jaw. "I love you too. Yet, I am afraid."

He pressed his brows to her. "I will not hurt you. Never fear to be with me."

With unsteady fingers, she pushed aside the shawl draped over his shoulder to expose his chest. She let her fingertips follow the line of his bare arm, heating his skin.

"Lalitha—" Dushyant's voice caught in his throat. Her fingers traveled to his collarbone, and his chest rose and fell more quickly than usual. "There is no need to rush. We can take things slowly." He hoped he had the strength to refrain from what his body craved.

"I want this," she whispered and swallowed.

He smiled at her. "And I possess neither the will nor the wish to resist you." He reached out and began to undo her hair until it tumbled down to her waist. He let his fingers comb her silky tresses.

She stood to remove her sari and let the fabric fall to the ground. Dushyant gulped as he gazed at her beautiful curves and crevices, realizing that he would never get tired of looking at Lalitha.

"Come here," he said in a low voice. In an offering of her trust, Lalitha moved toward him. He pulled her onto his lap, and she nestled her forehead against his neck. Burying his hands in her hair, he inhaled her sweet scent. "I have imagined this countless times." His hands settled on her slender waist.

She leaned in and brushed her lips to his. "And?"

It felt delicious to be kissed by her. "You are more beautiful in the flesh, and I love you with every drop of my blood."

"Then I must protect you from spilling it." She embraced him, and the heat of her hands on his bare back shocked him. He kissed his way down her throat. She shivered under his touch.

His heart lurched in anticipation. He was not remotely prepared for the way she felt around him. He savored the smoothness of her skin, the softness of her body, the saltiness of her lips, all incredibly new yet familiar. They became one of the heart as their bodies molded into each other. She opened herself to him in an unbearably intimate way. Trusting him. And he was willing to give her anything. Everything. He lost memory of who he was before because, at that moment, they were united as man and wife.

* * *

DUSHYANT WAS JOLTED out of his sleep by an elbow in his ribs. Lalitha snuggled against him, her body bent to his. With overflowing love, he watched her chest rise and fall. Her hand fell across his chest in a possessive way he felt oddly appealing. Creased silk sheets rested at their feet.

Her nose rubbed his arm, and she yawned sleepily. Then her eyes fluttered open like the wings of a bird.

"You mutter things in your sleep," she said, her palm on his chest, all shyness from last night gone.

Dushyant gazed at her in embarrassment. "What did I say?" When was the last time he'd shared a room with anyone other than his guards?

She grinned. "Nothing coherent. Something about your father. My name." She nestled against his arms. "I liked that part."

"Lalitha," he said softly. "I like saying it." He pushed her hair off of her forehead. "I cannot wait to take you to Vidarpur."

Her fingers rubbed his earlobe. "Tell me all about Vidarpur, both the good elements I can cherish and the bad ones we should fix. And I cannot wait to meet your sisters. They can reveal your secrets that will take me years to dig up." Her eyes twinkled in the morning sun as words tumbled out of her.

Dushyant laughed. "Don't believe everything they tell you."

"Only the parts I can use to make fun of you." She gave him a haughty look and then spoiled that gaze by leaning to kiss him tenderly.

His love for Lalitha expanded limitlessly. Dushyant knew it would fill his castle with laughter, bring light to the dark foreboding shadows, and chase away the ghosts that haunted him. The freshly risen sun painted her room an impossible gold. In that vibrant color, Dushyant saw the shape of his future with Lalitha by his side.

Tomorrow was only a promise. Only today existed in reality. Dushyant returned her kiss with ardor, grateful for every moment he spent with Lalitha.

ACKNOWLEDGMENTS

I love reading romance novels. I have devoured all of Jane Austen's novels. In our chaotic world, there is something comforting about a Happily Ever After ending. To the romance authors who inspired me, thank you for sharing your stories with the world and for inspiring me to write my own happily ever after tale.

This Historical Romance series is based on the ancient Indian custom, Swayamvara. During a Swayamvara, a bride chooses her groom from the assembled suitors. Here is how Kalidasa, a medieval Indian poet, describes a swayamvara in The Dynasty of Raghu, an epic poem:

> *The princess chooses. The princely suitors assemble in*
> *the hall: then, to the sound of music, the princess*
> *enters in a litter, robed as a bride, and creates a*
> *profound sensation.*

Kalidasa, the ancient Indian poet, was born in the kingdom of Magadha. I used a fictionalized version of Magadha in my Land of Magadha trilogy. King Vikramaditya of Ujjain was a patron of Kalidasa's art. Can you imagine the court of King Vikramaditya when Kalidasa staged one of his plays? The king and other royalty would gather around to watch. The actors wearing elaborate costumes would sing and dance to the sound of live music. Kalidasa predates Shakespeare by about a thousand years, so much of his life remains hidden in mystery and legend.

The precursor to present-day Holi celebrations, the Vasantotsava festival is a celebration of the arrival of spring. Poet Kalidasa describes the festival as a time when the "*earth is fragrant with new flowers.*" Ratnavali, the classic Sanskrit play by Emperor Harsha, has vivid descriptions of this festival, and I used them as my reference for this story.

While other poets wrote about royalty or divinity, Ilango Adigal wrote about two ordinary women in the Tamil Epic called Silappathikaram (Tale of Anklets), composed in the 5th century. The anklets of Princess Lalitha described by Dushyant in this tale are similar to the anklets at the center of this epic. Reading and appreciating these ancient epics and poems that have withstood the test of time is truly a blessing. The creativity and imagination of these ancient authors has been instrumental in shaping my writing style and helping me refine my craft.

Priya and Mary, thank you for reading the chapters as I wrote them. Your constructive feedback was invaluable. Melina, Neesa, and Jodie, thanks for reading an early draft of this novel. Thanks to your thoughtful feedback, this story is many folds better.

I would like to express my heartfelt gratitude to Ranga, Devina, Devi, Uma, Smita, Sushma, Kalpana, Seetha, Priya, Nanda, Brian, JR Jean, Meera, and many others, for their unwavering support and encouragement throughout my writing journey.

I would also like to extend my thanks to the local author community, Sarah, Theresa, Dennis, and others, for their invaluable guidance, motivation, and support. Thanks to Toni Cox for editing and proofreading this book.

To my husband, who puts up with the countless hours I spend writing and plugs my books to complete strangers, I could not do this without your support. To my daughters, who inspire me to be a better human being and write these courageous female characters, I still have not found the right words to express my love for you. To my Amma, who has read all my novels, and to my Appa, who still reads daily, thanks for nurturing my love of reading. To my brother, cousins, and extended family, thanks for believing in me.

Finally, I would like to express my sincere appreciation to my readers, whose support and enthusiasm for my writing have kept me going through the ups and downs of the writing process. Your kind words and encouragement have meant the world to me.

Thank you all for your support, guidance, and encouragement. I am forever grateful for your role in making this book a reality.

ABOUT THE AUTHOR

The stories I read growing up inspired me to write. I am interested in historical fiction and within that society, examining the human heart in conflict. I like to place my female characters in difficult situations and see how they learn to survive with no actual power. And watch my male characters fall in love while fighting for king and land. I love exploring the struggle between love and duty.

I live in California with my family. Visit me at annabushi.com to learn about upcoming books.

Thank you for reading! If you enjoyed this book, I would love it if you let your friends know so they can experience the adventures of Lalitha and Dushyant. You can also leave a review so that other readers know what they're getting into when they pick up this book!

This royal Indian saga weaves a tale of destiny and danger, forbidden love and courtly intrigue.

Heir to Malla is the first book in the epic Land of Magadha trilogy.

* * *

War of the Three Kings - Book 2

Jay promised not to kill him a decade ago. Now he stands between Jay and the throne.

Crown Prince Jay has grown into a legend with all his triumphs on the battlefield. While he is away helping a neighboring king, Jay is unaware of a new enemy who has emerged back home.

Jay fought with Nakul many years ago, but he believes the bitter past is behind them. Unknown to Jay, Nakul covets his crown. With chaos brewing in his realm and the lives of his people in peril, Jay stands exposed to danger as he cannot tell friend from foe.

Neither is Jay aware of the grave secret that binds him and Nakul together. Plunging into a conflict that might result in destruction, is he ready to pay the price for triumph? His failure would result in death— his and the kingdom he vowed to protect.

Malla siblings, Meera and Jay, return to face the consequences of their actions in War of the Three Kings, the second book in the epic trilogy, Land of Magadha.

Perfect for fans of historical fiction like Wolf Hall and Ponniyin Selvan or lovers of fantasy like Baahubali and The Lost Queen.

* * *

Burden of the Crown - Book 3

Blinded by despair, they fail to see the foe plotting their ruin.

His people revere him for the prosperity he has ushered. His enemies cower on hearing his name. Then, disaster strikes King Jay. He drowns in grief, forgetting his duty as a king.

When tragedy strikes, Meera thinks it is punishment for her past mistakes. One, in particular, rattles her. When she sets out to right her wrongs, she doesn't know if she can make up for the biggest mistake of all.

Anger festers in Jay's heart, threatening to ruin all he holds dear. The pain Meera inflicted on the one who captured her heart haunts her. A dangerous enemy seeking to seize the throne uses this opportunity to cause chaos in the kingdom.

Their foe has anticipated their moves to stay two steps ahead. Will the siblings heed the troubling signs? Or will they cause the downfall of their kingdom?

Burden of the Crown concludes the epic trilogy, Land of Magadha. Malla siblings face their gravest threat yet in their mission to protect their kingdom.

www.ingramcontent.com/pod-product-compliance
Lightning Source LLC
Chambersburg PA
CBHW051141190726
48290CB00006B/1942